THE
BELL
Messenger

**Center Point
Large Print**

**This Large Print Book carries the
Seal of Approval of N.A.V.H.**

THE
BELL
Messenger

ROBERT CORNUKE
with ALTON GANSKY

CENTER POINT PUBLISHING
THORNDIKE, MAINE

This Center Point Large Print edition
is published in the year 2009 by arrangement with
Howard Books, a division of Simon & Schuster, Inc.

The text of this Large Print edition is unabridged.
In other aspects, this book may vary
from the original edition.
Printed in the United States of America.
Set in 16-point Times New Roman type.

ISBN: 978-1-60285-370-6

Library of Congress Cataloging-in-Publication Data

Cornuke, Robert, 1951-
    The bell messenger / Robert Cornuke with Alton Gansky.
        p. cm.
    ISBN 978-1-60285-370-6 (library binding : alk. paper)
1. Treasure troves--Fiction. 2. Family secrets--Fiction. 3. Large type books.
    I. Gansky, Alton. II. Title.

PS3603.O7685B45 2009
813'.6—dc22

2008039481

Writing requires a unique kind of solitude—
and for a social creature like me, it is even
more of an ordeal. The writing, rewriting,
research, dreaming, frustration, and elation
are woven into the tapestry of the literary
work that follows.

The families of those who write are the most
worthy recipients of any dedication. They are
as much a part of a book as the author.

I dedicate this book to my loving family.
They are all my unabated joy.

—BOB CORNUKE

THE
BELL
Messenger

APRIL 9, 1865
CROWLEY FARM, VIRGINIA
7:36 A.M.

MUD.

A miserable earthen broth mingled with decaying cornstalks and brown rain. Mud in someone else's cornfield. Mud in someone else's state. Tate loathed it.

Four long, grueling years ago, he had longed for a field soaked with rain. People called him farmer then. Now they called him Lieutenant Jeremiah Tate. The title came with the blue uniform he wore, tattered and reeking from too many days of sweat, too many miles marched. The morning fog made the smell worse.

The gnarled roots of a fallen oak appeared from the mist, like a twisted hand rising from the fallow field. Lieutenant Tate turned to his men. "We rest here."

"We're lost, ain't we?" Corporal Larimore made his last sucking strides in muck and sat on the spine of the old oak.

Tate didn't answer. He massaged his pounding temples, trying not to think of the twenty men killed the day before—twenty good men now prostrate and silent, felled in the glint of clashing

Confederate and Union bayonets among the thunderous roar of artillery. Now only six remained, along with Tate's wounded horse, as if that were consolation. By sundown, they would all probably be dead. Tate led the limping horse to a shallow stream trickling a short distance away.

Snap!

A thatch of reeds in a marshy draw to his right rustled. Tate's eyes swiveled toward the sound. He dropped the reins and crept back to the fallen oak.

With one hand, Tate shoved Larimore down, still holding his Sharps carbine tight in the other. His men dropped to the sodden earth, their faces to the mud, and crawled on their bellies for cover behind the moldering tree.

Snap!

Tate's elbows sank in the cold earth, and he struggled to keep mud from fouling his Sharps.

A deer, a mature buck, bolted from the foliage, leaping, sprinting, changing direction, and flinging mud from its hooves.

"Venison, Lieutenant. Fresh meat." Larimore spoke in a tight whisper. He started to rise.

"Stay put," Tate ordered. "Something spooked it."

Tate understood the impulse. It had been his first instinct to rise and shoot when the buck appeared. His half-starved men had nothing more than hard biscuits for food—food that Larimore had taken to calling "teeth dullers." Regardless of his overwhelming desire for meat, the war had made Tate cautious.

"Too late now," the young corporal moaned. The deer disappeared in the morning fog. "The way he's moving, he's probably in Atlanta by now."

Tate raised his gloved hand, fingers spread—a sign to his men to stay put and be silent.

They remained pressed tight to the dead tree. Then Tate saw it—the ghostly form of a man emerging from the same stand of reeds. A man in a gray uniform.

The soldier took three strides into the open, raised his rifle, and fired. It was a shot made in desperation. The buck had vanished.

The gun's report echoed, pounding in their ears. A second later, three other soldiers emerged, stopping at the side of the first. To Tate, they looked more tired and gaunt than his own men. Even in the dim light he could see that their gray uniforms were battle worn and ragged.

They stood like a clump of trees—right in the open.

Such stupidity.

Tate raised his Sharps over the old oak and sighted down the barrel. From the corner of his eye, he saw his men do the same.

There could be no mercy—not in this war. It would be a close shot, an easy kill.

As if making a simple statement instead of a command, Tate uttered, "Fire." Rifle hammers fell, igniting gunpowder, and sent a fusillade of .52-caliber minié balls into their targets.

The white discharge of rifle smoke mingled with the moist air and shrouded their sight. A cry rose from the field. As wisps of smoke dissolved, two of the gray-clad figures lay contorted and motionless in the muck. Another man was sitting, legs apart, head tilted at an awkward angle. A moment later he fell backward. The last man to move was thin and small. He staggered, clutching something to his chest with one hand and staring at something on the other. Tate knew the other was blood. The man's chest had been Tate's target, the silhouette in the V groove of his rifle sight. The bullet had met its intended mark, punching a hole in the soldier's rib cage. The Reb collapsed, then curled in the mud.

Why do people die so slowly?

Seconds seemed like an eternity, each man frantically reloading in case other Confederates hid close by. Tate strained his ears to hear everything. He heard the creek gurgling, the excited breathing of the men next to him, but nothing else.

Tate slowly stood and approached the bodies. His men followed. *Engagement*, Tate reminded himself. War involved bloody engagement. These men were not victims, they were dead by necessity. They were the enemy. He struggled to find satisfaction in the fact that he had done his job, and done it well, but he felt hollow.

The first man Tate reached lay facedown in the muck. Tate rolled the corpse over with his foot.

Larimore walked up from behind and laughed. "Looks dead as a stone, Lieutenant."

The soldier lay on a bed of brown cornstalks and stared at Tate through one unblinking eye. Mud obscured half his face. A glistening, diamond-shaped red hole marred the man's forehead.

The second soldier lay on his side. Tate could see where the minié ball had entered his back and torn a hole through his coat, shirt, and flesh. Tate judged him to be in his early twenties. Despite the mud-caked beard, Tate bet the soldier had been a ladies' man. Strong features, blue eyes, and broad shoulders must have attracted his fair share of female attention.

"Better hurry and get what you can, Lieutenant."

Tate watched Corporal Larimore and the others pull objects from the dead men's coats and forage through their pants pockets.

Pointing a bloodstained finger, Larimore grinned. "That shot-up feller over there was kind enough to leave me some tobacco, a snip of jerky, and this." He stopped his pillaging and held out a photograph of a woman standing next to a padded chair. Young and clad in a long black dress with white frills at the neck, she struck a dramatic pose. "A handsome woman, I'd say. A real looker. I wouldn't mind making her acquaintance. Do you think she'd hold it against me that I killed her husband?"

"I think you're going to burn in hell, Larimore."

Larimore laughed. "I think we all are, Lieutenant. Yes, sir, I do believe we all are."

For the first time, Tate agreed with the man.

Larimore looked over Tate's shoulder. "If you want to get the best for the taking, you'd better start searching the bodies."

Tate ignored him, turned, and stopped in mid-step. The dead soldier he had shot was still holding something to his chest. It wasn't death that stunned Tate, it was the young face—a face that had yet to meet razor, an innocent face. Although he wore the gray of a Confederate soldier, he was no man of war. He was a young boy. His uniform didn't fit; the shirt hung loose and bore the dark brown stain of blood shed earlier—most likely from another soldier who had died in a field hospital.

"He's just a boy."

"What's that, Lieutenant?" Larimore had returned to probing the jacket of the dead man.

"We killed a boy. Can't be more than fourteen years old."

"Boy or no boy, you wear those grays and you can expect someone is going to try to kill you."

Tate lowered himself to one knee. The lad's face projected serenity and calm, as if he had died in his own bed, with his mother close by. Tate wiped away bloody drool from the boy's chin.

The lad's eyes opened at the touch.

Tate swore and shot to his feet.

The boy coughed. Frothy pink fluid bubbled between his lips.

"Don't talk, son. It'll only make things worse." Tate figured the boy had only minutes to live.

"Take the Bible." The words were faint.

"Save your strength." Tate knelt again and rested a hand on the lad's shoulder.

The boy forced words from pale lips. "A dry rain cometh if you do not take the book." The words could barely be called a whisper. The young Confederate pushed the Bible toward Tate with shaking hands.

"I have no want of the book, boy."

"The book has want of you."

Tate took it. The lad closed his eyes. Air gurgled from the hole in his chest. The air stopped with the final breath. It was over.

"A poor way to die. I'm sorry it had to be you." Tate paused. "I'm sorry it had to be me."

He rose, took a ragged breath, and addressed his men, who continued to search the bodies for anything of value. "Move out. Their own will bury them." He turned his back on the four corpses that, minutes before, had been men with lives and loves. After four years of war, maybe they were the lucky ones.

JEREMIAH TATE

chapter 1

I T STOOD LIKE a decaying monument of a bygone age, a time when travelers wearied from hours on the road took refuge within its stucco and wood-trimmed walls. That was before the freeway had diverted traffic from Nevada Avenue, giving travelers a choice of newer, less dingy places to stay. A World War II–era building, the Galaxy Motel had aged poorly.

Gary Brandon parked his Triumph motorcycle next to a chain-link fence that the wind had decorated with papers, grocery bags, and other trash.

He felt sullied just being there.

Glass from a broken whiskey bottle, sand and grit scattered by years of desert wind crunched beneath Gary's feet as he walked across the parking lot and made his way to room 12. Cigarette smoke that permeated the wood trim and walls seeped through the partially opened window. Gary paused at the door and raised his hand to knock. The door was as battered and beaten as the man he had seen yesterday, the man he knew to be inside the room. The knob looked loose, and a heel print clung to the door's faded paint, telling a story of some previous violence. The rattling of an air

19

conditioner sucking hot desert air couldn't mask the loud snoring that filtered through the cracks around the door frame. Daniel Huff—Uncle Daniel—was sleeping off a bender.

Gary lowered his hand and considered walking away. Not wanting to wake Uncle Daniel seemed as good a rationalization as any. Instead, he shifted the cardboard box he held under one arm, raised his hand again, and knocked hard.

The snoring stopped.

Gary pounded the door.

He heard a muted "What? Huh? Hold . . . hold on a minute."

The groaning protests of old bedsprings leeched outside. Gary straightened and waited for the door to open. He was the tall one in his family and the only one sporting blond hair. He looked nothing like his uncle, who was short, dark, wore weathered skin like an old suit, and had a big nose that appeared to be pecked over by birds. More than appearance separated the two. Gary had finished college and anticipated his future; Uncle Daniel had never gone to college and drank his future from dark-colored bottles with names like JACK DANIEL'S and WILD TURKEY on the label.

Gary chastised himself for thinking such thoughts about a family member, but his uncle gave him little reason not to. He didn't know his uncle well; perhaps if he did, he'd have more to go on than brief encounters and tainted, whispered rumors from his mother and other family members.

The door opened, and Uncle Daniel winced at the bright day. He took a step back. So did Gary, pushed by the pungency of booze and unwashed skin. Daniel's eyelids cupped syrupy fluid, and webbed red capillaries, ruptured by forty years of whiskey, spread across his cheeks. He ran a hand through oily, matted, gray hair that bore a tarnished halo of nicotine yellow and scratched the black and gray stubble dotting his chin.

"Gary. Good to see you, and that's the truth. Real good, son. I was hoping you'd come by today." Uncle Daniel paused and lowered his head, like a dog caught snitching food from the dining room table. "I'm real sorry about your graduation party last night. It was last night, wasn't it?"

"No problem, Uncle Daniel. I'm glad you came by."

"Your mom didn't seem all that glad to see me." Daniel massaged his wide belly through what had once been a white T-shirt. A stain from an unknown red sauce marred the area over his sternum. "She's never been happy to see me."

"May I come in?" Gary had to force the question through his lips.

Daniel stepped to the window and pulled open the curtain, allowing sunlight to invade the self-imposed darkness. A disgusting odor of curdled milk fermenting in an open carton on the dresser filled the room.

Daniel moved to the bed and swept a pile of rumpled clothing to the side. He sat and nodded to the room's one chair, situated next to a table tattooed with knife-drawn graffiti and cigarette burns. Gary set the cardboard box on the table and lowered himself onto the seat. The chair wiggled beneath him, and he wondered if his next seat would be on the floor.

Daniel pointed at the box. "I see you brought my gift back. It's not polite to return a gift."

"Uncle Daniel, I need you to tell me how you got this stuff. It must be worth a lot."

Daniel gave a nod. "It is, and it's all yours now."

"Where did you get this?"

His uncle rubbed his face, making a sound that reminded Gary of sandpaper on wood, and yawned. "I found it. That's treasure, and I want you to have it."

"Found it where?"

"Saudi Arabia. Back when I was working the oil rigs. Good money, miserable work. That's when I came by it. I found a ruby, too, but I sold it off; drank it away in a month's time. Dumb thing to do, but that's me: patron saint of stupidity. I knew if I sold any more of that stuff, I'd just guzzle the proceeds. I wanted to keep the rest as my retirement fund." He chuckled at the last words, as if they had been the punch line to a joke. "It's better that you have it."

"If you need it for retirement, then why give it to me?"

Daniel shifted his gaze to the stained carpet, as if his life had been written on the worn green shag. "It's not every day you graduate from college, boy."

Gary removed the lid and gazed into the box, as he had done a dozen times since Uncle Daniel pressed the whole thing into his hands the previous night at the graduation party. Nothing had changed. The box still held an odd assortment of objects: what looked like an ancient gold Egyptian scarab, a gold ring, and a Bible with a hand-scribbled date of 1751 on the inside front cover.

Gary reached inside and gently removed the gold ring. He held it up and said, "It's real gold. It might be some kind of ancient Egyptian artifact." He suddenly wasn't sure he had been told the truth, at least not the whole truth. "Uncle Daniel, I need to know how you got this stuff. I'm not sure I should keep it."

Again, Daniel hesitated before speaking, narrowed his eyes, and tilted his head to one side, as if by doing so memories would slide into place. "Okay, let me see if I can tell this." He shifted his weight on the creaky bed and leaned forward. "Several years ago, I was working in Saudi Arabia for Arabco Oil Company. One day I was heading back to Tabuk, driving my Jeep across the desert. I hate that desert, Gary. I really do. It's unforgiving and has no mercy for anyone but those born there. Anyway, I was doing my best to find an asphalt road. I got lost. To make things worse, my Jeep overheated and I needed to let it cool down. The sun was a scorcher, a real cooker. Sitting in the Jeep exposed to that sun would have fried my brain.

"I saw a cave on the side of a hill and figured I'd make use of the shade. I stopped the Jeep, left the radiator hissing, and made for the cave. As I neared the cave, I noticed an old water well. In Arabia there are hand-dug wells that date back centuries. There it was—just a hole in the ground rimmed with rocks. A rope hung down the gullet of the thing, just like you'd expect. I pulled it up and found a water-filled camel's stomach tied to the end."

"A camel's stomach?" Gary struggled not to make a face.

"Yeah, that's how they do it. I took the bag and made my way to the cave. The cave was bigger than I expected. I took a long hit off of the water bag. It tasted gamey, but I didn't complain."

He paused as if waiting for Gary to say something. When he didn't, Daniel continued. "I poured some of the water over my hair and face. It dripped on the sandy cave floor, washing away a thin layer of sand no bigger than the size of my hand."

Once more, his eyes focused on something in the past and many miles away. He licked his lips as if tasting the water he'd described. Gary gave him the time he needed to recall the next event.

Daniel chuckled. "Something shiny caught my eye. Gold shines like nothing else, Gary. There ain't no mistaking it."

Uncle Daniel's voice weakened as he unfolded the events. Gary had always considered him untrustworthy, and his mother's comments had led him to believe that his uncle loved exaggeration, but now the man's body language, tone, and distant gaze belied all that. It could be a wild tale made all the more wild by years of whiskey lubrication, but somehow Gary began to believe what he was hearing.

Silence reigned for a second, then Daniel came to, blinked several times, and reached for a dirty glass on the nightstand—a tumbler with two inches of amber liquid. After two long sips, Daniel fumbled for a pack of Marlboros and a battered Bic lighter. Seconds later a gossamer blue cloud rose to a ceiling already yellowed with nicotine. Gary hated the smell of cigarette smoke.

After clearing his throat, Daniel slipped into the past again. "I didn't move. Not at first. I looked out the cave opening to make sure no one was watching me. I felt a little paranoid. I reached into the damp sand and plucked out that gold ring you have. I pushed more sand to the side. An inch away from the ring, I touched the ruby I told you about and next to it the bug made with gold."

"The Egyptian scarab."

"That's right. The gold scarab." He shook his

head. "I couldn't believe it then, and I barely believe it now. I don't remember getting on my hands and knees, but there I was, pushing dirt around like a kid in a sandbox, wondering what else I might find. I found that old Bible a couple inches deeper down. I don't know what a Christian Bible was doing in a cave in Saudi Arabia, but then, I don't know what the other stuff was doing there, either. I just kept searching. I figured someone had buried these things in a real hurry."

The next words came as a whisper. "I dusted off the Bible and opened it to the first page. It was full of old letters and notes." He fell silent for several seconds. "On the first page, I saw words that looked to me like they had been written by someone's finger—a finger dipped in blood." Daniel looked at Gary with an expression that asked, *Is this too much to believe?*

Gary retrieved the Bible from the cardboard box and opened it. His eyes fell on the only words that matched his uncle's description.

KILLED HERE WITH FREDERICK—
FOUND IT ALL
EMILY IN WHITE—R.C. COOPER, 1921

"I searched the rest of the cave, but that's all I found. It left me pretty confused. How do a Bible and a ring and a ruby and that scarab thing get buried in a cave in the middle of the desert? It beats me."

"What did you do next, Uncle Daniel?"

"Ah, you're getting interested now. I tucked those things in my pockets and the Bible down my shirt and strolled back to my Jeep. I returned the water bag to the well, but not until I made sure the radiator and my canteen was plenty full. The Jeep started just fine and I pulled away. I hit the gas so hard it almost tore the hide off the tires. It took me an extra hour and lots of luck, but I found the asphalt road I had been looking for."

"This R.C. Cooper, whoever he is, must have buried these things and died nearby." An uncomfortable emotion churned in Gary. The story presented a problem. "These are not yours to give."

"Not mine to give? I found them; I can give them away if I please."

Gary leaned back in the chair and rubbed his forehead. "These things belong to the family of R.C. Cooper, not to us."

Daniel's frown furrowed like freshly tilled farmland. He reached for the glass with the amber fluid. His hand shook.

Gary spoke softly. "We have to do everything we can to find out who R.C. Cooper was. If we don't try, then all we're doing is stealing property that belongs to the man's family . . . assuming he had a family."

Daniel's head swiveled back and forth. "Are you really related to me?"

Gary took a firmer tone. "Uncle Daniel, this is

the right thing to do. It's the right thing for me and for you."

Daniel stubbed out the cigarette with more force than Gary thought necessary. He turned his face to the window.

Gary sighed and looked at the Bible. He flipped through it and let his finger fall on a page in the Gospel of Matthew. "I want to read something to you."

"I ain't much for Bible reading."

"Just listen." Gary tilted the Bible to get light from the window. " 'For what is a man profited, if he shall gain the whole world, and lose his own soul? Or what shall a man give in exchange for his soul?' "

"So?"

"Do you know what it means?"

Daniel grunted. "You're the college boy—you tell me."

"It means that there are things more important than riches and treasure. And for me, it means that before I keep any of this, we are going to do our best to find the true owner."

Daniel took a deep breath and stared into Gary's eyes but said nothing.

"You know I'm right about this."

Tears brimmed in Daniel's eyes. "You should know . . . never mind. It doesn't matter." He waved his hand, as if dismissing the whole conversation.

"What doesn't matter?"

"There's no easy way to say this, but you have to know. I have cancer, Gary."

The announcement punctured Gary's heart. "Cancer?"

"I'm afraid so."

"What kind of cancer?"

"No good kind of cancer, that's for sure. The doctors tell me I got about four months left, give or take. Not that it matters—I've messed my life up pretty good. I always figured I'd die before my time."

Gary rose on shaky legs. "Cancer? Terminal cancer? Is that what they said, Uncle Daniel? Are you sure they used the word *terminal*?" He paced the little room. He had seen his uncle only a handful of times over the years, but despite the man's problems, Gary always felt that hidden inside the rough alcoholic resided a basically good man.

"If you're asking if there might be some kind of mistake, then you can quit asking. I'm dying. No mistake."

Gary returned to the chair and eased himself down. His stomach twisted into a knot. "I'm so sorry, Uncle Daniel. I don't know what to say. Does Mom know?"

"No, and I don't want you telling her, either. I haven't been much of a brother to her. She's got every right to be put out with me. Telling her would only give her one more thing to worry about." He raised the glass to his lips and drained the remaining contents. "This is just between us, Gary. And I mean everything. Not just my sickness, but the stuff in that box I gave you. That's just between us. Got it?"

Gary "got" it all right, but he didn't want it. Still, it was a dying man's wish.

"Yes, I've got it."

chapter **2**

APRIL 9, 1865
UNION CAMP SOMEWHERE IN VIRGINIA
EARLY EVENING

SCORES OF UNION campfires dotted the rutted, muddy dirt road. The sun had settled behind the blue hills, and the evening took on a soothing quiet after a long day of avoiding sniper fire and listening to cannon rumble in the distance. They walked past a line of twenty corpses, whose bare, marble-white feet stuck out from under bloody canvas tarps. A few men were sitting by a small pile of boots and worn shoes, trying to find a pair better than their own.

"Where are we?" Tate asked the men.

"Doesn't matter much, does it?" one of them answered.

"No, I guess it doesn't."

Larimore stepped to Tate's side. "You know, if

you give me that there Bible, I bet I can trade it for some tobacco."

Tate glanced at Larimore. He knew what the corporal meant—he could coerce some fresh-faced recruit in camp to buy the book for more than tobacco.

"I guess I'll just be keeping it for now, Corporal."

"Suit yourself, Lieutenant. I'm just trying to do you a favor. You thinking of selling that book yourself, or you just bothered about shooting the boy?"

"I'm thinking about being alone."

"Cheer up, Lieutenant. We made it to a camp, and it's a Union camp at that." Larimore chuckled.

Something caught Larimore's attention and he moved away. Tate was glad to be rid of him.

They straggled single file into the camp. Now a man poked a stick into a struggling campfire rimmed with rocks. The smoky fire licked at a damp limb that Tate assumed had been foraged from the wet forest. All the other fires in camp were spitting columns of sparks into the night. Tate had passed several of those fires and noticed stacks of split-rail fencing, probably stripped from a nearby abandoned farm. Judging by the damp logs in this fire, there hadn't been enough wood to go around.

Three men surrounded the smoldering glow, waiting for the wood to catch. Each of the soldiers goaded the struggling flames with sticks. Tate would have preferred one of the more successful fires, but cold men had left no room for him and his men. This would have to do.

"Mind if we share the warmth?" he asked.

"What warmth?" A short man with his arm resting in a bloodied sling scowled.

Tate rubbed his hands together. "It's been a long, wet day, and we're a bit chilled."

The others said nothing. Tate took that to mean yes. His men shouldered in and raised palms to the struggling flames. For a long while, no one spoke.

Tate couldn't ignore the recurring image of the boy clutching his chest, then falling to the ground. He couldn't scrub away the boy's dimming voice or exorcise the strange words. Tate took the Bible from his jacket and scraped off some dried mud. He looked at the group, studying their empty, dark expressions as they stared into the meager flames.

"I shot a boy today," he began. "He was young, about fourteen. His dying words were, 'A dry rain cometh if you do not take the book.' Anyone know the sense of it?"

One of the other men, a captain with a gray-peppered beard and a patch over his eye, held out a hand and snapped his fingers. "Give it here, Lieutenant. I'll have a go at it. I'm a pastor by trade and a soldier by need." He gently took the Bible and held it like it was a familiar thing. He leaned into the weak firelight, flipping through the pages.

Tate waited, chewing at an annoying chunk of dry skin peeling from his lower lip.

The captain held the Bible close to his one good eye. Seconds later he said, "Here it is: book of Amos, chapter four. The passage speaks of God bestowing life-giving rain to those who follow Him and sending no rain to those that don't. Seems plain enough: a dry rain is coming to all that do not return to God."

The captain studied the passage again. "The Bible has many such stories. The Lord gives rain as a blessing and withholds it as a curse. It seems the boy was giving you warning that you should repent and follow the Good Book or your life will be as a dry rain. Since they were the boy's last earthly words before the Almighty carried him home to glory, I'd ponder mightily on what he asked of you, that's for sure."

Tate took the Bible back and stared at the page.

The captain asked, "You know the Lord, son? You a praying man?"

"I prayed once when my wife and son were sick with the pox. I prayed long and hard, but the Lord didn't see fit to listen then, so I don't see that He has any want to listen now."

"Well, this boy you killed seems to have a different take on things. Dry rain is a bad thing, Lieutenant."

"After this war, I won't be putting hand to plow ever again, so I don't see that I have a need of rain—dry or wet."

The captain frowned. "Maybe that boy was God's own prophet. Ever think of that, Lieutenant? I'd take care about dismissing him so lightly."

Tate held out the Bible. "I don't want this book. If you're a preacher man, you need this Bible more than me."

"Seems that the boy you killed sees it as you owning it, or maybe that the Bible now owns you." The captain returned to goading the fire with his stick. "It's a terrible thing to dishonor the last wish of a dead man—especially if the dead man was killed by you."

Tate grew weary of talking and started to put the Bible back under his coat. A thin rectangular photograph slid from its hiding place and fell to the ground. He picked it up and held the portrait toward the fire. The flickering light danced on the image, like sunlight on the ripples of a pond.

Centered in the photograph sat a middle-aged woman of humble dress. Her dark hair was pinned in a tight bun. Her hands were folded in her lap and resting on a Bible. Tate wondered briefly if the Bible in the photograph was the same as the one he held. He turned the image over. Someone had penned the words: *Emma Bell, Petersburg, Virginia, 1859.*

The simple words landed heavy in his chest. He

held the photograph of the dead boy's mother. Depression, darker than the night, enfolded him in cold fingers.

A noise from down the road rolled through the trees. It sounded like a cheer. The soldiers around the fire turned as a man astride a horse galloped their way, weaving around wagons, men, and fires, shouting all the while. At first, Tate couldn't make out the words, but as the rider drew close, he heard it clearly. He just didn't believe what he was hearing.

"It's over, boys! It's all over!" the man bellowed. "Lee surrendered to General Grant at Appomattox Court House today." His voice was raspy and failing. Tate could only guess how long the messenger had been shouting the news.

Tate knew they were close to Appomattox Station. He trotted to the man on the horse and seized the beast's bridle. He gazed into the smiling face of the messenger. "Say it again, Sergeant. Did I hear you right?"

The messenger coughed into his gloved hand. "You heard me right, Lieutenant. We'll be sleeping in our own beds and eating Momma's sweet corn bread real soon."

Tate released his hold, and the messenger galloped through the camp, heralding the news. Cheer after cheer went up.

Tate didn't cheer. He thought of the four men who hadn't needed to die. He thought of the boy.

Not only had they died on the last day of the war, they had died in vain.

He looked at the picture . . . and at the Bible. He thought of the boy's final words and wondered what it all meant.

chapter 3

MAY 23, 1865
WHITE OAK ROAD, PETERSBURG, VIRGINIA

SQUINTING AGAINST THE glare of a late spring afternoon sun, Lieutenant Tate pulled his horse to a walk and rode slowly to a pair of shirtless boys gathering bricks from the rubble-strewn road. A diminutive, narrow-chested man, with wide eyes and a trickle of sweat escaping from beneath his wide-brimmed parson's hat, stood to the side.

"Need lots of brick," the man snapped. "The faster you work, the sooner you get done."

Tate reined his horse to a stop and slipped from the saddle.

The boys paused to scrutinize Tate, then returned their attention to tossing bricks into the wheel-barrow.

"Afternoon," Tate said, touching the brim of his worn and dusty hat.

The parson didn't return the greeting. Instead, he looked Tate over as if he could read the visitor's life story printed on his blue uniform. "Going to build back the church—and it may even last a spell if y'all don't cannon us again." The clergyman scowled.

"War's over, Parson."

The preacher dabbed at his sweaty brow with a red kerchief. "Some wars are never over. What's your business in our town?"

Before answering, Tate turned and untied a canvas sack from his saddle and removed the Bible he had accepted from the fallen Confederate boy. He opened it and handed the portrait to the pinch-faced man.

"Emma," the clergyman murmured after only a glance. "Emma Bell." He handed the daguerreotype back to Tate. He offered nothing more.

"And?"

"What do you want with the widow Bell, eh?"

"I have something that belongs to her." Tate offered nothing more.

The preacher eyed Tate again. "Never guessed Emma knew a Yankee." He appeared to weigh his thoughts, then said cautiously, "Well, she's up this road a mile or so." He motioned north. "Brown brick house. Leaning arbor out front. Can't miss it."

"I thank you, Preacher."

"A word of advice." The preacher's expression softened. "I suggest you be careful riding around in that uniform. The good Lord may be quick to forgive us our transgressions, but people around here aren't very tolerant of Yankees."

Tate smiled. "Don't work them boys too hard. They might grow up to be some of your deacons." Tate returned to the saddle and jabbed his heels into the horse's ribs. A noise caught his ear as the horse cantered off—the sound made by someone spitting in his direction. He hoped it was one of the boys.

He didn't look back.

The widow Bell's home stood just as described by the parson: a small brick building with an arbor that looked ready to collapse. He tied his mount to the porch rail and made his way up the steps to the front door. The porch groaned softly under his boots. It took a minute for him to find his courage. He had ridden into battles and endured ear-splitting cannon fire, but this frightened him more.

Tate rapped on the door.

A second later he heard footsteps and the slow release of a metal latch. The door opened slightly, allowing a sliver of sunlight no wider than a knife blade to slice into the shadowy recesses of the house. A faint voice crept out. "Leave me alone."

Tate leaned closer. His words came out more like a prayer than a statement. "I'm real sorry to bother you, ma'am. I'm Lieutenant . . . I'm Jeremiah Tate. I've news of your boy."

"My boy's dead. I need no more news of it."

"Yes, ma'am, I know. I was there when he died."

The door creaked open an inch. Daylight painted the woman's face. "What do you mean . . . ?" Her dark eyes widened at the sight of his uniform.

He raised the leather-bound Bible to the gap in the doorway.

The bereaved mother moved a hand to the door's edge. Tate watched her fingers squeeze the sunblistered wood, her bony hand steadying her slight frame. The gap widened. She stared at the black book, the edge of its pages tinged russet from her son's blood. She opened the door the rest of the way and stepped onto the porch, shielding her eyes from the sun's glare.

In the full light of day, Tate could see the toll the war and the loss of a son had taken. She appeared haggard and twenty years older than her picture. To his eye, she was thinner, more ceramic doll than flesh and blood. She wore a black dress and a frayed brown shawl.

The widow looked into his face with an expression he could not describe. Her eyes seemed to burn with anger one second, then cool to forgiveness the next. She looked at him, then the Bible, then at him again. It struck Tate that he gazed upon two women in one body: a mother broken by loss and a woman torn by the same hatred that ripped apart a nation. Time might have helped her reach beyond a heart worn raw with grief, but the unexpected and unwanted presence of someone responsible for her loss—a Yankee soldier—forced the pain to the surface again.

Tate's mind wandered to the men's bodies he

had left for others to bury. He'd reasoned that other Confederates would find the soldiers and do their own a proper burial. It was war, and he had no time for such matters. But what if the dead Rebs were still out there, sprawled among the cornstalks . . . rotting? He fought off a shudder.

Tate just wanted to return the Bible. It seemed the right thing to do—the very *least* he could do. But the woman, gutted by grief, had fixed her full attention on him. It felt as if she had nailed his boots to the boards of the porch.

"I was there when your son was killed." Tate lowered his head. "He died in a battle. My men . . . well, they came upon him and some others . . . and . . . they killed . . ." He closed his eyes and started over. "I'm the one who killed your son, ma'am." Just saying the words skewered his heart.

Tate opened his eyes to see Emma Bell press back against the doorframe. She wilted, like a paper doll left in the rain. "He wrote me and said you'd be coming. I never believed it till now." She seemed to grow weaker with each word. "You. You are *that* Yankee from that cornfield, ain't you?"

A foul taste soured Tate's mouth. "Yes, ma'am. I'm afraid I am."

"I'm doing my Christian best not to hate you, Yankee. That there book you hold teaches that I am supposed to love my enemies, but that commandment goes down bitter right now. I ain't feeling any love." She turned away. "I haven't felt love for a long time."

"I understand, Mrs. Bell. You have every right to hate me. I can't hold that against you."

She shook her head. "What you done to my Elijah . . ." Tears began to well up. "Elijah, he'd be angered fierce at me if he knew how I felt so poorly towards you." She tightened her lips, as if about to offer a faint smile. She didn't. "I'm suspecting you are a good man. I can see you are sore in the heart for what you done, else you wouldn't of come here today. My boy could see that in your eyes and in your soul. Elijah was that kind of a boy to see such a thing. He saw no enemies in blue or gray uniforms—only lost souls that needed harvesting." She moved a hand across her face, pushing away tears.

"Ma'am—I have no words."

"Mr. Tate, my boy, Elijah, didn't die in that cornfield like you think. He died in the home of Jonathan and Beth Crowley, who own the farm where you shot him. Elijah was sorely wounded, but I guess you know that. They thought he might have a chance of living, but he passed on four days after you shot him."

Everything within Tate froze. "Four days? No, ma'am. That can't be. I was certain he was dead. He spoke to me, then I watched him die in that old cornfield."

41

"Yankee, you're wrong—just plain wrong. Oh, Lord above, how I wish it all weren't so."

Tate's heart stopped; his lungs refused to draw air. He stepped to the railing at the edge of the porch and leaned against it. "No. He was dead. If he wasn't, then I left the poor boy . . ." He turned back to her. "No, he was dead, I tell you."

"Mr. Tate, my boy lay in that field for hours until the Crowleys come by and took him to their home. I'm ever in their debt for that." Emma turned her eyes away from the sun-washed day, as if trying to believe it wasn't so. "He must of been told by God Almighty that you would return that Bible."

Tate's stomach cinched and his grip on the Bible slackened. He barely noticed the thud it made on the wood planks. It took the motion of Emma slowly bending to pick it up to pull him back. She rose, holding the worn book in one hand and the copperplate photograph of herself in the other. She studied her image.

"That woman died right along with Elijah. She moves, she breathes, but she's every bit as dead." Rivulets of tears flowed down her cheeks.

She placed the photograph in the Bible, carefully, reverently. "He left school one day and walked along with our troops, carrying this Bible, telling them about the Lord. He was all of fourteen. Too young. Not a man but not a child. I couldn't tell Elijah not to go. I tried, but my words fell on deaf ears. He felt called by God. Not even a mother can question the ways of the Creator. Elijah just knew he had to go. His mind stayed made up. He was a strong-willed boy. Things being the way they were, they would of called him to fight soon enough, I suppose. I figured that having Elijah give our men a word from God was better than him sending a ball of lead into the enemy."

Those last words had the impact of a shot to Tate's chest.

"Your name and town were written on the back. That's how I found you."

As he fumbled for what to say next, Emma turned and retreated into the house, then reappeared an instant later. She held out a piece of paper in a tremulous hand. Tate took it and read.

To the man who kilt me.

The wind blows where it wishes and you hear the sound of it, but cannot tell where it comes from and where it goes.

So it will be with your own life.

You will surely come to find my ma's picture and try to return the Bible to her, but I want you to have the Holy Book and be the wind that carries forth the word of our Lord and be God's messenger as I have been.

It shall be a blessing for all that come to have this book and read its words, for in that day they will surely save lives and give life. But if anyone who has this book and does not follow the Lord, then I fear a dry rain cometh.

Elijah Bell
April 13, 1865

The handwriting was clear and steady, all except the signature. That came from a trembling hand. Someone had helped him pen the letter—Beth Crowley, Tate assumed—and young Elijah had signed it himself.

Tate lifted his eyes and dredged his mind for the right words to say. He failed. He had shot many a man in battle and had never been concerned about it—until now. He had taught his men that "any fretting about killing only slows a man's finger to the trigger." Now he grieved more than he'd thought possible.

"The men he traveled with gave him a name," Emma said with a glimmer of pride. "They called him the Bell Messenger. I know he was real proud of it, but he was most proud that he was able to preach the gospel and comfort many souls before they died." She turned away from Tate and stepped back in the house. "The Bible is yours, Mr. Tate," she said. "Elijah gave it to you and it would be wrong of you not to take it. You will surely have a dry rain come—my boy was a prophet of God and told you those words as a blessing and a warning." She turned back to him and held out the Bible.

44

"You take it now. You take it and the letter and go."

Tate took it in hands that never before had known trembling.

Emma Bell closed the door behind her. Seconds later, Lieutenant Jeremiah Tate heard the muffled sobs of pain only a mother torn with grief could cry.

chapter 4

GARY STOOD TO leave the motel room. His uncle eyed the bottle on the nightstand. When Gary reached the threshold, he glanced back to see Daniel nimbly unscrewing the metal cap.

Returning to the glaring sun, Gary slid on a pair of sunglasses and walked across the parking lot to his motorcycle. His mind was numb with the talk of treasure and dying. What to do now?

He slung his leg over the bike and sat, lost in thought. The sun scorched the pavement. Sweat spread across the back of his shirt.

He opened the box and poked at the objects inside, trying to believe the story he had been told and finding it hard. He removed the old Bible and thumbed through the weathered pages once more, stopping at an old, yellowed letter. Carefully unfolding it, he read. The tragedy of the message touched him, as did the courage of the writer. Gary couldn't imagine writing a note to the man who had mortally wounded him, let alone encouraging him to undertake a godly mission.

He put back the letter as he found it and flipped through more pages. He saw several handwritten notes and dates. Most were names with the birth and death dates of previous owners scrawled with different quill tips—strange, unknown letters in different handwriting styles and ink colors. The dates reached as far back as the 1700s, in England, and ended with R.C. Cooper's death message written in blood.

Gary returned the Bible and replaced the lid on the mysterious objects. He had an uncanny feeling that somehow these items would change his life.

Four hours later, Gary sat at the desk in his bedroom at his mother's home, studying the notes and letters in the old Bible. He had little to go on. The letter from someone named Elijah Bell seized his attention. Bell seemed as good a place to start as any.

He dialed the county recorder's office in Petersburg, Virginia, a number he'd received from long-distance information. Two transfers later, a woman with a soft and pleasant voice asked how she could help him.

"My name is Gary Brandon, and I'm trying to locate a man named Elijah Bell. He may have lived in your county and possibly owned property there."

"You said, 'may have.' Do you mean to say that this person no longer owns property?"

"His family might. I don't know. The Bell I'm looking for lived in your area in the 1860s."

There was a pause. "That's a long time ago, Mr. Brandon. Such records are not easy to find."

"Yes, ma'am, I know, but I thought local governments kept that kind of information in their archives."

"Yes, we do. You wouldn't believe the kinds of records we have."

"Then you'll be able to help me."

"I'm afraid not, Mr. Brandon. First off, I'd need more information than the name Elijah Bell. The real problem, however, is the time such a search would involve. I'd have to do a hand search, and we're a little too shorthanded here for me to be gone from my desk that long. No, I don't think my supervisors would appreciate that."

"I know I'm asking a lot," Gary said, "but the information is very important."

"All information is important, Mr. Brandon. So is time." She paused again. He got the impression she had covered the mouthpiece with her hand. He heard muffled conversation but couldn't make out the words. She came back on. "Some people hire researchers to comb the archives. You could do that."

"How would I do that?" Gary tried to keep the frustration from his voice.

"It just so happens, my daughter has done that kind of work. She's a history major at the college. Smart as they come."

"Mother!"

The new voice was clear and young. Gary assumed the speaker stood in the same office as the clerk.

"Your daughter?"

"Yes. We were just about to go to lunch."

"And I'm starving. Let's go."

Gary started to speak again but heard, "Here, you talk to him."

A second later a woman with a decidedly younger voice said, "This is Yvonne Kiel. I'm sorry about my mother."

"Don't be. She's just trying to help."

"Maybe. How can I help you?"

Gary repeated what he had told the clerk. The woman on the other end of the phone listened patiently. "I charge one hundred dollars to do a search like that. Does that sound fair?"

"I'm sure it's fair, but I don't have much money. I just graduated from college. I'm afraid I'm not at my peak earning potential. In fact, I'm not even employed yet."

"I'm sorry to hear that. Maybe we can work together another time."

"Wait. Don't hang up. Look, just listen to the

story for a minute, then we can talk about money."
Before she could object, Gary poured out the story
of the Bible found in Saudi Arabia, then added,
"You're in college; you know how it is."

He heard a long sigh. "Okay, I'll do it for fifty
bucks, but I can't go lower."

"Thank you. You won't regret this."

She chuckled. "I've heard that from men
before."

chapter 5

FOUR YEARS.

Too long. Much too long.

Tate pulled the reins, bringing his mare to a stop,
and gazed at his home for the first time in four miserable years. A forlorn chimney rose from the
charred remains left by looters, squatters, or other
culprits known only to God.

He slid from his mount and released the reins,
letting the horse chew freely in the knee-deep
grass. After walking across the pasture, he stopped
at a tiny mound and let his gaze fall to a weathered
plank lying across the grave. Removing his hat, he
stared at the board and the dim letters he had
painted so long ago. Sun, wind, and rain had nearly
obliterated the words, but Tate didn't need to read

them to know what was there. Years of weather couldn't erase the names from his mind. He pulled the weathered board from a tangle of weeds and hammered it back into the soil with a rock.

His wife and young son lay buried beneath that board, having died on the same day years earlier, two more victims of the smallpox. Before laying them to rest, Tate had placed his son alongside his wife on a canvas tarp and placed her arms around the boy. He'd then wrapped them and buried them. After tamping the dirt smooth, he had set the grave marker facing east to receive the morning sun. Three days later, Fort Sumter was cannoned, and he had left to enlist in the Union Army. There was nothing left on the farm to hold him.

He turned to the remains of what had once been the place he called home. For a brief time, the charred remains disappeared, replaced by the clapboard house he had constructed with his own hands. A woman with fawn-colored hair, blue eyes, and a smile that dimmed the sun stood on the narrow porch, an infant bundled in her arms.

The next second the image was gone.

Tate slipped to one knee and placed the palm of his hand flat against the cool sod. He looked to a slate-colored sky and whispered, "Here lies the only love I will ever know, and You took them." He closed his eyes. "But I pray to You, if there is such a thing as prayer, that You will not fight me anymore. I'm tired and only want to go far away from here. I want a new start. I will be selling this place and leaving for good, so take care of my family here . . . When I go, I'd be obliged if You would not find the need to follow."

In the following days, he sold his farm to his neighbor, a Mennonite with six boys who didn't fight in the war, because they believed God was "most against it." From the farm that was no longer his, Tate headed for New York City to catch a ship. The newspapers ran ads from the railroads. They needed men of all abilities in California to build a railroad that would stretch across America.

If he had his way, he would become one of them.

JULY 24, 1865
NEW YORK CITY

On the day of his departure, Tate climbed the gangplank of the SS *Eureka*, moored at the Hudson River shipping berth on North Moore Street, his only possessions stuffed in a canvas sack. Minutes earlier, he had given his horse away to a chance-met boy standing by the dock.

"This is a good horse," he'd declared. "She's been with me the whole war and limps some from taking grapeshot at Shiloh, but she'll walk the day and never come to slow."

He'd placed the reins into the surprised lad's hand, then gently scratched the horse's forehead. "This here boy's a bit lighter in the saddle than me and won't be as much a bother." He hoisted the canvas sack over his shoulder, turned, and started for the gangplank.

Within the hour, the *Eureka*'s furnace was fired red hot, the boilers sending up tumbling black smoke from the two stacks located fore and aft. The people gathered on the docks waved hats, handkerchiefs, and parasols while shouting their good-byes over the occasional shrill whistle blast. Although most smiled, their positive expressions could not hide the fear Tate knew many felt—the fear of never seeing their loved ones again. For some, he imagined that fear would come true.

The only boat that Tate had ever been on was the flat-bottomed, rear-paddle wheeler that had ferried him to Pittsburgh Landing at the Battle of Shiloh. The water then was shallow and muddy, but the ocean he was about to steam over would be deep blue, with a horizon that stretched forever.

The engine gained steam, and the two enormous side-mounted paddle wheels began to turn. Tate felt a vibration crawl through his feet, up his legs, and into his chest. Crewmen cast off lines and the boat slipped from the dock and into the cold, green, current-driven waters of the Hudson River. It was the start of a grand adventure, and for the first time in years, Tate smiled.

Passengers dressed in finery strolled along the deck, vying for an early social presence. By late afternoon, a cutting easterly wind raked across the river. The spinning side wheels labored to press the ship's bulk through mounting swells. Passengers hurried to their cabins. Tate had no doubt they were pulling chamber pots close to green faces.

Unlike most of the other passengers, Tate felt no ill effects from the unfamiliar motion of the ship. Instead, he felt content. Passengers hid in their cabins or retched over the rail. All were too busy to bother him.

For several hours, he stood on the forward deck watching the churning sea, but as the sun sank into a clump of pink clouds on the western horizon, exhaustion took hold. Since becoming a soldier he had not slept well, and when he did sleep, fitful dreams played in his mind. But here there were no fire-spitting cannons on the horizon, no rifle sights trained on him by an unseen foe. That night he slept soundly for the first time in more than four years.

In the following weeks, the *Eureka* steamed around the Florida peninsula and across the Gulf of Mexico. The vessel stopped briefly in Panama to take on supplies, but a cholera epidemic kept everyone confined to the ship. The captain hugged the coast, passing Rio de Janeiro, and by the second month at sea they had rounded South America's icy Cape Horn and started the long final push north for San Francisco Bay.

For two months, Tate kept to himself, hardly

offering a word to any passenger. He knew the other travelers considered him odd and rude, but he didn't care. Some of the unmarried women offered a smile, but he didn't give as much as a nod in return. Hour after hour, he sat on the forward winch cowling, inhaling the salt-laced spray from the pounding hull, a spray that slowly washed away the stench of war that had clung to him.

A new life awaited him. At least he hoped so.

chapter **6**

SEPTEMBER 26, 1865
OFF THE WEST COAST OF CENTRAL AMERICA

TATE LOWERED HIMSELF into a slatted deck chair and watched as the steamy jungle of Central America passed by the starboard side. He let his eyes draw in the deep greens of trees and bushes, none of which he could name. The tropical sun that normally warmed the humid air and baked Tate's skin seemed to be napping. The air had turned cool, cool enough for Tate to wear his coat.

Minutes passed in leisure and he was happy to let them go. So far the trip had been medicinal for his tormented mind. Being somewhere where no one knew him or his past proved liberating.

With no idea how much time had passed by, Tate opened the thick black book that rested on his lap. Aside from finding the photo in the Bible, he had not bothered to open it since his visit to the widow Bell. He didn't know why, but he felt the need to carry it with him on his frequent visits to the deck. He sat in the same chair, at the same place he always sat, and stared at the undulating sea. Maybe it was boredom, maybe it was some unseen inner call, but he held the Bible in his big hands and felt comfort in it.

He flipped through the pages, recognizing the names of a few of the books, ones he'd heard in his infrequent visits to church as a boy. Page gave way to page, but Tate read none of the words. Minutes rolled into an hour as Tate shifted his eyes from page to coastline to ocean to Bible.

The day changed with the passing hours. Already dim skies grew dark and sullen. Bruise-tinted clouds cast deep shadows on the ship. What had been a gentle breeze became short, sharp gusts. Tate appreciated the change. He was changing everything in his life, so why shouldn't the weather be as fickle?

"You a preacher man?" The voice, barely perceptible over the singing wind brushing through spars and rigging, came from behind Tate. He didn't need to look to know that it belonged to a child.

Tate turned and saw a young girl wearing a summer dress and a cranberry-colored bonnet. It was an awkward moment. Tate held no social graces and he could not recall the last time he had spoken to a young girl.

"Excuse me?"

"My name's Ruth Stiles. Are you a reverend?"

"No, missy. I ain't no reverend."

The girl tilted her head. "Then why are you holding a Bible? It's not Sunday."

Tate considered the black book. "I'll admit it's an odd thing to do."

The girl fidgeted and held up a thick book with a worn cover. "I'm reading *The Arabian Nights*. My father bought it for me. Someday I will go to Egypt and see the desert."

Tate studied Ruth's smiling face. "Ain't you a little too young to read?"

"I'm not young. I'm eight years old and I read all the time. My momma taught me to read before I went to school. The teachers taught me more about reading. I like reading. I like school. Did you like school?"

Tate feared that the girl would jabber the day away, so he reached in his coat pocket and removed a thick cut of bread he had taken from the galley. He handed the slice to the girl, then pointed to the sky. "I bet those white gulls would be most grateful for something to eat."

Ruth grinned, took the bread, and ran to the railing. Tucking her book under one arm, she pulled chunk after chunk off the bread and flung it over the side. Occasionally a gull would snap a piece in the air, but most were content to retrieve the offerings from the churning water. As he watched her, he felt an unusual sensation on his face: a smile.

Over the next half hour, the wind rose in intensity, fluctuating from breezes to gusts that raked through his hair and fluttered the pages in the open Bible. Tate glanced at Ruth, who had moved from the front rail to the side rail near the wheelhouse and where a freight wagon bound for Sacramento stood lashed to the deck. Ruth leaned against the rail and stared into the green water. The gulls that had circled her head minutes before had disappeared.

Movement on the deck drew Tate's attention from the child. Crew members scurried about moving wooden chairs, spittoons, and tables inside the main hold.

The ship pitched up, then to the side. The wind continued to grow in intensity. The sea tumbled, tossing white mist into the air. The already gray sky darkened faster than Tate thought possible.

He studied the faces of the crew. He had seen the same dread on the faces of soldiers preparing for battle . . . as they watched the enemy move large cannons into place. Lightning scratched across the sky. The air thickened with the smell of brine borne on wind-driven mist. The ocean grew more forceful with each rising swell.

A handful of passengers remained on deck. Most had gone below when the wind picked up.

"Excuse me, sir." Tate gazed into the face of a young crewman. "The captain has asked that all passengers return to their rooms. There's a storm ahead."

Tate rose. "You expecting it to be big?"

"There's nothing to worry about, sir. Storms come up along here this time of year. Everything is going to be fine." But the sailor's face said something different.

"I ain't worried, son. Just trying to get a handle on what's ahead."

The ship rose in the bow, then dropped a second later.

"Please, sir. If you don't mind—"

"I'm going. I'm going—"

"Ruth." A deep voice called the little girl's name.

Tate looked to where he had last seen the girl. She stood near the rail, her book clutched in her hands. "Here, Father."

Tate watched the man run to the girl. She grabbed the railing to steady her legs on the rolling deck. "We have to go below! We have to go now." He grabbed her arm.

Overhead, sails snapped in the wind. Lightning cracked and the deck pitched again.

Tate started across the deck just as the ship shuddered and cut to port. Tate assumed the captain had ordered the change in direction to better greet the oncoming swells, but the sudden motion sent Ruth and her father to their knees. They struggled to their feet. The girl's knees were bloodied by the rough wood deck.

The ship shuddered again as a large swell slammed against the bow. The craft twisted to one side, then the other. Another wave crashed into the ship, sending earthquakelike jolts down the deck.

The noise of cracking wood cut through the blast of sea and wind. Tate snapped his head around in time to see a starboard cleat rip loose from the deck—a cleat used to secure the freight wagon. A second later, another cleat gave way. The big carriage slipped free and rolled across the slanting deck toward the man and girl.

"Watch it!" Tate sprinted toward the two.

Again the deck rolled and the man staggered backward, his arm extended, stretching for his daughter.

Ruth reached for him. The inches between them became a distance too far to span.

Tate crossed the short space that separated them on legs that struggled against the pitching deck. He shot past the fallen man and seized Ruth around the waist, lifted her from her feet, and yanked her close as the freight wagon bore down on them.

He spun, putting his body between the careening wagon and Ruth, then slipped to the side. The leading corner of the wagon caught Tate on one shoulder, forcing him to turn. Pain shot through him and he wondered if lightning had hit him.

With his other hand, Bible still in his grip, he covered her face, and tried to put as much distance as possible between her and the massive, rolling object. Although a glancing blow, the force of the impact was enough to drive Tate sideways into the wheelhouse wall. He used his body to cushion the impact for Ruth but hit the wall with enough force to drive the air from his lungs.

A crunching squeal rang in his ears as the wagon slammed into the deck structure, fracturing the wood siding and caving in a portion of wall as wide as the wagon itself. As the ship slipped over the crest of a swell and nosed into the wave's trough, the wagon pulled free. Tate struggled not to fall forward. Wood splinters flew through the air, propelled by a gushing hiss. Just then the freight wagon snapped the distant railing, flew over the gunnels, and dropped into the churning sea.

Boiler-driven steam shot from a split pipe, striking Tate and the girl. The scalding mist caught Tate's hand—the hand that was clamped over Ruth's face. Ruth's muffled cry gurgled from beneath Tate's tight hold. He stumbled away from the pierced steam pipe, then fell, still holding Ruth. He landed hard, and his head bounced off the solid teak deck. Something thick and wet matted his hair and moistened his neck.

The dark and angry sky gave way to black.

chapter 7

GARY BRANDON SAT on the edge of his bed in his upstairs bedroom reading the old writing in the margins of the Bible he'd inherited. The reddish-brown cursive print looked odd. The ink flowed from a quill held by a purposeful hand that gave no hint of hurry: *I shall die by a rope, but I hope to someday live again by a cross.* Gary wondered how such simple, brittle symbols of consonants and vowels could relay the mind of the person long after he had died. He thought of his own mortality for the first time in his young life.

He took a pen from his desk, clicked it open, and wrote his own name in the front of the Bible, next to some Chinese letters. He then wrote, *I will find the answers to this riddle. Then I will be able to rest, knowing I have done the right thing.* As he finished writing, he wondered if anyone would read his name and words in the future and what they would think of his strange inscription.

The ringing of the phone downstairs filtered through the door of his room.

His mother shouted up the stairs, "Gary, you have a long-distance call."

He leapt to his feet. This was the call he had been

waiting for. He picked up the extension in his room.

Yvonne's excitement poured through the phone, undiminished by the hundreds of miles that separated her from Gary.

"There was a woman with the same last name you gave me. Emma was her first name. Emma Bell. She lived in Petersburg at the time you indicated."

"Really?"

"Of course, really. I wouldn't waste the money on a long-distance call if I weren't certain. She lived on White Oak Road."

"During Civil War times?" Gary reached for a pad of paper and began making notes.

"As I said, she lived in the time frame you gave me, so yes, during the Civil War. She also bought some land at that time and later deeded it to the city to be used as a park."

"A park?"

"Yes. Well, I went to the park and found a stone monument. It was so overgrown with vines I almost missed it. I pulled away the ivy—and chiseled on the face of it were these words . . . you ready?"

"Yup. I'm writing down everything you say."

"Okay, I'll go slowly: *Elijah Bell fell silent upon the sod as another now carries his sacred rod. It was the words of his final will that Jeremiah Tate be his messenger still. Mother, July 1865.'*"

"Incredible."

"I asked around. No one knows what those words on the stone monument mean."

"I think I do. Listen." Gary took the Bible and plucked out the yellowed note tucked inside. He read it aloud.

Yvonne gasped. "So, if I have this right, someone named Jeremiah Tate killed Emma Bell's son, Elijah. As a memorial to her boy, Emma Bell had those words chiseled on the stone. The question is, who was Jeremiah Tate?"

Gary thought. "I think I may know."

He flipped open the Bible and found the words in flowing brown ink: *The Messenger Jeremiah Tate died June 12, 1866, in San Francisco.* He read the words to Yvonne.

"That's some Bible you have." She fell silent, then said, "I have a university professor who knows everything about the history of this town. His name is Dr. Lester Burke. If anyone can find our Elijah Bell, I'm sure he can. Maybe he can also shed more light on Tate. I'll call him and see if he'll meet with me."

"I'm afraid that's going beyond what my fifty dollars can expect."

"Well beyond, but it's this kind of stuff that turned me into a history major. You've got my curiosity working overtime."

"Should I apologize?"

"Not yet, but keep one handy in case I end up wasting my time."

"I have several ready."

chapter 8

TATE'S EYES FLUTTERED open. He could see the hazy light of the lantern in the hand of a woman. The light swayed in tempo with the roll of the ship. The engines were silent; the only noises were the eerie slap of water against the hull and the creaking moan of timbers grating against each other.

He felt woozy, in pain, and uncertain about where he was. He tried to speak, but his throat was too dry. He licked his chapped lips. A distant roll of thunder told him the storm had passed.

He tried to sit up, but the sudden motion made his head pound and his stomach roil.

"You just stay where you are."

He looked into the face of a woman with delicate features and clear blue eyes. She sat on a chair next to the bunk in which he lay. She returned his gaze. Her red hair rested in a tight roll on the top of her head. She sat on a stool beside him, holding a threaded needle. His aching head oozed blood from the back of his scalp, and he felt its warm stickiness in his hair. He followed her advice.

He touched the back of his head. "I'm bleeding."

"That you are. You should have stayed unconscious a little longer—this is going to hurt most unfavorably."

Pain fogged Tate's mind. "I'm . . . I'm afraid that I'm a little confused."

"That's to be expected. A man's head and a ship's deck were never meant to meet so abruptly. Take a moment, then I'll help you sit up. I can't do this when you're lying down."

"What are you intending with that needle?" His voice was raspy.

"Fixing your busted head. I need to close the wound." She stood. "Give me your arm. I'll pull so you don't have to do all the heavy lifting yourself."

"No, ma'am. I think I can manage well enough." Tate sucked in a lungful of air and slowly pulled himself into a seated position, draping his legs over the edge of the bunk. The room twisted and tilted. He couldn't tell if the motion of the ship or his pounding head caused his queasiness. Everything hurt—especially his head and hands. He struggled to remember what happened. "The storm . . ."

"Mostly gone, but the sea is still having its way with the ship. I think it might let up soon. That's the way squalls work."

"How would you know?" Tate's eyes lost focus.

"Because I've sailed once before. Not this far, but enough to learn a couple of things."

"That a fact?"

"It is." She stood and moved to Tate, pausing just

long enough to catch her balance. "Please lower your head, sir."

Tate did.

"Now turn it to the side so I can reach your wound."

Again he complied. He felt her brace her body against his shoulder, then pinch his split scalp together, then plunge the sewing needle into the hairy flesh. He winced as she slowly pulled the string through his skin and returned the needle a second later for another jab.

Minutes passed in painful slowness, the ship rocking beneath him, and the woman struggling to remain upright while sewing his scalp shut.

Finally, she stepped back. "I told you it would hurt." She withdrew a wet cloth from a pail on the floor. "Here, hold this to your head. It will help some and loosen that dried blood."

"Who are you?" Tate struggled to keep his stomach down.

"My name is Mary Connor." She hoisted a bottle of whiskey from the floor, removed its cork with her teeth, and spat it out. "You may remove the cloth." She poured a stream of stinging alcohol over the wound.

Tate gnashed his teeth. "I could use that whiskey better on this side of my head." He reached to take the bottle and saw bandaged hands. He looked at the wrappings. Pink, swollen, curdled skin pressed out of the bloody cloth strips.

He tried to force the fog from his mind. "What . . . what happened?"

Her answer didn't come immediately. Instead, she picked up Tate's Bible from its resting place on a narrow shelf attached to the wall. She held it close to the candle, as if reading the cover for the first time.

"You were holding this Bible when you snatched that young girl from in front of the runaway wagon." She shifted her gaze from the black cover to Tate's face. "This holy book, along with your hands, became a shield from the escaping steam. It would have disfigured her bad for sure. She got some burns on her neck and on a patch of arm, but her sweet face is as God gave it at birth. If you hadn't had this Bible, the steam would have marred her for life."

Tate's mind drifted to a front porch in Petersburg where he'd read a letter that said, *It shall be a blessing for all that come to have this book and read its words, for in that day they will surely save lives and give life.*

"How is it that you know so much about doctoring?"

"My father was a physician, and I used to help him some in his office."

Tate waited for her to tell the story. She offered no more about her past, and he asked nothing more.

"That Bible you hold—it come to me in . . . an

67

unusual way." He held up his bandaged hands and studied them. "Perhaps you should open it. There's a letter held in its pages."

Mary found the folded paper easily. She removed it and returned the Bible to the narrow shelf.

Tate felt relief when he saw the document. "I just wanted to make sure it was still there and undamaged. Can it still be read?"

"Yes. The steam did it no harm." She held the paper so he could see the writing.

"That's good. That's real good."

Mary turned the document so the letter faced her, then stopped. "I'm sorry. I'm being nosey. I'll put it back."

"No, please read it. I want you to. After all you've done for me, you deserve to know why I carry that book."

Mary bent toward the candle and read aloud, " *To the man who kilt me . . .* '" She halted after reciting Elijah Bell's name. "You killed this man?"

Tate broke eye contact. "Yes, ma'am, in the war—except he weren't no man. He was just a boy."

"Would I be too forward if I asked you to tell me about it?"

"Ain't much to tell, ma'am. He was in the wrong place at the wrong time and in the wrong uniform. Had I known he was a young'un, I wouldn't have taken the shot. I don't make no excuses about it, but . . . I do think about it more than I care to. I suspect I'll be thinking about it the rest of my days." Tate took a deep breath. "You sure you want to hear this? It ain't pretty, and I take no joy in telling it."

Mary returned to her seat. "If you don't mind, sir."

Tate let his eyes drift to the letter Mary held gently in her hands. Ten minutes later the telling was done.

She lifted her gaze. "Boy or not, these are prophetic words. By amazing grace he gave a holy inheritance to you, and now his gift has given life just as he said it would." She dropped her gaze to the document. "You killed a prophet in that cornfield, and now you have become the messenger. You are His anointed one, the messenger of God Almighty."

chapter 9

SEPTEMBER 26, 1865
BELOWDECKS

THE GREEN SEA was still agitated three hours after the storm had passed. Whitecaps danced on the surface. Scores of seasick passengers leaned over the rail as the crew spent the next two hours securing shifted cargo and making repairs to the damaged wheelhouse. They worked with practiced speed and had the ship seaworthy before the sun dipped below the jungle-choked horizon.

Tate was glad to be under way. A large part of him wanted to help with repairs. It didn't feel right for a man to sit around while others worked, but the bandages on his scalded hands reminded him of his injuries, as did the searing pain that came with every move of a finger.

The engines remained off-line for the better part of two days, but that didn't keep the captain from continuing. Under his orders, sailors raised the sails and the ship resumed its course.

Tate spent the next several weeks in his cabin, self-sequestered from crew and passengers. He had no taste for pity and no stomach for the kind of gratitude heaped upon heroes. He had done what he did out of impulse. The war had held his instinct to the whetstone, sharpening it as he had once sharpened his sword.

Mary Connor's daily visits were bittersweet. The times he did venture out of his room, he caught snippets of gossip and facial expressions that said more than words could.

"You shouldn't come to my room," Tate once said to Mary.

"I'll have none of that hogwash. I am here doing what needs to be done. I pay no attention to tongue wagging."

"But, Mary—"

"And I'll not be hearing any buts from you, Mr.

Tate. Now you just let me see those hands of yours."

Every eight hours, Mary removed soiled linen wrappings; cleaned the raw, seeping skin; and applied new bandages. She also took it upon herself to feed him, something he allowed for only a week. After that, he insisted that he could hold a fork on his own. What he didn't admit was the pain the action caused.

Three weeks after the accident, Tate could button his own coat. Never had he dreamed he would consider such an act a significant victory.

NOVEMBER 7, 1865
SAN FRANCISCO BAY

San Francisco Bay glistened under a late-afternoon sun, its waters emerald green and decorated by tiny wind-driven whitecaps. Tate felt glad to be free of his room, free of confining bandages, and free of the ship that had been home for too many weeks. He also felt a great sense of accomplishment in packing his belongings and carrying them topside without help.

A forest of masts and ascending spires of smoke greeted him. Steamers and sailing ships choked the bay. Eager to see family and friends, passengers pressed against the dockside rail as the big ship slid next to the Jackson Street Pier, their eyes scanning the gathered crowd for familiar and long-missed faces.

Tate had no friends or family waiting for him, so he didn't bother to search the throng on the wood pier. Instead, he let his eyes drift along the water that still separated the ship from its place on the dock. This close to the pier, the water bore garbage and discarded waste. It also held a body.

Tate seemed to be the only passenger who saw the corpse bobbing facedown in a tangle of debris and seaweed. The body wore a blue silk tunic. White-soled, black satin shoes stuck out from baggy pants. A long, braided pigtail trailed from the back of a shaved head.

A deckhand who had followed Tate's gaze elbowed him and laughed. "Too many Chinese around here anyway."

Tate didn't respond. He shifted his gaze to three excited boys trying their best to retrieve the body by throwing a rope on it but not having much luck.

Deckhands and their pier-side counterparts pulled the ship to rest alongside the dock and low-ered a wide gangplank in place. Tate took his place in line, made his way to the pier, and waded through the crowd. Before he had finished ten paces, he felt a tug on his pants leg.

"This is to feed the birds." Little Ruth held out a piece of bread, most likely taken from the morning meal. Overhead, gulls sang in piercing screeches.

"Hello, Miss Ruth."

"This bread is for feeding the birds. Just like you taught me."

Tate took the bread and slipped it in his pocket. He smiled. "Thank you. I'll be sure the birds get it."

She looked at his hands. "Do they hurt?"

Tate raised them to his face, then lowered them again. "Some, now and again. They've taken their own sweet time healing, but they're doing all right now."

"My neck is better, too—"

"Ruth." A man ran toward them. He wore an expensive suit.

A woman in a broad, flowing, bustled dress trailed him.

They pushed their way through the crowd until they reached Ruth. Tate recognized the man as Ruth's father. He assumed the woman to be her mother.

"She ain't bothering me none. She's only being polite and returning a favor. You brought her up good."

"I know. It's just that after everything, well, we don't want her out of our sight." His voice came out clear and strong, yet he seemed embarrassed.

"I understand. She's a right fine child."

"Yes, she is." The father took a deep breath. "Do you have children, Mr. Tate?"

"Had. My son and wife died a long time back."

"I'm truly sorry." He broke eye contact, letting his gaze fall to his daughter. She continued to smile at Tate.

Ruth looked at her father. "He says his hands are much better."

He placed a hand on her head. "That's good, my dear. That's very good."

Tate gave the man time to form his words. Ruth's father started to speak, then stopped.

Tate gave a short nod. "I suppose I should be moving on. I wish you and your family well." Tate looked at Ruth. "And you, young missy, don't you forget to feed the birds every now and again."

"I won't."

"Wait," the man said. "I want to apologize to you."

"You owe me no apology."

"We are not ones to be social, Mr. Tate. We are a proud and private family. Ruth here is our only child, and we will always be beholden to you." The man held out his hand and Tate took it. Fresh whole skin met rough and scarred flesh. "I'll never forget what you have done and, with the grace of God, I will in some way repay you."

"Thank you."

"I should have introduced myself. I am Judge William Stiles. This is my wife, Clare. I am to take a position on the bench here in San Francisco. It's a federal appellate court—"

Clare interrupted. "What my husband is trying to say, Mr. Tate, is that we owe you so very much for what you did for our little Ruth. There's no telling what would have happened to Ruth if you hadn't . . ." She began to cry.

"I don't deserve no thanks, ma'am. I just did what a man's supposed to do."

Clare stepped forward and hugged Tate, gently pressing her face into his shoulder. The embrace lasted only a second before she backed away. "We regret not telling you all this sooner. I mean, while you were recovering and all. We should have come by to offer any help we could, but we heard you wanted to be alone."

"We wanted to respect your privacy," Judge Stiles added.

"God bless you, Mr. Tate," Clare said. "May God watch over you as you watched over our Ruth." Clare wiped her cheek with the back of her white-gloved hand.

The couple turned and walked away, Judge Stiles leading Ruth by the hand. Tate caught the eyes of the girl's turned head just as the family melted into the crowd. Ruth waved with her free hand.

Tate resumed his course, finally pushing through the milling throng. A familiar voice stopped him midstep by calling his name.

Mary moved past several dockworkers. She held something in her hand. Behind her walked an elderly Chinese man.

"Mary?"

"Please read this after I have gone." She pressed an envelope into his hand.

"What is it?"

"Don't ask so many questions," she said, like a

mother scolding a child. She would have pulled off the imitation, too, if it hadn't been for her broad, warm smile. "It's a letter that I want you to read in private." She fixed her eyes on his. "Please know that I will always be there for you if need be."

Mary squeezed his wrist, as though trying to communicate something that words could not. She released her grip, leaving the letter in his hand. "You are the prophet now."

Then she turned and walked away. The Chinese man followed.

Nearby, Tate saw an old Mexican woman wearing a red scarf and selling yellow roses. There were only three left. Tate bought them all and sprinted after Mary. He called her name. When she turned, Tate held the tiny bouquet in his brawny fist.

"I hope you like roses." It took a moment before he could say the rest. "I don't know if I will ever see you again, but I thank you for all your help and the doctoring, too."

Mary took the flowers and lifted them to her face. "Can't remember a time I got flowers." She turned them, catching the yellow petals in the sunshine. "One flower will forever remind me of our first meeting, the second will remind me of how God will use your life, and the third will remind me of a day to come when we will meet again."

Then she turned her back on Tate and walked away.

chapter **10**

JUNE 26, 1980
PETERSBURG, VIRGINIA

YVONNE KIEL PARKED her car at the westside curb of White Oak Street, in front of a church bearing a bronze marker tinted green from years of exposure to the elements. Through the patina she read: FIRST CHURCH OF CHRIST. DESTROYED BY UNION FORCES IN THE ATTACK OF PETERSBURG, NOVEMBER 1864. REBUILT FROM FALLEN BRICKS BY REVEREND MICHAEL BARNES IN 1865. She studied the plaque, letting the words remind her that she stood on what had once been a battleground. Buildings and lives were ruined, but out of conflict something new had arisen—a resurrection of life and purpose.

A dozen strides away stood a single-story, well-kept Craftsman-style home, proud of its suit of brown paint, accessorized by white fascia and bargeboard, and equally white trim around the French pane windows. She covered the remaining steps in short order, ascended the wide wood stairs that led to the covered front porch, and knocked on the door. A tall man with a sparse tuft of white hair answered. He wore casual clothing: beige slacks, black polo shirt, and slippers that looked as if they had endured a thousand miles of walking. He stood with a round-shouldered stoop—the effect, she assumed, of age and countless hours poring over historical documents. Yvonne had expected something different. Each time she'd seen Dr. Burke, he'd been wearing a dress shirt and tie. Why she expected him to dress that way at home she didn't know.

Dr. Burke was one of the rare professors who made history come alive for Yvonne. She had sat in his classroom and listened as he described the joy of his research, of sitting on his front porch gazing onto a street that had once been a passageway for generals and their armies; of soldiers, young and fresh faced, who would never return.

"Professor Burke," Yvonne said with an outstretched hand. "I'm Yvonne. I phoned you earlier. Do you remember?"

"Well, of course I remember. I'm old, not stupid. You're the one who wanted information on Emma Bell."

"Yes, sir, that's right."

"You're one of my students, aren't you?"

"I'm taking your class on Colonial America."

Burke squinted through his eyeglasses, then shook his head. "Oh, wait." He removed the spectacles. "My reading glasses. Great for reading but not for looking at faces." He looked her over again. "Yes, yes, I remember you. You sit at the back of the class. I'm not much with names. I've seen so many students over the last forty years that all the names run together. Faces, however . . . I still have an eye for faces. Espccially pretty ones."

Yvonne felt her face warm. "Um, thank you, sir."

"Well, come in. We'll sit at the dining table. I've just made some sweet tea. May I pour a glass for you?"

"Yes. That would be wonderful."

He escorted her through the short foyer to the dining room, motioned to a chair, then moved through a doorway that Yvonne assumed led to the kitchen. "Have a seat at the table. I'll be right back." He walked with a slight limp, something she hadn't noticed in class. On the walls hung wallpaper with a print of Grant and Lee at Appomattox Court House. A china hutch, as old looking as the house itself, stood next to a side-wall. On the hutch rested a photo in a decorative silver frame. Instead of sitting, she moved to the hutch and picked up the picture. The photo displayed a sepia image of a young couple: a tall, stoic man in an ill-fitting suit and a much shorter, smiling woman in a white gown. *A wedding photo.*

The man she recognized. It was the image of her host and professor taken decades earlier. The background showed a flower garden bordered with a white picket fence.

"That was taken a long time before you were born."

Yvonne jumped and turned. Burke had returned to the dining room carrying a tray with two glass tumblers and a pitcher of tea. "I'm sorry. I didn't mean to pry." She returned the photo to its resting place and stepped to the table.

"You weren't prying. People who love history love old photos." He set the tray down and poured tea into the glasses. "I know I've looked at my share."

"That's you in the photo, isn't it?" She took a seat in one of the side chairs.

He nodded. "My wedding day. Almost fifty-five years ago." He sat and handed a glass to Yvonne. "We were only twenty when we married. I hadn't even finished my undergraduate work. Elizabeth couldn't wait. To tell the truth, neither could I. I went to school in North Carolina. We had a simple ceremony at a friend's house. I promised her a big wedding once we got on our feet, but she would have nothing to do with it. Said she needed only one ceremony in her life."

His attention drifted, and a curtain of silence descended between them. Yvonne let the man have his memories.

"She died ten years ago. I miss her."

"I'm so sorry."

He raised a hand. "Everyone dies, young lady. We historians know that. We spend our lives studying people who went to their graves a long time ago. That brings us back to your question. You want to know about Emma Bell."

"Yes. I'm helping someone with a little research."

"I'm afraid no one knows much about her. Her son, Elijah Bell—well now, he's a different story. Many consider him the most famous soldier who came from these parts."

Yvonne removed a pen and a notepad from her purse.

Burke rubbed his chin. "We have letters from soldiers who knew him. Most of the letters describe the war and how much they miss being home; a couple mention Elijah Bell. He was quite young, you know. Still in his teens. Nonetheless, he made quite a reputation for himself: walking headlong into battle with the soldiers day after day; sitting in camp with them waiting for the next battle. Several letters call him the boy preacher. Some called him the Bell Messenger; others called him a prophet of God. When he preached from the Bible he carried, he was something else."

"So he was religious." Yvonne sipped her tea.

"That's one way to put it, but it takes more than religion to drive a young man like that into the middle of a war. Those who heard him said whenever Bell stood on some wooden stump or a spit of rock and raised his Bible, they expected fire to rain from Heaven."

"How does someone as young as Bell get such confidence?"

Burke shrugged. "I'm sure it had something to do with the tensions of war and his religious fervor."

"So Bell was a soldier-preacher."

"No, not a soldier at all. The same letter that described the boy's preaching said he never held a rifle, only a Bible."

"Not something you expect to see today." Yvonne made a couple of notes.

"It's sad, really. So many with great character die so young."

"Life is so unjust." She made the quip without thought.

"Not entirely, young lady." Burke slipped into his professorial tone of voice. "Life is overflowing with injustice, yes, but life itself is not unjust. We historians don't study the past because we're afraid of the future; we do so because the past *tells us the future*. It's a warning siren to what will happen if we repeat the past. Do you understand?"

"Yes, sir. I think I do."

"Five days a week, I stand in front of my students knowing that most of them would rather be somewhere else. History is not as popular as other subjects. Even the history majors seem bored at times. Maybe I'm not an exciting teacher, but I know the value of history. It's my passion."

"You're a great teacher, Dr. Burke. I find your classes fascinating."

He pursed his lips. "Then why do you sit at the back of the class?"

"Less distraction, I suppose. I sit in the back of all my classes."

His gaze made her uncomfortable. She didn't like talking about herself. "Back to Bell."

"Right. The business at hand. The boy died at the end of the war, shot in a skirmish with Union soldiers. One of the men's journals said they had been so starved that some stripped bark from trees and chewed it just to keep from going mad."

"How horrible."

"War is always horrible, especially if it is fought on one's own soil. It can also be terribly ironic. Technically, the war was already over when Bell died in a farmer's house a few days after he was shot. Word of the cessation of conflict spread fast, but not fast enough. If word had come a day earlier, the boy might have been spared and lived a long life."

"Farmer's home? He was killed in someone's home?"

"No. He was shot while in a farmer's cornfield. A family named Crowley found him and tried to nurse him back to health. He died in their house."

Burke rose and stepped from the room, returning a short time later with a manila folder. He sat and drew a plastic bag from the folder. "I bought this letter at a Civil War artifact auction five years ago. I buy everything I can of historical value if it relates to this town. This letter is from your Elijah Bell, written to his mother on the day he died. What do you see?" He pushed the letter, still in the plastic protector, to Yvonne.

"It looks like it is written in a woman's hand. It's not the kind of penmanship I'd expect from a teenager."

"Very good. It was penned by Mrs. Crowley."

"The farmer's wife?"

"Yes. The first paragraph confirms that fact. Read it aloud."

She lifted the letter and turned it so the sunlight filtering through the dining room window struck the paper. The ink had paled over the decades and the paper had yellowed. Still, the graceful pen strokes remained legible. She read aloud. " *'The boy is too shallow in strength to write any and has barely the breath to speak, so I will do my best to relay what he intends.'* "

"Rips out the heart, doesn't it?"

Yvonne agreed.

"Continue."

Yvonne swallowed and braced herself.

"Dearest Mother. I will not see the morrow. My wounds received three days ago are the cause of my demise. They will send me to a better place. A man will assuredly bring my Bible to you. He is the man who kilt me, but, Mother, please find the grace to forgive him. I received

a whisper from my Redeemer at the very moment that the man stood over me. He was to have the book. Mother, I love . . .

"The letter stops there."

Burke said, "I've read that letter many times over the years. It never fails to move me." Moisture dampened his eyes. "Isn't it interesting that people who start wars never seem to die in them?"

"I've never thought of that."

"If you continue to study history, you will have many such thoughts. This is our job as historians: to think the thoughts others will not."

Yvonne slid the plastic-sealed letter back to Burke. "Thank you for showing me this."

"The park down the street is named after Elijah Bell."

"I've been there. There's a stone marker."

"I've seen it many times; always thought it poetic. You know, I've never put the two together, but Tate must be the Yankee who shot young Bell."

"That's true."

Burke gave her a puzzled look. "How can you know it's true?"

Yvonne couldn't help smiling. "The Bible tells me so."

"The Bible?"

"I have an acquaintance who owns the very Bible that Elijah Bell carried. There is a notation about Jeremiah Tate."

Burke's eyes brightened. "You have the Bible Bell carried?"

"Well, I don't, but the person I'm doing research for does. Can we find anything else about Tate?"

"If he was in the Union Army, I can find him. Tell me what the Bible says about Tate."

"The inscription says he died in San Francisco in 1866, but I don't know why or how."

"Okay, young lady, you just gave an old man something to do. I will find your Mr. Tate. I first read that stone marker at the park when I was a boy and have always wondered who Tate was and why Emily Bell chiseled his name in stone."

She thanked him again and started to leave.

"Ms. Kiel? Do you know what a historian does?"

She turned. "I think historians keep the dead alive."

"That is exactly what we do. Bell and Tate will live again, if only on paper."

chapter 11

NOVEMBER 7, 1865
SAN FRANCISCO, CALIFORNIA

NEAR THE WHARF'S edge, Tate noticed a blue sign dangling by one chain, flailing in the stiff breeze. The Thunderbolt Saloon resembled the other buildings lining the waterfront: dirty, worn, and in need of paint. Tate had seen worse. He pushed through the door.

Moments later he sat at a wide, heavily marred bar with a frothy beer in a mug that had obviously held such cargo countless times before. The pub was dark but clean. The rough-cut floorboards formed an uneven but steady surface, only a third of which squeaked when Tate stepped on them.

It took a moment for his eyes to adjust to the dim light. Outside, the sun eased toward the horizon, but paper shades over the bar's two windows kept the glow and reality of the outside world at bay.

Before he had finished the last swallow of beer, the bartender, a jowl-laden man with moist, tired eyes, laid down another mug, white foam and gold fluid sloshing over the rim. Tate smiled. The man knew how to draw another coin out of a customer. He didn't protest.

As the beer touched his lips, he felt a tap on his shoulder. Tate took his swallow, set the mug down, and turned to see an old man—with a gap-toothed grin and red eyes with the lower lids resembling canvas bags—staring at him.

"Can I help you, old-timer?"

"You be looking for a room, I suspect." His words rode on a wheezing exhalation.

"You'd be suspecting right."

"Good. So happens that beds are real hard to come by in this part of town. Especially after a ship like yours pulls dockside, if you know what I mean."

"For a price, I am sure you can find me a place to sleep the night."

The gap-toothed grin widened. "Finish your drink, friend, then follow me. I got just the hotel for a gent like you."

Tate drained the rest of the beer before following the old man into the street.

"This way." The old man pulled a wad of shredded tobacco from a tin and tucked it in his mouth, making one cheek bulge.

They moved through the growing gloom, stepping over the broken bottles and discarded sardine cans that littered the roadway.

"This way," the man instructed again as he stepped past the broken bricks littering the entry and much of the street.

"No tricks, old man."

"You don't trust me?"

"I don't even know your name."

The old man laughed. "Names aren't important, stranger. You have nothing to fear from a weak old man like me."

They walked a quarter mile by Tate's estimation. The old man stayed close to the waterfront buildings, Tate kept his distance from doorways and alleys—just in case. He took every step with caution, his eyes peering into shadowed alleys.

"Here we are." The man spat a stream of brown goop to the ground.

Tate stood before a two-story clapboard building

that most likely had been built a half century before. Most of its windows were broken, the front door hung open and at an angle, and the wood steps leading to the lobby rested a foot farther from the door than anyone would have designed. White letters painted above the door declared the place to be Ocean View Hotel. Beneath the sign were painted the words: FOR DISCERNING CLIENTS.

"I know it ain't much to look at, but it's better than sleeping on the streets. We had a real shaker four weeks back. The earthquake took several buildings right to the ground. This one fared better. You can take it or you can leave it; there'll be others to have it if you're not of a mind."

"Are you the owner?"

He spat again. "Let's just say I'm renting the place out for tonight."

Dust rose with every footfall as Tate let the old man lead him up stairs that angled more sharply than they should. On the second floor, they turned left and entered a room that was little better than a cave. Dim light spread along the floor and partway up one wall. The reddish light poured through a hole in the wall that had once been a window. Tate poked his head through the opening and saw the remains of the window, shattered in the back alley below.

Pressed against the far wall rested an iron frame and a bare mattress that reminded Tate of a sway-back horse. The only other furnishing was a straight-backed chair with most of its spindles broken.

"I know there ain't no window to keep out the wind, but you'll be out of the rain if there is any to come."

"It'll do," Tate muttered. He dug his bandaged hand in his pocket and then dropped forty cents in the man's outstretched hand. The hand trembled. *Too long without a drink?*

"I thank you, sir."

"I could use a candle or two."

The old man nodded, slipped from the room, and returned with two candles, each nearly burned beyond use. Tate thanked him and the old man was gone.

Alone again, he sat on the badly bowed bed and retrieved the letter Mary had given him at the docks. Since it was too dark to read, Tate withdrew a match from his coat and lit one of the candles.

Dear Mr. Tate,
Please know that I consider you a messenger of the Lord who saved darling Ruth from a harm that is unimaginable to my heart. I remain ever pledged to help you in any way that I can. It is of no concern for me as to how great your need, for I will remain, as always, diligent to assist you in any requirement that my humble abilities may provide.

You may find me ever in the Lord's presence, and in His good service, at the Mission of Mercy on Sacramento Street, San Francisco.

Humbly yours,
Mary

Tate returned to the Thunderbolt Saloon around nine the next morning. At this hour, he longed for a meal more than warm beer. Other patrons showed less concern, crowding the bar like men dehydrated by a week in the desert. They were a mixed lot, ranging from clerks in white cotton aprons, miners in threadbare overalls, and fancy men in hats and gloves and carrying silver-tipped canes.

Behind the bar, a frustrated barkeep struggled to keep up with the rapid orders barked his way. Tate tried to wedge himself between a thick-shouldered dockworker and a one-legged man with a hickory crutch. The lame man whacked Tate's shin. With a spit on the floor the man barked, "Federals took my leg at Chickamauga, so I'm not inclined to let them take my place at the bar."

Tate gave up the struggle, deciding to watch several men play cards at a table in one corner. Perhaps the chaos at the bar would subside. A bearded, surly, short man with a blue-tinted cheek gathered in his freshly dealt cards and fanned them open.

"You in, Blue Mike?" A large man with a

weathered, bronzed face framed in a matted, peppered beard asked the question.

So the man's stained skin had become a nickname.

"Of course I'm in. I'm always in." The man called Blue Mike tossed two coins on the table.

Blue Mike held his cards tight to his chest, shielding them from his opponent. Both men wore dingy hats that slouched on their heads. Buckskin patches covered their trousers. A knife and two pistols hung from Blue Mike's belt, as did a fat leather tobacco pouch. The other player bore similar weapons. Tate wondered how often a friendly game turned otherwise.

From where he stood, Tate could see that Blue Mike had two cards facedown in his lap and barely covered by an elbow. Cash and coins formed a mound in the middle of the table.

"That's it?" The man laughed. "I gotta raise you jus' to keep things interesting." He tossed two paper bills on the table. "Or is that too rich for your blood?"

The jab didn't seem to bother Blue Mike. He matched the raise and returned the favor by adding three more bills of his own. As he tossed down the bet with one hand, he scooped the hidden cards from his lap with the other and tucked them neatly in his hand.

His opponent clawed at his beard with gnarled fingers that looked as if they each had been broken more than once. "I guess I call."

Blue Mike thumbed out three jacks faceup and parted his lips in a grin, revealing tobacco-stained teeth.

With no show of emotion, the other player stood and fanned out four queens and a lone one-eyed king. "What are the odds?"

Blue Mike slid a hand over his elk-boned knife. A second later, he released his grip, stood, and moved toward the door.

The winner scooped up his money and laughed. "Railroad men—they're an easy lot."

Railroad man? Tate said to himself.

Tate went after Blue Mike and found him already halfway across the street, where he had stopped to kick at several feral cats pawing at a discarded ham bone.

"Hey." Tate stepped into the street. "Blue Mike, isn't it?"

"Who wants to know?"

"The name is Jeremiah Tate. You work for the railroad."

"Why you asking?" His words came out harsh.

Tate couldn't blame Blue Mike for being in a bad way. He had just lost a good chunk of money to a better cheater.

"I am looking for work."

Blue Mike looked him up and down. "You sure? The work on the rail line is hard. Most white men don't take to it."

"I ain't been harmed by hard work yet."

"I'm in town to get drunk and play cards, but tomorrow I'll take forty Chinese and ten Irishmen up to the high tunnels. I guess I could make room for one more. Considering you ain't Chinese or Irish, you seem sober enough."

"Thanks. Don't worry none. I've endured my share of hard work, and I'm not the sort to complain much."

"What'd you say the name was?"

"Tate. Jeremiah Tate."

"I'm guessing from your accent you ain't from around here."

"Pennsylvania. Harrisburg."

"Harrisburg. Never been that far east. You a soldier boy, I suspect?"

"Not anymore."

"There will be a flat-bellied steamer dockside in the morning. Don't miss it if you want work. I don't wait on any man."

"I'll be there."

Blue Mike kicked at the cats again, scattering them in a chorus of hissing yowls before he marched away.

chapter 12

TATE FOUND THE rear-paddle steamer moored along the dock, just as Blue Mike had said. A narrow plank bridged the gap between boat and dock. At the foot of the gangplank, Blue Mike was making notes on a piece of paper. A line of men waited with sacks hung over their shoulders. Ten men stood at the front of the line. Tate assumed them to be the Irish workers Blue Mike had mentioned. Behind them three times as many Chinese men stood in queue, each with his head bowed. Tate walked to the back of the line. He caught the railroad man's eye.

"Tate. Get up here with the white men."

Tate stepped forward, and Blue Mike motioned him to the front of the line. No one protested.

"Jacob Tate, right?" Blue Mike's voice rolled down the dock.

"*Jeremiah* Tate."

"Right. Jeremiah. You sure you want to hook up with us? I ain't turning back if you change your mind."

"No need to worry about me."

"Go aboard. The man up there will show you where to stow your gear."

95

Tate placed boot on plank without hesitation or regret.

An hour later, the paddle wheeler was under way. The Irish workers had gathered in the ship's parlor, drinking heavily and laughing loudly. The Chinese congregated at the stern, some squatting and fanning a fire laid on bricks and heating a black kettle of tea. When Tate walked by, they averted their eyes. Tate did what he had done on the ship that brought him to San Francisco: he found a quiet spot at the bow and watched the water part before the wood hull.

"Second thoughts?"

Tate turned to see Blue Mike. "No. I like quiet."

"Can't blame a man for that. Don't do much socializing myself. Unless, of course, it involves whiskey, cards, or yelling at the Chinese."

"Why you got such a disfavor with the Chinese?"

"Look at my face, Tate. Look at what those Chinks did to me."

Tate stared at the blue stain scarring the man's cheek.

Blue Mike opened a leather pouch and poured a line of tobacco onto a thin square of paper on his palm. He then licked the edge before his fingers nimbly rolled the smoke. "I don't mind telling what happened. Me and three Chinamen were reloading for a seam blast on the Comstock Lode. That's in Nevada. Made Virginia City what it is.

96

Mount Davidson was thick with silver ore. My job was to free it from the ground. We set our powder and was making ready for the blast. A spark—maybe an ember from the previous blast . . . don't really know, touched off the black powder. I woke up fifty feet down the tunnel. I was alive. Them Chinamen that were close to the explosion got blown to kingdom come. Me, I got this here tattoo of blue powder on the side of my face. People been calling me Blue Mike ever since."

"That a story or advice?"

Blue Mike returned his gaze to the churning water at the bow and lit his rolled cigarette. "Both, I suppose."

"I'll try and remember. I don't know much of mining or railroading, but I lived through four years in battle. Maybe I can live through this."

Blue Mike took a hard drag from his smoldering tobacco. "A man like you, with all that war experience and being an officer and all, would make a good supervisor. Can't be having a white man do the same work as those Chinese. I think I'll make you head of the Chinks. They're going to need a little kicking, and maybe you're the man to do it. Always remember that some spit from the devil can move more rock than anything else."

Tate nodded and thought of the strange Asian men with the long, braided pigtails draped down their narrow backs. He thought of the dead Chinaman he had seen when his ship pulled into port. Like him, they were men out of place and far from home. Tate had no idea what drove them here . . . and didn't know what drove him, either.

In Sacramento, Tate and the others exchanged the smooth sailing of the paddle wheeler for a lurching service train that chugged up serpentine grades, with clacking metal wheels clinging to steel rails. Tate wondered what awaited him. All he was sure of was that his days would be dominated by hard work and danger as Chinese crews blasted away cliffs of ice-polished granite to make rail beds like the one that coursed beneath him.

Cobalt skies hovered over green pines, tall spruce, and splintered rock spires. For a portion of the journey, the train paralleled the churning American River, water on a journey of its own from mountaintop to the Sacramento River to the bay at San Francisco, the place he had left not long ago.

In late afternoon, the locomotive discharged its last bloated head of steam from the two massive side pistons, and the metal beast jolted to a stop.

"Welcome to high camp, friend." Blue Mike stood. "Some call the place the devil's backyard." His ragged-tooth smile made Tate uncomfortable. "It ain't much, but it's home for you, soldier boy."

Tate leaned out the open train window and saw men working the side of the mountain like ants on an anthill. Along the track, slightly built men labored under wide, pointed straw hats that bobbed with every motion. None bothered to look at the newly arrived train or those who stepped from its confines. Some had picks and shovels, and those who didn't gathered, with their bare hands, fragments of rocks that were chipped by pick or blasted by dynamite.

Tate rose and followed his new boss.

Blue Mike hopped from the train, stepped to a pile of broken tools, retrieved an ax handle with a ragged end and slapped his palm with it. He turned his attention to the newly arrived Chinese workers. "Get in line! Step it up. I want to see a single line. Let's go!"

Men poured from the coaches, prodded by Blue Mike's orders. Any man who moved too slowly for his liking gained momentum from a shove, a kick, or a swat with the ax handle. Tate could see the pleasure Blue Mike took in tormenting the new arrivals, especially the Chinese.

Once the Chinese workers had formed a long line, Blue Mike took a position in front of them. It reminded Tate of his days in the army. An old Chinese man took a place next to Blue Mike.

"My name is Blue Mike. What I say goes." He stopped and the old Chinaman spoke, matching volume and inflection. "Next to me is No Chew. He is your number one coolie."

Again the old man translated, except Tate heard

him give his name as Lo Chew. Since the translator had no teeth, the nickname made sense.

"From this moment on, you will do as I tell you. No Chew will handle your pay, your food, and anything else I tell him. Cooperate and you will earn your pay and maybe even a little opium on Sundays for relaxation. If you cause me any grief—" He raised the ax handle. "Then this will be your reward."

It was clear the men understood. The fear on their faces was proof enough for Tate.

The Irish were assigned three men to a tent—the Chinese, eight to a tent.

On the trip up, Tate learned that the Irish would be supervisors or do the skilled jobs such as setting the timber for beamed trestles or laying masonry. The Chinese would do the rest of the raw-bone labor.

Tate's assigned tent was tucked in a draw near the edge of a rocky spur that jutted over the roaring American River. He stopped to look about. He had never seen such mighty mountains, and his eyes could barely drink in the sight. Snaking along the sheer granite cliffs was the rail-bed road carved from solid granite more than a thousand feet above the river. In the dwindling minutes of sunlight, the soaring diorama of mountain peaks looked like islands jutting from an ocean of shade. It was a sculpture beyond what Tate thought even God capable of. He inhaled the smell of pine sap and mountain air.

Tate pushed aside the closed flap and stooped to enter the tent. Once inside, he dropped his canvas sack next to a pile of pine boughs covered in rags. The prickly mound would be his bed. A deer leg hung by a hemp rope from a center pole and canvas sacks of beans and flour rested on the floor. A short, red-haired man was squatting in front of a smoking, mostly rusted, potbellied stove, feeding it green sticks. The man stood and greeted Tate. A smile parted a red-stubble beard.

"James Mahoney is the name," he said, his tongue lacquered with a thick Irish brogue.

Tate shook his extended hand. "Tate. Jeremiah Tate."

"Pleased to meet you, Mr. Tate. I hope you don't mind sharing a space with the likes of me."

"It's all right by me. Must say, you Irish were the best fighters in the war."

James laughed and picked at the pine sap sticking to his palms. "I prefer running away from a fight. I come from a long line of cowards. Besides, I have a winsome face that is too kind to the eyes of any woman. I should never want to mar it in a silly brawl."

Tate grinned. He liked James straight off.

chapter **13**

NOVEMBER 9, 1865
CAPE HORN RAILROAD CAMP

YUEN STOOD IN the long line with his countrymen and felt his knees go weak. The bellowing man with the oak handle continued to bark threats. At sixteen, Yuen knew he was one of the youngest to arrive in camp.

The Orientals had exchanged stories of their lives, but every account seemed to mirror the one before. He was no different. Like the others, he had been a poor worker in the rice fields of the drought-stricken South China province. His land of Guangdong suffered a more severe famine and drought than most others. Yuen had labored hard there just to earn enough food to stay alive. In his village, Yuen saw one man eat weeds from a pond—the only food he could find. Yuen himself strung beans on a string and looped it around his neck each day—that was to be his only food while working long, tortuous hours, bent over humid rice paddies.

While walking to his tiny home, Yuen saw a white waxed-paper poster nailed to a tree in his village. The note was from a Hong Kong brokerage house. It read:

MEN WANTED TO BUILD A RAILROAD. AMERICAN RAILROAD INTEREST NEEDS WORKERS LIKE YOU. GOOD PAY AND FOOD. JOIN YOUR BROTHERS WHO HAVE MADE MUCH WEALTH. MANY REWARDS FOR HARD WORK.

Yuen read the poster several times. The prospect of earning enough money to support his family was tempting. It meant leaving his country to travel to another land but, he reasoned, it couldn't be worse than it was here.

Yuen's father rejected the idea of his son leaving for America. He had heard Americans were tall, fat, evil men with green eyes and faces covered in red hair . . . vile people who seldom bathed and cared nothing for their ancestors.

"What of Kim Doh?" Yuen said. "Have you not told the story many times of how he left the village sixteen years ago to go to California and dig gold from the ground? Did he not return a wealthy and respected man? Did he not buy the entire village ducks and chickens and make a meal for all to enjoy?"

"Yes, I have told that story, but I never believed it would put thoughts of desertion into the mind of my son." Yuen's father could be harsh, but he had always been fair.

Yuen didn't let up. "Did he not speak of American wizardry, of steel boxes that could spin cotton, of boats pushed by machines, of news printed on paper? He told of strings of glowing lanterns that burned all night, and of coaches that shook the earth as they carried people from town to town."

"He did say all those things."

"Was he unwise to go, Father?"

Yuen's father did not reply.

The conversation carried into the night. Yuen reasoned with his father, who fought back with excuses for why Yuen should stay, but even he didn't seem convinced of his position. Yuen's mother listened in silence. She was not allowed to speak and communicated her opinion through tears.

"Father, fortune has not been with us. We work hard, but the rains fail. We have remained honest and proud, but war and misfortune have taken what little we have. I must do what I can."

By morning, his father, weary and worn by circumstance and grief, consented. "If it is to be that you return with wealth, return also with honor."

"I will, Father."

The day he left, Yuen's mother came to him as he packed some rice and dried pork strips in a bag. It was all he had to keep himself fed on the long journey to Canton. She kept her eyes low, hiding her tears. "I will never see you again."

"No, Mother, you are incorrect. I will see you when I return in much honor and wealth."

"I am only a woman, but I am wiser than the

crow. I will never see you again, my son." She lifted a black-lacquered box and held it forward. "Please. Take it."

Yuen removed it slowly from his mother's hands and opened the box. Inside rested a tiny white teacup, cradled with dried paulownia flower buds. The purple flowers surrounded the cup, providing a protective cushion.

"The cup is from my mother, who received it from her mother, and she from other mothers for three hundred years. It is for you to take to give to your wife, who will give it to her daughter. It is all I have from my past and the only thing I can give for your future."

"Mother, it is too beautiful and precious a thing to take on such a long voyage."

"Take the cup for good fortune. It will help you remember me."

"I could never forget you. I am doing this for you and Father." Yuen closed the box.

Before he could say more, she scurried away. He heard her choke back a sob.

The good-byes were short. The pain of separation and the realization that this might be the last time they held each other made a lingering farewell impossible. Yuen walked from his home, stopping only once as he crested the ridge to look back upon the anemic, terraced rice fields that clung to the sides of twin knobby hills. There he saw, jutting up from some aged twisting banyan trees, the pavilion of his ancestors, which would await his return.

After several days' walk to Canton Harbor, he arrived at the dock. An anchored ship there would carry him across the big sea to America. The Shanghai–New York Trading Company owned this scarred vessel. A man in San Francisco named Cheong Moon had paid his forty-dollar passage, a fee that had to be repaid from Yuen's early wages.

To Yuen's eye, the ship looked old and worn. He had not expected better, but the sight of the scuffed and weathered hull made him apprehensive. Perhaps at one time it had served a great purpose: perhaps it had been a warship. But now it was a lumbering mail vessel sailing between San Francisco and Canton. He guessed it to be over two hundred feet in length, with four towering masts that seemed to scratch the sky. It sat low in the water, lower than Yuen thought wise, but he was no sailor. He would have to trust those whose business it was to sail over the deep.

A thick-set Chinese sailor with several angry-looking skin cancers on his neck led Yuen and a dozen others to the ship's forward compartment. A ladder led into the ship's bowels, and Yuen joined a hundred and fifty other men and women bound for the land known to all Chinese as Gold Mountain. The compartment was large and spanned the width of the ship, but it was not large enough to hold comfortably the scores of desperate people longing to begin a new life in a new land. A smell of urine and old feces made Yuen gag, and the realization that the ship had yet to leave port only made his foreboding worse. The smell had to be an old odor, from the previous crossing. It could only get worse. It was as if the ship were a long-dead whale, washed ashore by the tides and now home to scores of homeless men and women.

Rats scurried around the feet of the travelers, occasionally taking a tiny bite of human toe or ankle. No bunks hung from walls; no mattresses cushioned the floor. The only beds were wafer-thin palm leaf or rice mats and a few canvas hammocks that hung bunched together from overhead beams. There was not enough room for a man to crawl.

The first night's meal was dried fish and insect-infested bread. At home he had little to eat but noodles, rice, and occasionally vegetables. It wasn't much, but it was better than what he held in his hand.

Six large barrels of water lashed to the aft deck had to be rationed for the long journey. Boiling the precious liquid for cooking was forbidden. The only luxury came in the meager amount of water allowed for steeping tea.

Yuen stared at the dried fish and buggy bread, then passed the bowl to the man next to him. He refused to eat it. The sights and smells had robbed nearly everyone of an appetite.

Then the seasickness came and new, vile smells hung in the thick air of the compartment.

Each day, Yuen pulled the black box his mother had given him from his travel sack. He carefully opened it, and the jasminelike smell rose to his nose. He inhaled the soothing fragrance of the paulownia flower buds, cradling the teacup like a parched man downing fresh water. Each time he closed his eyes, he forgot the shouting, the rocking and rolling, the sweltering, humid heat of the compartment and lost himself in the intoxicating fragrance of home. Then he would close the box and return it safely to the sack, curl up on his rice mat, and listen in the dank, opium-smoke-laced hold as men clicked tiles in unending games of Mah-jongg. Others preferred to gamble into the night by scooping a handful of beans from a wooden bowl, removing four, then guessing at the remaining as odd or even. The chatter often erupted into shouting and arguing that lasted until the morning light.

For endless weeks, Yuen tolerated each day, reminding himself that every minute brought him closer to his goal. His only work for the time was to survive.

Yuen's ship arrived at the Jackson Street pier in San Francisco two months after leaving China. There were no crowds to greet the arriving Chinese—only boys trying to rope a dead man from the bay's frigid water. A short distance away rested a moored side-paddle wheeler.

Yuen's fellow passengers slowed their exit from the ship, every pair of eyes fixcd on the floating corpse.

A shout jolted them. "Have good sense or have bad fortune."

The warning boomed from a fat man who stared at them through one eye. The other eye looked glued shut. Even at a distance, Yuen could tell that the eye was gone. Beneath the eye was a dent where a cheekbone should have been. Much of his head was shaved and a black queue swayed over his back with each step. Several scars lined his pockmarked face. Clearly, the man had endured rough treatment.

Whatever painful handling he had received, it hadn't broken his spirit. He marched up the gangplank as if the ship were his own. The gluttonous man wore what looked like an expensive red silk robe. With him walked a tall man, several years older than Yuen and wearing black, baggy silks. He also wore a coat. Both of his hands were plunged into the pockets, as if he hid something ominous. Yuen guessed him to be a bodyguard.

Once at the top of the gangplank, the fat man looked at the gathered Chinese and frowned. He nodded to his companion, who said, "You will listen. This man is Cheong Moon of Sunwui district of Kwantung Province. You will do all he says without question. To defy him would be unwise." The bodyguard stepped to the side and bowed before Cheong Moon. Yuen and the others followed his example.

"Sit!" Cheong's voice was higher than Yuen expected, almost feminine, but there was nothing soft or gentle in his tone or manner.

They sat without question.

Cheong studied them. "When you die, I promise that your body will be taken back to China to be buried with your ancestors. When you die, we will scrape all the flesh from your bones and dry them in the sun. I will make certain that your bones are wrapped in silk and taken to your families for proper burial."

He stared at Yuen, then continued. "In return, you will work till your arms are unable to lift, then you will lift more, and you will do so without complaint. You will also promise me to repay all the money I paid for your passage here, plus the interest on your debt. If you do not pay, then you will never see China again and your bones will never know the Celestial Kingdom. If you do not pay all that is owed, you will end up dead and floating in the bay with the fish or, maybe worse, like the turtle on his back."

Yuen lowered his eyes and tried to drive the image away. No one spoke.

Cheong Moon raised his voice. "The whites will call you 'coolies' and 'celestials.' You are nothing but dogs to them, slaves to build their railroads and work their mines and clean their clothes. They do not know that we are the rightful owners of the oldest civilization on earth. The whites are the youngest civilization, but they have plenty of money."

He lowered his voice. "These whites are drunk with pride, but I humble them and take their money because I know their ways." He scanned the group with a penetrating stare, as if he had the power to see right through their hearts. "You will never know the ways of the whites, so you must do exactly as I say if you want to live long and earn money to take back to China. Do you understand?"

The seated men mumbled their response.

"Good. Get up. Follow me."

Yuen and the others rose, formed a line, and marched down the gangplank to the pier and to eight mule-drawn wagons lining the dock. Yuen trailed the line and was the last man to board. The wagons carried them to a dark building in an area populated with other Chinese and only the occasional white. Someone in the wagon knew enough English to read a street sign: Dupont Street. Inside the building, Yuen saw soiled rice mats covering a dirt floor. Soured garbage filled the corner of the room and the stench of urine assaulted his nose.

Cheong stepped in, holding a camphene lamp high over his head. "You will sleep here tonight. Do not go out. Robbers and killers wait around every corner." He smiled and left.

Yuen heard the click of a lock securing the door.

He had crossed the sea to become a prisoner. Working his way to a side wall, he sat and lowered his head into his hand and struggled to keep his courage alive.

There was no light and no ventilation. Odors from scores of men permeated the room with stale breath and the smell of bodies too long without a bath. Yuen had hoped for food, but no one came with a meal.

With no room to lie down, Yuen slept sitting up, waking every few minutes to some unknown noise or to the weeping of men close to losing their minds.

Tomorrow will be better. Tomorrow I begin a new life that will bring honor and wealth to my family.

He hoped he wasn't lying to himself.

chapter 14

JUNE 30, 1980
PHOENIX, ARIZONA

YVONNE RATTLED INTO the phone's mouthpiece, her mind racing faster than her words could travel over her tongue. "Your Mr. Tate was in the Twenty-third Pennsylvania Infantry Regiment. He was fighting under Grant the last days of the war. That would be in the same area that Elijah Bell was shot. My research shows Tate died of smallpox just two days before he was supposed to be hanged."

"You're kidding," Gary said.

"Nope. I'm dead serious . . . sorry. What I mean is: Tate was tried in front of a circuit judge for San Francisco."

"Why? What'd he do?"

"They charged him with killing three men, a Chinese woman, and a Tong leader named Cheong Moon. The records say he started a fire that led to their deaths. For some reason, he was only convicted of killing the three men. I searched the newspapers from that time. It was big news in 1866."

"They still have copies of newspapers that old?"

Yvonne sighed. "Major libraries keep copies of newspapers. Most in San Francisco were burned in the fire after the great earthquake, but some survived and were later stored on microfiche. The reports we have state that Tate pleaded guilty and said nothing in his defense."

"This is strange."

"You got that right. It was as if he wanted to be hanged. Fortunately, Dr. Lester Burke found an article detailing the whole trial. He thinks the trial was a setup. The jury deliberated for only fifteen minutes before returning."

"Wait a sec. You said Tate pleaded guilty. Why would there be a jury?"

"Can't hang a man without a jury trial."

Gary took notes as she spoke.

"Gary, are there other markings in the Bible?

Anything else that might help us understand what happened?"

"Just some names and records of births and deaths going back to the 1700s."

"Tell me about the names."

"Mary Connor from San Francisco. Then there's an inscription about an orphanage for a Ruth Donahue who died in Egypt."

"Those names will be almost impossible to trace unless we can find a connection to Tate."

"Maybe I can find more information if I go to San Francisco," Gary said.

"That seems like a lot of effort. The Bible is that important to you?"

"It's more than the Bible. Besides, it may be the only way to learn more about Tate and Mary Connor."

"Okay, this is none of my business, but when you hired me, you told me you had very little money."

Gary hesitated. "I was being honest. I've just graduated from college, so I have no job and very little money. However, I've received some graduation gifts from family members."

"Ah, graduation money. A time-honored practice."

"It's only five hundred miles to San Francisco from Phoenix. I can make it in nine hours or so. I'm sure I can find a cheap hotel and live off McDonald's and Taco Bell for a couple of days."

Yvonne said, "What else can I do?"

"You've already gone way beyond for the little I paid you."

She chuckled. "I'm afraid your mystery has me hooked. It's a personality fault shared by history majors. I'm going crazy trying to figure this out. I want to do more."

"Okay, I'll take whatever help I can get. How about trying to find out something about Mary Connor or Ruth Donahue in Egypt?"

"I'll do what I can."

chapter **15**

DECEMBER 11, 1865
CAPE HORN RAILROAD CAMP

A MONTH HAD PASSED since Tate arrived at high camp. A dry wind now swept up from the south. Tate had learned well from the Chinese how to blast away the high cliffs. The men who taught him were the proud descendants of those who had built the Great Wall of China and the fortresses in the Yangtze gorges. The strange men respected the tall man whose eyes showed concern every time one of the Oriental workers had been lowered over the lip of the cliff.

The first time Tate had seen the act, he'd been certain he was watching a man about to die. The taut rope that held the worker was lashed to a red, woven-reed basket—the man's only support. The basket's occupant would swing a heavy steel hammer with one hand and strike a single jack drill in the other. For hours he would work chipping a hole in the uncooperative rock.

When the worker had pounded a hole deep enough, he would tamp black powder into it. Once a string of holes had been hand-drilled into the rock face, workers, still hanging in their reed baskets, would light the fuses in unison. Men up on the ridges would then haul the baskets up before the mountain heaved and the face fell away in an ear-pounding, teeth-rattling explosion. After cold mountain breezes scrubbed the air clean of dust and smoke, laborers below would scurry to fill the long line of pushcarts with the fallen and shattered granite. The rubble would be dumped into ravines as fill.

Tate had seen the procedure many times over the weeks, yet it never ceased to amaze him—and frighten him.

He stepped to the edge now and looked down the sheer and jagged edge of the freshly fractured mountain to where the Chinese workers were gathering chunks of stone.

Yuen paused and gazed up the face of the cliff. A tall white man stood at its edge, looking down upon him and the other workers. Yuen moved his gaze to his blistered, bloody, and cramped hands. For a moment, he allowed himself to wish for work in the rice fields. He shook off the memory, determined not to slow. Others around him also suffered, but none complained. Yuen loaded his bucket, straightened, and turned to carry it to one of the waiting carts. As he turned, he stepped into Blue Mike. His boss staggered back two steps. Yuen dropped his pail.

Yuen immediately bowed his head and stared at the ground. His heart fluttered in his chest like a frightened bird. He waited for the fury. Perhaps the large man would understand that it was an accident. Perhaps he would forgive—

Something hard struck Yuen on the head. He felt his head snap to the side and fire race down his neck. Daylight grayed.

"Clumsy Chinee! I'll teach you to plow into me."

A hand grabbed his collar and Yuen stumbled across the rubble as Blue Mike pulled him forward and with a shove sent him staggering back.

Yuen tumbled down the sharp slope like a rag doll, sliding to a patch of loose rock thirty feet below. Yuen felt his head hit the ground and his body roll. The grayness in his eyes turned black.

Yuen opened his eyes slowly and row a line of Chinese lowering themselves in a human line held together with outstretched arms gripped hand to hand. He raised his head. Warm blood had pooled beneath his ear. Scorching pain ran up his right arm. He forced himself to focus, and when he did, he saw a white, jagged bone poking through his skin. He lowered his head and lay still, certain that death waited just minutes away.

He felt movement. He heard voices—Chinese voices. Yuen opened his eyes to see several of his fellow workers attempting to carry him up the steep slope. Every movement sent pain through his shuddering body.

Once again, the day dimmed as darkness pressed in from the edge of his eyes.

Yuen welcomed it.

Before slipping into unconsciousness again, he saw the tall man at the top of the cliff watching . . . watching . . .

On the windy ridge, Tate watched it all and was sickened by the sight of it. It wasn't the first time he had witnessed Blue Mike treat the Chinese with such cruelty, but as always, he would say nothing. Trained as an army officer, he had been taught never to challenge the command of a superior. It was a code of war that extended to the rail lines.

That night, as the sun dissolved into the western canyon, spilling dark shadows into the green valley, Tate made his way back to his tent. Thick clouds crawled along the darkening sky.

The day had made him bone weary, but he reminded himself that his life was ten times better than that of the Chinese workers. He paused to watch the smaller men work their way along the uneven ground to their overcrowded tents. On several occasions, Tate had walked through that section of camp. He knew what awaited the men: water-filled barrels that formerly held black powder would be made available by Lo Chew. The men would strip off their shirts in the crisp air and crowd their shivering bodies around the big oak casks brimming with steaming liquid. Each held a wood bowl in an outstretched hand waiting to scoop a bowl of bathwater.

Next was a meager meal and tea. Tate thought it odd that he had spent four years of his life in a war over slavery, only to come to California and see free men treated as slaves . . . as nothing more than beasts of burden.

Tate, in his tent, sat on a pine stump next to a flickering lamp and listened to the wind tear at his flimsy shelter. The cast-iron stove in the corner radiated warmth and the pot on top started to wobble as the coffee reached a frantic boil. Tate pulled out the Bible from his canvas sack and found two letters folded inside—the one from the boy he had killed and the other from Mary. He carefully unfolded Mary's letter, as he had done many times before, and again thought of her kind face.

James ducked inside the tent flap, stomped mud and dung off his boots, interrupting Tate's thoughts. He raised an eyebrow when he saw the Bible on Tate's lap. "I didn't know you were a man of the book."

Tate kept his eyes on the letters in the Bible.

James asked, "Mind if I have me a look?"

Tate nodded, closed the book on the letters, and handed him the Bible.

"My father was a Protestant preacher in Belfast. I never told you that, did I?"

"No," Tate said.

"I don't talk about it much. He died young. I was still a wee lad. I never heard him preach, but my mother loved to read the Bible to me." He opened its covers. "It was wrong for the Chinese boy to be hurt like that today. Last month Blue Mike hit another boy over the head with his ax handle because the lad stopped to get a drink. You saw what happened?"

"I did. Weren't pretty."

James seemed to sadden. "Blue Mike almost killed him, and not one man did a thing about it. Not one thing." James returned his face to the Bible and resumed flipping pages. "You ever read the book of Exodus?"

"Can't say I have."

"The book tells of Moses. Did you know that Moses once killed a man?"

"I heard tell."

"Then you know that an Egyptian was beating a Hebrew slave and Moses came to his rescue, killing the Egyptian." He handed the Bible back to Tate. "No one should let a man beat another, white or yellow skinned."

James stepped to the stove and poured two cups of coffee. He handed one to Tate. "Let me ask you something. How many men did you see killed in the war to set the Negroes free?"

"More than I care to remember."

"And now we all just looked on as a young man was almost killed. We did nothing about it. Didn't raise a finger. Didn't say a word."

Tate's muscles tightened. Just because he had the same thoughts didn't mean he liked hearing it from another.

"God did not give you strength so you could only fight a war and build a railroad," James said. "He gave you strength so you could also defend the weak."

Tate set the Bible down. "That a fact, is it? I don't recall you doing anything when Blue Mike was pounding that boy's head in."

James frowned and nodded. "True as the rain, that is. I already told you, Mr. Tate. I am a coward and small of stature, not fit for any fight. But you, my friend . . . you are a big, big man, and I sense you are a man who would never stand by and allow a boy to die."

"I find it best to mind my own business. You might find it a wise rule to follow."

"Boss man, please to help!"

The voice came from outside the tent flap and bore a heavy Oriental accent.

Tate ducked under the tent flap. Lo Chew stood just feet away, dancing from one foot to the other and slapping his arms to drive away the night's cold.

"What's wrong, Lo Chew?" Tate asked.

"You come. You help. Boy hurt bad. Boy need help."

"Boy?" Tate said but knew the boy Lo Chew had in mind.

"Yuen. Mr. Blue Mike hurt him bad. You come. You help."

"All right, all right. I can't do much, but I'll take a look."

Tate exchanged a glance with James, and the three men made their way through the cold night past row after row of Chinese tents. Up the way, along the tracks, they saw the orange light of torches leading to the upper tunnels from where rumbling concussions of black-powder chargers rolled down the valley all night long.

At the end of the line, in the last tent, Tate and James found several men leaning over the slack body of Yuen and wringing moisture from a wet sponge over the young man's forehead.

Lo Chew sighed and pointed. "We all offer tea, apples, rice-wax tapers, and joss sticks—hoping that the Celestial gods will help him, but he not get better." Lo Chew placed a hand on his own arm. "Yuen break arm like dry stick."

Tate stepped in the tent and studied the boy. He lay on a dirty mat. A stream of pink, foamy drool ran from his mouth. A jagged end of bone protruded from the skin just below the elbow.

Lo Chew's face slacked. "You fix. You make better."

Tate bent and looked over the injuries. He had seen many men wounded in battle, some worse than Yuen, but he knew it was bad for the boy. Tate turned to James. "I'm not any doctor—can't do a thing for him."

"You've seen this kind of damage to flesh in the war."

Tate pressed his lips into a thin line. "Seeing ain't the same as fixing. God takes whoever He wants, when He wants, and there ain't much we can do about it." Tate stood and faced Lo Chew. "I fear for the boy, but I can't do much."

chapter 16

DECEMBER 12, 1865
CAPE HORN RAILROAD CAMP

TATE HAD HEARD the service train's whistle countless times, but this time was different. The banshee squeal echoed up the valley again, carrying urgency with every blast. Tate had finished dressing by the time the first piercing sounds rolled through the camp. He pulled on his second boot and charged through the flaps of his tent, almost colliding with James.

"We got big trouble, Jeremiah." James's face was tense.

"Where?" Tate didn't need an answer from James. He saw the slow-rolling motion of black smoke as thick as pudding in the sky.

"Fire. Down the embankment and along the river. Probably started before dawn. I'm guessing a spark from the train's stack."

Wind, laced with burning wood and sage and spurred by the fire-heated air, raced through the camp.

"This wind ain't going to make things any easier," James said.

The train whistle sent a dozen more frenetic blasts into the air. Tate faced James. "Get the Chinamen."

An explosive noise that reminded Tate of a distant cannon's report rumbled through the camp.

"What was that?" James looked ready to faint.

"Tree trunks exploding, most likely. Now get. We need our crew."

"Where should I bring 'em?"

Tate pointed at the column of curling smoke that rose and spread across the sky like engorged thunderclouds.

James groaned. "I was afraid you were going to say that." He left in a full trot, a rag pressed over his face.

Tate marched toward the fire, consumed with purpose and devoid of panic. With every step, he took in more of the hellish sight. He had been in many battles and knew this to be a fight they couldn't win. When he neared the embankment, he saw the snaking line of fire at the base of the ravine along the river. It lapped at grass, chewed on brush, and devoured the bark of pine trees. It grew more ravenous with each gulp of wind.

The train whistled again and again, mingling in the air with ash and heat and smoke. The noise of panicked men filled the air. But Tate had heard such things before. He had heard rolling explosions of cannon, the sharp blasts of rifles and handguns, the cries of wounded and dying men, and the orders of officers. He drove the sounds from his head and focused on the blaze.

The closer he came to the fire, the more he despaired. The flames made the air as hot as that in the stove in his tent. Smoke burned his lungs. He stepped to the brim of the embankment that led to the rushing river below. Several teams of Chinese waded into a whirlpool inlet along the river's edge, scooping bucketful after bucketful of water from the swirling eddy, then carrying them to the fire. Water sloshed from the pails as they ran.

Numerous footfalls drew Tate's attention. James jogged to where Tate stood. Behind him were fifteen Chinese and three Irish. "Got here as fast as we could."

"Tate!"

Tate turned to see Blue Mike lumbering his way. Lo Chew followed on his heels, barely able to keep pace.

"You and your men get down there and help them Chinese fight this thing," Blue Mike ordered. "I want you to meet this fire head-on. I want it stopped right here, right now."

"No."

Blue Mike blinked several times, as if he had never heard the word before. "Tate, you do as I say."

Tate shook his head. "Can't be done that way. You're going to kill us all if we do a fool thing like that. The wind is gathering from below and changing direction faster than we can speak a word about it. We would be swallowed in the flames for sure if we tried to take her on in a frontal attack."

"Tate, this ain't no war—"

"It is, for sure. I've been watching the ways of this fire. It is a fearsome thing, and it can leap fifty feet in just a second or two. It can't be stopped."

Blue Mike stepped forward, his large jaw set tight. "I don't have time for this. It ain't soldiering."

"Yes, it is, and you better know who and where the enemy is before you go charging at them." Tate pointed at the fire. "Look at it. You ain't going to beat that down with a few buckets of water. Not even if we had twice the men we got."

"I never took you for a coward."

Tate could not believe the raw stupidity of the man. "Mike, if you fight the fire, you lose. You lose the battle, and you lose good men. Worse, you probably lose the camp and all the trestle work done this far." He stared into the darkening sky swirling with falling ash. "Let the fire take the trees, let her take the brush, but if we are smart, she'll not burn the trestles." He looked at Blue Mike. "That's all you really care about, isn't it?"

Blue Mike's eyes moved across the advancing fire. "I want you to do this my way. You hear me? My way!"

"Those are prideful words from a man set on killing more than stopping this thing."

"You got a better idea?"

"Yes."

Mike took a step back and crossed his arms. "If you got a plan, then spit it out."

"Lo Chew," Tate said, "tell your people to take their buckets to the bridges. Tie ropes to the buckets and lower them into the river. I want those bridges real wet from the top of the trestles to the rails. Keep dousing them. Don't let up until the flames are licking at your heels, then run."

"Yes, boss. I understand."

"Let the forest burn for all we care, but those trestles will not go by fire."

"Yes, boss man. I understand."

"Go now, Lo Chew."

Tate shifted his attention to James. "Jimmy, have

men put the black powder in the carts and have the mules haul them to the deep tunnels. Take the powder in deep so it won't catch a spark."

"Got it."

Tate glanced at Mike. Mike spoke no words, but his eyes said plenty.

In short order, men had been redeployed to protect the bridges and move the black powder to the safety of the tunnels.

The wind whipped the flames along the river, sending ash high into the air, only to fall later like a ghostly snow matting the ground.

Tate moved to the bridge closest to the flames. The fire approached, and Chinese and Irish alike dropped buckets over the edge and into the coursing water below, pulling up the heavy load as fast as they could. Blood ran from the hands of the men as rough hemp wore away flesh.

Tate pulled his shirt over his face to reduce the amount of ash he inhaled. Already his head hurt from breathing the foul air. On the bridge, the air was worse, thick with toxins and soot. The sky darkened with billows of smoke that blocked out the sun. What light pierced the tainted air appeared blood red.

Tate joined James, helping him draw up a bucket. The workers spread water from the pails on as much exposed wood as possible. Tate's lungs burned from the exertion and dizziness made him stagger.

After two hours, the wind shifted, driving the fire away from the bridge and up the far canyon wall. During the hours that followed, much of the fire burned itself out, the wind having forced it to travel over already consumed ground. The fire had come close enough to ignite one of the lower trestles, but a dozen Chinese fought it off, leaving only damage that could be repaired in a day. By nightfall, Tate felt confident enough to return to the untouched main camp but left men to keep an eye on the wind and what stubborn flames remained.

Tate couldn't remember having worked so hard or having been so tired.

James walked next to Tate, his face black with soot. Gray ash, cooled by the coming night, fell from the sky. "Looks like a dry rain falling, don't it?"

The words snapped his mind to the image of a foggy cornfield three thousand miles away, to the last day of the war and young Elijah Bell bleeding into the mud. He thought of the boy, of his words, of his strength in death. His ears heard the words again, as if they were uttered fresh from the pale lips of the lad he'd shot—words about a dry rain coming. It was as if the words of Elijah Bell had come true. Another boy came to mind. A boy from a distant land lay hurt and dying in a tent not far from where Tate now walked. He thought of the favorable wind that had just saved them. It was as if God were whispering in his ear.

Again, words heard long ago came to mind. "All that come to have this book . . . will surely save lives and give life." *Give life.* Something needed doing. For the first time since his war with God and the Confederate states had started, Tate knew what he had to do.

chapter **17**

'LL BE TAKING the Chinese boy to San Francisco." Tate stood in the rough-sawn wood shack that served as Blue Mike's cabin. The roof of the structure had been shingled with flattened kerosene cans.

"That a fact, is it?" Blue Mike said.

A halo of cook smoke clung to the ceiling. Mike didn't bother looking up from his breakfast of flour, water, and salt, swimming in sow-belly fat simmering on the stove. The fire had turned it brown and stiff.

"It is. He's in bad shape because of you."

"That Chinee got what he deserved."

"He's just a boy."

"He ain't no boy; ain't no man, neither. He is just another lazy Chinee that got what he deserved." Mike spooned some of the slop from the sizzling pan into his mouth.

"His arm is busted up bad and he's bleeding. If he doesn't get doctoring, he'll infect and die for sure. I know of a Christian mission in San Francisco—on Sacramento Street. They'll take him in and tend to his arm."

Mike shrugged. "No one is going anywhere; we got a railroad that needs building."

Tate tensed. "A woman named Mary knows me from the ship I took from New York. She will see to it that the boy is cared for."

Blue Mike wiped his runny nose with his sleeve and sniffed. "You got ears, man? He's only a Chinee boy, not a man like you and me. He's a yellow devil, if you hadn't noticed. We got a thousand Chinee 'round here, and if he dies, we got someone to take his place before his body begins to cool."

Tate removed his hat and pointed with it, nearly shoving it in Mike's face. "I'm taking the boy to San Francisco, leaving with him this morning on the service train."

Mike shoved the edge of the hot pan into Tate's chest. "You ain't going nowhere with that Chinee boy. You'll stay here and do the work I hired you to do. Now get out."

The heat from the pan pushed its way through Tate's shirt. He slapped the pan aside with the back of his hand, sending gruel splattering against the raw-timbered wall.

Blue Mike's face reddened. He spit out a morsel

of unchewed food as he yelled, "You taking the side of a Celestial over me, when it was me that gave you this job?"

"I left another boy to die in a muddy field once. I won't leave this boy to die now."

Mike spun and poked his finger at Tate as if it were a knife. "You do and I'll—"

Tate sent his fist into the man's face. Blue Mike dropped like a shot deer.

Five minutes later, Tate found the boy sitting on the floor of the tent he shared with several others. Yuen's arm was splinted with two thin shavings of peeled firewood that were bound with rags. A piece of rope served as a sling. His face twisted in pain, but he said nothing. Lo Chew sat near the boy helping him drink tea.

"Can you get up, son?" Tate asked.

Lo Chew translated.

"Yes."

Tate stepped to Yuen and helped him up. The boy writhed in pain, and Tate had to steady him to prevent him from crumpling to the floor like an empty flour sack. "You just have to make the train." He paused. "I know it's not going to be easy."

Again Lo Chew translated. Yuen nodded and smiled weakly.

The cold morning breeze greeted Tate as he and Lo Chew helped the boy past the workers and toward the train. The rumble of the coal-fired boiler digesting fuel rolled through the air and clouds of black smoke rose from the stack. Soon the train would leave on its daily scheduled supply run to Sacramento.

As they walked across the road that separated the train from the Chinese portion of the camp, workers stopped and bowed to Tate in a respectfully long bend at the waist.

"What are they doing?" Tate asked Lo Chew.

"They honor you. They now call you Sheming."

"Shem . . . what does that mean?"

"It mean, 'Man Who Give Life.' They very grateful for you. Much impressed because you fight fire like wise man. You saved lives with mind that is smarter than crafty fire. They honor you because you help hurt boy Yuen."

"I shouldn't get respect for doing what a man ought to do."

"You not like other white men. I have seen white men shoot Chinese man and laugh. We are as animals, as workers no better than a beast. You see Chinamen as men, not yellow, not white, but a person like all others."

Tate nodded, embarrassed by the words.

"There is much favor on you. Much good will come of your life. I see luck in each step of the trail you walk."

Tate saw no need for more words. With each stride he felt the spine of the Bible in the sack that held his few belongings. It rubbed against his side, and for some reason it gave him comfort.

They paused at the set of steps that led to the passenger car. Yuen started up, then stopped on the second step. He said something in Chinese and Lo Chew held out the bag that contained the boy's belongings. Tate stepped out of the way. As the bag was transferred from one hand to another, it slipped from Yuen's grip and fell on the first step, then tumbled to the hard ground.

Tate didn't speak Chinese, but he recognized a gasp and an exclamation when he heard them. Yuen looked horrified at what had fallen from the bag. A white teacup lay under the black wood box with a sprung lid. Dried purple flowers poured from the box onto the ground. A gust sent seed pods tumbling into the foliage along the tracks.

Lo Chew knelt and carefully lifted the cup and placed it in the damaged black box. The cup had survived the fall with only a chip in the handle.

Lo Chew handed it to Tate. "It is luck-fortune if we go through life with only a chip and do not break."

Tate took the box and slid it into Yuen's sack. He helped Yuen into the train and to a seat. Tate sat next to the window. Through the glass he saw Blue Mike approach. The line boss looked at Tate and sniffed at the trickle of blood under his nose. He stood on the dry flowers and seeds strewn on the ground. As the train began to pull away, a hard rain began to fall.

chapter 18

JULY 1, 1980
NEAR BAKERSFIELD, CALIFORNIA

A T THREE THAT afternoon, Gary pulled off Interstate 5 north of Bakersfield. He still had four or five hours more to travel before reaching San Francisco. The ride from Phoenix had gone smoothly but hours on the back of a motorcycle were taking their toll. He had left home eight hours earlier and had stopped only once for fuel and a brief fast-food lunch. Although young and in good condition, the monotonous vibration of the old motorcycle had left him stiff and sore. He needed a break.

He pulled his motorcycle to the side of the road at a plywood fruit-and-vegetable stand. As he dismounted, he felt his joints creak. He walked to the fruit stand, the hot sun beating on his back and neck, and surveyed an array of green plastic containers set in neat rows under the shade of the stand's plywood roof. He found a small basket of fat San Joaquin strawberries.

The Mexican merchant stood nearby spraying lettuce with water from a hose, his stubby finger pressed over the opening. When Gary lifted the basket of strawberries, the man said, *"Un dólar."*

It seemed a reasonable price. Gary removed a

single from his wallet—a wallet that held four hundred dollars, a gift from his grandmother for graduating with a bachelor's degree in economics—and paid the man.

For Gary this was a grand adventure, a hunt through the past, a mystery he could solve. He felt more freedom than he had ever known. The horizon seen over his motorcycle's handlebars was his new friend and the old Bible in his backpack was a map to an unsolved mystery that could change his life forever.

With purchase in hand, he returned to his old Triumph and set the container on the vinyl seat. The day was hot and Gary's hair felt glued to his scalp by sweat and the constant pressure of the helmet he wore. In Bakersfield, a sign at a used-car dealership had given the temperature as 105. The pavement below his feet felt closer to 130. He reminded himself that Phoenix was hotter.

He popped a strawberry in his mouth and enjoyed the fresh sweetness of the fruit. As he chewed he saw a roadside pay phone and decided to place a collect call to Yvonne. She accepted the charges.

"Where are you?" Her voice said she felt glad to hear from him.

"Not far outside Bakersfield. Do you know where that is?"

"No, I've never been to California, but I promise to look it up on a map."

"It's in the central part of the state. I've still got a lot of miles ahead of me."

"Doesn't sound like much fun."

"Of course it is. What could be better than tooling around on a motorcycle in the summer sun eating ripe strawberries with the juice trickling down my chin?"

"How about a comfortable chair in the shade of an old Virginia oak and sipping some iced sweet tea like a Southern gentleman with nothing spilling out of your mouth?"

"Okay, you got me." He took a bite of another strawberry. With his mouth still full he said, "Where's your sense of adventure?"

"All my adventures happened long ago. I live in the past, in history books, when there was a time men didn't call women collect."

"I'm sorry about that. I'll pay you back."

"I've heard that line before." He noted the humor in her voice.

"Got anything new?"

"Yes, and I think it's good. Professor Burke did a little more research for us. He found a record that shows a Lieutenant Jeremiah Tate in action around Appomattox Station on April ninth, and there is also a Jeremiah Tate listed in the burial records at Murrell Lawn Cemetery."

"So that's our guy?"

"Maybe. I can't say they're the same man, yet. The name isn't all that uncommon."

"But there's a good chance that it is the same guy."

"Probably. I just can't prove it yet."

"You history types are a cautious bunch."

"Carelessness can ruin a career, and my career hasn't even started."

"Well, you're becoming my favorite historian."

He heard her laugh. "And just how many historians do you know?"

"Just you."

"I thought so."

Gary thanked her, and just before she hung up, she said, "You be careful out there, okay?"

"I will."

chapter 19

DECEMBER 13, 1865
SAN FRANCISCO, CALIFORNIA

THE SAN FRANCISCO fog rolled in with the tide, covering streets and buildings in a funerary shroud of dreary gray. Only twenty minutes earlier, the air had been clear and the setting sun had set the horizon ablaze. The thick, damp mist extinguished the sunset and made it difficult for Tate to see across Sacramento Street. He supported Yuen, weak from the hours of travel and fevered by infection, past buildings with strange pagoda roofs banded in carved ornamental red and black dragons. The streets were nearly empty, except for an old woman who slept on sacks of strange-smelling spices. Down the street, the hazy forms of drunken men staggered in various directions, like inebriated ghosts looking for their graves.

As he and Yuen moved slowly along the lane, Tate strained his eyes, probing each door for a sign that might read Mission of Mercy—the name Mary had written on her letter. Several blocks back, he had been told by a white man leaving a Mah-jongg gambling house that the mission was just down the street, but he had yet to find it. The signs were painted in gold-and-red-lacquered Chinese letters that Tate couldn't understand. He wanted to ask Yuen what the signs said, but he spoke no Chinese and Yuen no English.

When they passed the open door of a washhouse, Tate caught sight of a Chinaman inside holding a metal pan loaded with glowing embers. The man wore a black skullcap with the traditional pigtail. He sipped from a cup in his other hand and spit a spray of water onto the laundry while pulling and pushing the metal belly of the pan across a white shirt resting on a table. Beside him sat several bundles of other laundry waiting to be ironed. A boy squatted in a corner of the room, mending white sheets with a needle and black thread.

Tate moved to the door, still supporting Yuen each step of the way. At the threshold, he dropped his canvas sack and thumped on the laundry's doorjamb. The noise frightened a sleeping cat in the middle of the room; it hissed and sprang to its feet. The startled laundryman stiffened with surprise and stared wide eyed at the tall stranger in his doorway. The boy shot to his feet and slipped into the darkness of another room, his silk slippers whispering against the wood floor.

"Do you speak English?"

The worker shrugged and jabbered what seemed like nonsense to Tate. He extended Mary's letter and the man approached cautiously, still holding the cup of water and pan of smoldering coals. The laundryman glanced at the letter, then shook his head. Tate held little hope the laundryman could read the document, but he had to try.

The Chinaman studied Yuen, then pushed past Tate and out the door, motioning for them to follow. He sometimes moved faster than Yuen's condition would allow. Several times Tate had to call the man back.

Yuen groaned with each step. Tate could feel the heat from the boy's fevered skin.

Finally, the laundryman stopped in front of a two-story, white brick building with a black-painted front door. He poured what little water remained in the cup onto the street and tapped the cup on the entryway. Inside the dark home, a metal oil lamp appeared to float past the mullioned windows.

The door opened with a creak and the figure of a

thin, bent Chinese man in blue silk appeared in the doorway. He looked weary and aged. The queue down his back was long and gray, and a thin line of silver mustache curled from the sides of his wizened face. The laundryman spoke fast and glanced down at the letter in Tate's hand. Tate held it out and the old man took it, angling the nut-oil flame in his lamp to better see the words.

The old man looked at Tate, then at Yuen. His eyes lingered on the injured man. "The woman you seek is not here."

"You speak English." Tate felt a bit of hope.

"Yes. The woman you seek is not here."

"Is this the Mission of Mercy?" Tate moved closer to the door and stood just a foot from the opening.

"Do I know you?"

"No, but Mary does."

The man lowered his light. "I can speak no more of such things tonight." He started to close the door. Tate put his boot forward and the door halted at his step.

"My name is Jeremiah Tate, and I need to find the woman named Mary." Tate motioned to the boy. "He's hurt bad. Can't you see that? His arm is red with infection. Mary told me to come to this place if I ever needed help. Well, I need help."

The Chinaman examined Tate's eyes. "Tate? You are the one she calls the Messenger? The one who gives the life? The prophet?"

"I am. Well, she did call me Messenger."

"I am Dr. Ling. I am the mission's physician. You must now pray that God will put his hand of protection over Mary. With God's grace she will be here soon, if she has not fallen into the hands of the evil ones."

Tate had no idea what that meant. "Can we come in? We've been traveling and walking for too long."

Ling invited the two in. The laundryman followed, his smoking coal-bearing pan still in hand. Once inside, Ling lit another lamp. Flickering light fell on teak furnishings and a red Oriental rug that covered a worn plank floor.

"Sit him in that chair." Ling pointed to a straight-backed, padded chair that looked as if it may have once graced a fine home. Now it looked worn and tired of having held the weight of so many people.

Tate helped Yuen to the chair and lowered him to its faded cushion.

"Please hold this." Ling handed the lamp to Tate. "Hold it close to the boy's face."

Tate did. Ling studied Yuen's face. He moved his attention to the seeping, blood-soaked rags that served as bandages around the fractured arm. The smell of rotting flesh filled the room as Ling removed the makeshift dressing. The man from the laundry gasped and retreated to a corner. Tate had seen such horrors and worse during the war, but he still had to fight the urge to step back and turn away.

142

"What caused this?"

"We work on the railroad outside of Sacramento. A man there struck him in the face and the boy fell down a steep slope."

"How long ago?"

"It's been three days."

"Much time has passed. You should have brought him sooner."

Tate didn't respond. He already knew that.

A faint gasp made Tate turn. Mary stepped through the front door from the dark night, her hands raised to her mouth. She lowered her hands and approached. "Mr. Tate, this is a surprise. It is very nice to see you again."

"Mary!" His joy at seeing her surprised him. In the dim light, she looked as lovely as the last time he'd seen her on the docks of San Francisco. He thought of her letter, a letter he had read countless times.

She raised her hand in formal fashion and Tate took it. He noticed her eyes drifting to his white-scarred hands. "I see your wounds have healed."

"Thanks to you. I owe you a great deal."

She smiled, and if the light had been brighter, Tate guessed he could have seen her blush. "You owe me nothing, Mr. Tate. Caring for others should be the joy and obligation of everyone."

"I've missed you." His words tumbled out awkwardly.

Mary started to speak, but no words came.

A moan from Yuen brought Tate back. "The boy is hurt bad, and I figured he'd die if he didn't get help soon. I hear hospitals tend to whites and don't care much for his kind. I was hoping you could do something to help him."

Mary hesitated, then moved closer to the injured boy. Tate saw the darkening concern spread across her face as she exchanged glances with Ling. His expression told her what Tate already knew.

"We have to take the infected arm," Ling said apologetically. He straightened, still holding bandages that smelled like a dead animal.

Ling and Mary moved to a table in the parlor and cleared its surface. Tate realized they planned to do the surgery then and there. Several times he had seen limbs of soldiers amputated in field hospitals. The sounds, the odors, the horrid sights still haunted him. He wished to be someplace else—anyplace else.

With Tate's help, Ling and Mary carried Yuen to the table. With every move, he moaned in anguished pain. Perspiration beaded his brow like thick morning dew.

Yuen whispered in Chinese.

"What'd he say?" Tate asked.

"He wants to know what we are doing," Ling answered, then spoke to Yuen.

Yuen jabbered and wagged his head back and forth. He tried to sit up but lacked the strength. He spoke again.

Before Tate could ask, Ling translated. "He says he would rather die and that he cannot live with only one arm. He doesn't want to go into the Celestial Kingdom as half a man."

Again, Tate thought of wounded soldiers who had left an arm or a leg in a battlefield hospital. Those soldiers had also pleaded for the doctors to stop, but a sharp knife always advanced to flesh.

Tate placed a hand on Yuen's chest to keep him from trying to rise again. It took very little strength to hold the feverish young man to the table. Yuen gazed at Tate through swollen eyes. Nothing was said, but the communication was clear.

"Lay still. It'll all be over soon." Tate doubted Yuen understood the words, but his expression made Tate believe the intent got through.

Yuen turned his eyes to the peeling plaster ceiling. A trickle of tears ran down one cheek. He looked frail and gaunt. The gray bone of his arm poked through a red-purple hole that was hot with infection.

Mary shifted her gaze to Tate. "Do you have the Bible with you? The one the boy gave you on the battlefield?"

"Yes?"

"Please get it if you will."

"Do you really think that book has the power to save the boy, as you think it did for that girl on the ship?"

"No. I believe the Bible is only paper and print,

but the words on its pages hold a power beyond what our minds can ever know."

Tate foraged through his sack and retrieved the book, then handed it to Mary, who immediately flipped through it, her thumb resting on a page. "Here it is: Second Chronicles thirty-two. 'Be strong and courageous, be not afraid nor dismayed' . . ." She paused, then continued. " 'With him is an arm of flesh; but with us is the Lord our God' . . ."

"Mary," Tate began, "Yuen doesn't—"

Mary stopped him with an upraised hand. A second later, she spoke in unbroken Cantonese. Yuen tilted his head to face Mary. He seemed as stunned as Tate felt.

She closed the book, looked at Yuen, and spoke in Chinese. Ling translated. "This God I read about is a mighty God, a God who sits above all others. There is none like Him. He calms the sea. He breathes life into death, and He will listen to me when I speak to Him in prayer."

Yuen spoke, and Mary translated for Tate. "Will you pray to your God that my arm will not be removed from my side this night?"

Mary lowered her head for a moment. She said in English, then Cantonese, "My God has already answered that prayer. God knew that Dr. Ling is a most skilled Chinese doctor and is well trained in such matters. It is why you are here tonight. If God had not put it on the heart of Mr. Tate to bring you to us, then you would have soon died."

Again Yuen spoke, his words so weak that Tate feared they would be his last. "Is there no other way to live and be a whole man?"

Mary smiled, but her eyes betrayed her sadness. "Yes, but not in this world."

Dr. Ling glanced at Tate and then at Mary. He spoke from thin lips covering stubby, ill-spaced teeth. "You will need to hold him down; even with opium, it will be very painful. I will cut the arm off at the elbow with one smooth, round cut. The saw will sever the uncut tendons and bone, and a red-hot iron will sear closed the exposed veins. It should take only a minute."

The laundryman stood stiffly, moving only to fan air to the smoldering embers. In the pan was a heated piece of iron bar placed there by Ling. The doctor lit an opium pipe and handed it to Yuen. It was the only pain-numbing substance they had. Most soldiers Tate had seen go through an amputation were forced to drink lots of whiskey or were knocked out. The fortunate ones had chloroform that would put them into a temporary sleep. Some died from the misuse of the chemical. Dr. Ling had no chloroform.

The boy took it with his good arm and raised the white pipe to his dry mouth. Dr. Ling told him to inhale the smoke. The boy sucked in deep and coughed. The doctor whispered, "Breathe in the smoke again."

Within ten minutes, Yuen's eyes floated in a moony gaze. The old man gave his knife one last swipe across a leather strap, then placed the blade against Yuen's red, hot skin.

Mary pressed down on Yuen's chest. Tate was instructed to hold the boy's injured arm extended. The doctor nodded to both of them. Sweat trickled from his forehead and seeped into his eyes as he cut. Yuen's skin split open and folded outward. Nerves twitched and glistened in the oozing red. Blood from the artery spurted on Tate's face and shirt. Yuen arched his back, screamed, moaned, then went slack. His brown eyes appeared vacant. The saw blade separated the bone and cut the last stretched tendon. Tate held Yuen's severed forearm. Dr. Ling pulled the smoldering iron bar from the laundryman's pan of coals and placed the orange, glowing tip against Yuen's exposed artery and veins, searing them closed. Ling sewed the wound up with silk thread.

They had done all they could. Tate wondered if it had been enough.

chapter 20

JULY 2, 1980
SAN FRANCISCO, CALIFORNIA

ARY HAD SPENT the night at an economy motel an hour outside of San Francisco. After a brief breakfast, he made his way through swelling traffic and into the city. He went directly to the Murrell Lawn Cemetery, entered the chapel offices, and asked for the manager. A round, middle-aged man with receding hair met him in the lobby. The manager gave his name as Larry Tuttle.

After introductions, Gary asked for the location of Jeremiah Tate's grave.

"Let's go to my office." Tuttle led him down a short hall to an expansive room with a plush rug, large oak desk, and expensive-looking trim. Soft music filtered from overhead speakers. It was an instrumental of a hymn, but Gary couldn't identify it.

"Have a seat, Mr. Brandon." Gary did and Tuttle slipped into his high-backed black leather chair. "You said your relative is named Jeremiah Tate?"

"He's not a relative. I'm doing some research."

"Really? Research? May I inquire—"

"It's historical in nature." Gary hoped the short answer would be enough.

149

Tuttle seemed to take the hint. "When did Mr. Tate pass on?"

"In 1866."

"Yes, I guess that would make it historical." Tuttle turned to a computer, its monochrome green face coming to life, then typed in Tate's name. "We have everything on these new computers, even the really old records. Just had the system installed. I don't know how we got by without it. Anyway, if he's on our grounds, the computer will tell us." He studied the screen. "We have several Tates. Maybe there is a Jeremiah Tate—1866 you said?"

"Yes, sir." Gary shifted in his seat.

"Here he is." Tuttle jotted something on a notepad. "Jeremiah Tate, buried in 1866 in the old Chinese section of the cemetery and was scheduled to be relocated to the new section in 1972."

"What do you mean, 'relocated'?"

"As you can see, we have a very large operation and much of the original cemetery had to be relocated because of a freeway project that crossed through the edge of the cemetery. We moved—I say 'we,' but it was before I started working here, you understand."

"Yes, I understand."

"Anyway, about two hundred graves were relocated to make room for the new freeway. In their cases, 'final resting place' wasn't so final." He chortled at his own joke.

"Where is Tate buried now?"

"The ledger says he was buried in . . . odd. I didn't see that the first time." He fell silent as he studied the monitor.

Gary cleared his throat.

"Sorry. It appears that when the old section of the Murrell Lawn grave site was opened for relocation, there was no body in Mr. Tate's coffin. Still, the record shows that his grave was on that property. But as I said, there were no remains."

"No remains?"

"No corpse."

"That makes no sense."

"I must warn you that records from the mid-nineteenth century are not always reliable. You say you're not family?" Tuttle looked as if he had inadvertently revealed some fault on the part of the cemetery.

"No, I am not family, but it's important I find anything I can about him."

"The database shows that old Pavel asked to take the grave marker since there was no body to relocate."

"No body, but you have a grave."

"We had a grave, but it was vacant of any remains."

Gary leaned forward. "Who is old Pavel?"

"He used to work here. Started in the mid-to-late fifties, I think, way before my time. Anyway, he was still working when I first started. Real nice guy but talks a blue streak. Meticulous about everything. Keeps detailed records. Old Pavel often asked for anything unclaimed, and the headstone was certainly unclaimed."

"You say Pavel was responsible for moving all the coffins?"

"Yes, I'm sure some administrator was in charge, but Pavel would be the man actually doing the work and overseeing the laborers. Seems a disagreeable job, don't you think?" Tuttle looked back at the screen.

Gary rubbed his forehead. "Why would he take Tate's headstone?"

"Your guess is as good as mine. In any event, he asked for it and got permission to take it. We had no body to move, so we had no grave to put the headstone on."

"Let me get this straight," Gary said. "Back in the seventies, your company moves a bunch of graves, including Tate's, because the city needed the land for a freeway—"

Tuttle raised his hand. "To be accurate, Mr. Brandon, one doesn't move graves; one moves coffins."

"Okay, so your company moves the *contents* of several hundred graves, but in Tate's case there is no body, and the man you call Pavel took the headstone from the original grave site."

"That's about right."

"Any chance the body had just decomposed to dust?"

"No, the note says there was no body, no bones, not even a tooth—nothing. I wonder . . ." Tuttle picked up the phone.

"Who are you calling?"

"Susie Eastman. She maintains our records, including our paper files—" He stopped. "Ms. Eastman, this is Mr. Tuttle. I need a favor."

Gary smiled at the formality.

Tuttle listened, then continued, "I have someone here who needs your expertise." He explained the situation, listened again, then hung up. He turned to Gary. "She should be here soon. She's an organizational genius. She knows where every important paper is. Can I get you something to drink?"

"No. I don't understand. I thought the information was in the computer."

Tuttle smiled. "Our organization has been around for a long while. We have a database on every interment and grave location, but the database holds only the essential information. Notes by employees made during the days before computers are filed away. One never knows when one will need a particular document."

Time inched by as Tuttle spoke of the cemetery's history and the interesting people he had met in his job. Gary could do nothing but listen.

Ten minutes later, a matronly woman entered with a file folder in hand. Tuttle introduced them and the archivist left, but only after issuing a reminder to Tuttle that she wanted her folder back in the same shape she'd delivered it in.

Tuttle laid the file on the desk and opened it. "Ah, here we go. I knew Pavel would have made some notes." He read in silence, then, "Interesting. The coffin was simple pine and in bad shape." He looked up. "You know, today we place the casket in a concrete liner and place a concrete lid to seal it in. State law doesn't allow us to bury a coffin directly in the ground."

"That's very interesting. What does Pavel say?"

"He writes that the coffin was in bad shape. The lid had come loose. That's to be expected. One hundred and ten years in the ground can cause serious damage to untreated wood. Anyway, inside the casket, where he expected to find the remains of the departed, he found . . ." He looked back at the folder. "He found about a hundred pounds of— get this—sand and the scraps of what was . . ." He ran a finger along the line he was reading, ". . . *old Chinese rice bags. No human remains.*' Imagine that. That must have bothered Pavel for years."

"Pavel. I don't think I've ever met anyone by that name." Through the window, Gary saw the cloud-stuffed sky darken.

"It's Ukrainian. Pavel and his brother, Vlad, came to the U.S. when they were kids. Vlad worked here, too."

Gary hadn't expected a story about an empty coffin. He assumed it would be an easy thing to ride into the cemetery, ask for directions, and soon be standing over Tate's grave. "Where do they live now?"

"Well, Vlad is dead. Died two or three years ago. Pavel lives with his daughter in Laurel Heights on some side street off Geary Boulevard. By the way, he is very old, and the last I heard, he was pretty ill."

"Ill?"

"Heart problems."

"What's Pavel's full name?"

"Pavel Trafemchuck. You thinking of paying him a visit?"

Gary nodded. "Could I get his address?"

Tuttle studied Gary. "I'm not supposed to give out personal information on existing or former employees."

"I understand." Gary stood.

"You don't look like a troublemaker. Maybe I can make an exception in your case." Tuttle worked the keyboard again, then jotted down a note on a piece of paper. "He won't mind a visitor, he loves to talk. I'll warn you of that. Tell him we think of him often."

"I will."

A soft tapping at the office window caught Gary's attention. A light rain had begun to fall.

chapter 21

GARY, THANKFUL THAT the light rain remained little more than a drizzle, parked his motorcycle on Geary Boulevard in front of an older blue house in need of a handyman's touch. An old couch with stuffing peeking out in spots stood on the front porch. He set his helmet on the seat and walked to the front door. Two gentle knocks and a minute later a woman answered. She was as tall as Gary and had chiseled cheekbones and amber hair that curled just above her shoulders. He guessed her to be a couple of years shy of thirty. Gary introduced himself and asked to speak to Mr. Pavel Trafemchuck.

She didn't move from the door. "Who did you say you were?"

"Gary Brandon. I'm doing some research on a man who died in the mid-1800s. Mr. Tuttle at the cemetery gave me your address."

"I don't see how my grandfather can help you."

He explained about the empty coffin her grandfather had discovered eight years earlier. "I promise not to take up too much time."

She stepped to the side. "Come in. You'll have to forgive my caution. San Francisco has its share of weirdos."

Gary smiled. "Phoenix has quite a few of those, too. I imagine all big cities do."

"I'm Gina Alistair." She extended her hand and Gary shook it.

As he stepped over the threshold, the sharp odor of garlic assaulted his nose. His face must have reflected his shock. "I'm sorry about the smell. Grandpa has heart problems and garlic is an old Ukrainian remedy. He eats garlic on everything; he even smears it on toast." She shrugged. "This way. He's in the kitchen."

Pavel sat on a chrome chair in the kitchen, eating kielbasa slices layered on a roll smeared with garlic. Before him rested the sports section of the morning paper and from its perch on a scarred Formica countertop a radio played: *The results of the fourth race at Golden Gate Fields are official. Sharp-as-a-Tack wins; Little Harvey is second; and Poker Chip comes in third.* A half-finished cup of coffee sat to his right.

Pavel scratched a heavy mark through the names on the newspaper. "I shouldn't have bet on that old hag in the first place, Gina. He usually does well on a wet track, loves the mud, but today he ran like a rented mule." He didn't look up.

"Grandpa—"

"Don't start lecturing me, girl. I've heard it all before. I have a right to waste my money as I see fit."

"Grandfather." She switched to a formal and

firm tone. "This is Mr. Gary Brandon. He has come all the way from Phoenix to talk to you."

Pavel looked up. "From Phoenix?"

Gary took in the man. Painfully thin, his flesh drooped on his face and neck as if divorced from the muscles below. His skin seemed thin and bore the color of paper left too long in the sun. Rheumy eyes gazed back at Gary.

"Yes, sir. Just got in today."

"That's a long way to travel; you ever heard of a phone?"

"Grandpa, there is no need to be rude."

"I am too old to be polite."

Gina pursed her lips and scowled. The expression failed to convince. She moved to the radio and turned it off.

"I was listening to that. There are two more races to be run. Besides, I wasn't being rude, just honest."

Gina sighed. "I'll get the results later."

"Not the same."

Gary decided to intervene. "I don't mind waiting."

"You bet on the ponies, son?"

"No, I don't gamble."

He shook his head. "It's hard to trust a man who doesn't gamble."

"Grandpa!"

"Okay, okay." He directed his gaze back to Gary. "Have a seat. I'm just having some fun with you. I don't get many visitors these days."

Gary sat in a chair opposite Pavel. The old man had liver spots on the side of his face and more hair bristling from his nose than on his head. Gary could smell the garlic and coffee on his breath even though he sat several feet away.

"Grandpa, this man wants to ask you a question about when you worked at the cemetery. Mr. Tuttle sent him."

"What's to know? I dug holes and put them in; I dug holes and took them out. Not much to tell."

"Mr. Tuttle spoke highly of you. He said you kept great records."

"I did my job. A man is judged not by his job but by how well he does it. At least, that's the way it used to be."

"I understand that you occasionally relocated bodies."

"Sometimes. Not much call for that. Well, there was the relocation project back in . . . sometime in the seventies."

"In 1972," Gary said. "At least that's what Tuttle said."

"That'd be about right. If he says it was 1972, then I won't argue. What's that got to do with you?"

"I need to know something about a specific body you relocated."

The old man gave a garlic-laced laugh. "I can only remember the first body I dug up as a boy long ago. I don't remember much of the others. There were so many . . . hundreds of bodies."

"Which ones do you remember?"

"Like I said, I was only a boy, only about eight or so, still living in the old country, and I helped my father dig up a corpse. My father is the reason I got into the business. He dug graves in Kiev. I remember it well. It was a gray day, leaves blowing about, you know, like in the movies. My father took me to a cemetery—"

"Excuse me, sir," Gary interjected. "I'm sorry, but I was thinking about the time when you relocated the graves here in San Francisco. I'm looking for information on a man named Jeremiah Tate—" A hand touched him on the shoulder and gave a gentle squeeze.

Gina spoke softly. "He's hard of hearing. He also likes to tell stories of the old days back home. It's all he's got. I suggest you listen if you ever want an answer to your questions."

"Um, sure. Of course." He turned to Pavel. "Please continue."

The old man stammered, "I . . . I forgot where I was." He looked at his granddaughter as if confused.

"You were a boy and you were with your father and you dug up a body in Kiev."

"Of course. Well, we spent a good part of the morning digging up this man who had been buried the year before. My father was a friend of his. He knew the man had been buried with several bottles of vodka." He laughed, as if the words tickled his throat. " '*Good* vodka,' Father said. Anyway, my father and I thumped the top of the casket with our shovels and then I dug around the lid, clearing away all the dirt with my fingers. My father used his shovel to pry it open. The lid squeaked open and I saw my first skeleton. His skin was dried on the bones, but the meat was all gone. It scared me to death. The remains had four bottles of vodka, two cradled in each arm. My father took the bottles and handed them to me and then he lifted me up and out of the hole. He then held his shovel like a baseball bat and smashed the skull with the blade. 'That's for not paying back the rubles you owed me,' he shouted." The man's voice softened and his gaze shifted to events only he could see.

"I cried when my father yelled at the corpse," Pavel continued. "He said, 'We are even now, my old friend,' then took one of the bottles from me and returned it to the coffin, placing it under the skeleton's arm. 'You are forgiven,' my father muttered over and over as we shoveled dirt back into the hole. We didn't even replace the lid."

Pavel fell silent and Gary gave him the time he needed. The old man spoke again. "That reminds me of another story—"

"Grandfather, Mr. Brandon has traveled a long way. Don't you think we should answer his questions now?"

Pavel took the coffee and sipped but ignored the kielbasa on his plate. "All right, let's hear what the boy has to say."

Gary leaned over the table and folded his hands. "Do you know the name Jeremiah Tate?"

"Son, I've heard lots of names. Thousands. Tate?"

"Yes. Jeremiah Tate."

"Yes," the old man said slowly, as if dredging his shadowed mind, "Tate. Yes, I remember. His was one of the graves we tried to relocate. I remember because it was odd that someone with a white man's name had been buried in the middle of the Chinese part of the cemetery." He stared at the wall. "No body in the box, just sand inside his coffin and some old rice bags. Chinese rice bags."

"How do you know the bags were from China?"

Pavel fixed his eyes on Gary. "Because they had Chinese writing on them, that's how. My memory is fading some, but I'm not that dull in the brain just yet."

"Of course not, sir. I didn't mean to imply you were."

"Don't be so grumpy, Grandpa. He's just trying to get the details."

"You his lawyer, Gina? Let the boy speak for himself."

"The grave was marked Jeremiah Tate, but there was no body in that coffin?" Gary tried to get the man back on track.

"Not bone nor boot. I'm telling you that at the very least, a skull and teeth would be there; skulls and teeth last a very long time. Like rocks, they last hundreds and hundreds of years."

"So you then moved the coffin."

"No, why do a thing like that? There was no body, so why move an empty old box?"

"Okay, what then?"

"The coffin was a cheap pine affair. The man must have been poor; there was no craftsmanship to it. Two of its sides had caved in from the weight of the ground."

"So you found the open coffin in the grave?"

"Yes, when we tried lifting it, the bags of sand just fell through the bottom. Old coffins like that are usually light, since all that's in them is a decomposed body."

"Mr. Tuttle said you kept the headstone."

"Mr. Tuttle talks too much. Yes, I did."

"Why keep the tombstone?"

"I kept the ones no one wanted: the broken ones, the abandoned ones. Sometimes vandals work them over pretty good and it looks bad for the cemetery, so they replace them. I kept some."

"May I ask where the stone is now?"

The old man pointed to the backyard. "I used them to make a walkway to my garden. I am too old and sick to do any gardening these days. I used to garden all the time. I remember—"

"Grandpa, you're talking too much."

"All right. Instead of nagging me, girl, why don't you take the boy out back and show him?"

Gary rose.

"And turn the radio back on. Maybe I can catch the final race."

The rain had let up. Gary stood in an overgrown garden populated by weeds and flowers. A narrow path crossed the little yard and led to an old picnic table. The walkway was composed of a dozen or more granite headstones. Gary tried to find the inscriptions on the old markers, but all he saw was worn granite. He bit his lip and tried to conceal his disappointment.

"Turn them over, son. You're looking at the back sides."

Gary looked up to see the old man leaning his weight on an aluminum cane.

"Well, I feel stupid," Gary said.

"Don't," Gina replied. "It took years for me to realize what these were, and they still give me the creeps."

"You don't mind if I—"

"Go ahead. You've got my curiosity up." She stepped to the fence and retrieved a flat-nose shovel. Gary levered up the first stone and held it on end. It was from 1933 and he let it drop in place.

The next was a woman named Katherine. Again Gary let the stone fall back to its resting place.

"I hope you don't think my grandfather is macabre. He is a good man; he just doesn't like to see things go to waste."

"I don't think he's weird, just unique."

Gary took the time to sweep away the loose dirt with his hand, then pried up the next stone. Mud covered the letters, but he could see *TA*. His heart beat as if he had been jogging. He dropped the shovel to free both hands. Slowly he brushed away damp earth but succeeded only in spreading the mud.

"Wait," Gina said.

He watched as she moved to the house, took hold of the hose, and turned the valve. A trickle of water began to flow. She handed the hose to Gary, who washed caked dirt from the stone. Mud slipped away. In the gray, cloud-diffused light, Gary read:

JEREMIAH TATE
LT. 23RD PENN. CAVALRY
BORN FEBRUARY 4, 1831
DIED JUNE 12, 1866

The last line gave Gary a start.

THOUGH HE DIES HE LIVES.

chapter 22

DECEMBER 14, 1865
SAN FRANCISCO, CALIFORNIA

TATE OPENED HIS eyes to bright sun streaming through the window. The aroma of eggs and bacon wafted up the stairs. It was an aroma he had not experienced in a long time. Over the last few months, his meals had consisted of venison swimming in lard.

He swung his legs over the edge of the bed and stretched his back—a real bed, with smooth sheets and soft blankets. He fought a strong urge to go back to sleep.

Standing, he stretched again, then slipped into his trousers. He froze. There was a new odor, one not nearly as pleasant as frying eggs and bacon. He sniffed the air, then sniffed his arm. He reeked. His body odor clashed with the savory smell of breakfast. At the work camp, everyone smelled bad. No one complained, and after a while, no one noticed. But here, in a proper bedroom in a proper house, the stench was undeniable. If it was offensive to him, then his odor must gag Mary and Ling.

In the corner of the room stood a simple table supporting a washbasin and plain porcelain pitcher. Filling the basin with water from the pitcher, Tate washed with a square slab of soap, scrubbing his face and torso. Next to the basin rested a straight razor, and Tate made use of it. As he wiped the last of the soap from his face, someone knocked on his door.

"Mr. Tate, it is Dr. Ling."

Tate opened the door, still bare from the waist up. "Good morning, Dr. Ling."

Ling stood with a package wrapped in brown paper and bound by a string. He held it out to Tate.

"What's this?"

"A gift from Mary."

"A gift?"

"A new and clean shirt, Mr. Tate."

Tate untied the string, unfolded the paper, and held up the garment. "It makes one think about city living just to be clean."

"Chinese men like to wash every day, whether in the city or not."

Tate slid on the white cotton shirt and buttoned it to the top. "I am obliged for the shirt." He scooped up a handful of water and slicked back his black hair.

"Your meal is waiting, Mr. Tate. Mary is expecting you."

Mary looked up and smiled at Tate as he entered the kitchen.

Tate grinned back. "Thank you for the shirt."

"You are quite welcome. We can have your other

shirt cleaned. It is rather soiled from your walk through the city with Yuen, and the surgery."

"That shirt has seen a lot over these last months."

The kitchen buzzed with activity. Three Chinese women watched over food cooking in wide-brimmed metal pans. When they noticed Tate's presence, they immediately turned and bowed.

Tate gave a nod. "Good morning, ladies."

They resumed their work without a word.

Mary poured steaming coffee from a pot on the stove and set it on the kitchen table.

Tate thanked her and sat. "The smell sure gets a man's stomach growling, but I don't think I can eat all of that. I assume you're expecting guests."

Mary laughed. "It is part of our work. There are many hungry in the city. Some are homeless men, unable to work because of injuries received in the mines or on the railroad, like Yuen."

"How is he?" Tate sipped the coffee. It was strong and hot.

"He is resting. Dr. Ling stayed with him all night. He is in pain, of course, but the opium pipe Dr. Ling gives him helps."

"That's good. I had doubts he'd survive the night."

"He's not out of danger yet. It will be some time before he is up and around."

"I thank you for your kindness to the boy."

"It is what we do here. Not many white men would have bothered with someone like Yuen. You are remarkable."

"I just did what I thought was right."

"That, Mr. Tate, is what makes you remarkable."

The words embarrassed Tate. He changed the subject. "So you feed injured and homeless men."

"Much more than that. There are the orphans who wander the streets, the lame, the blind, those cast off by their families. The desperation in this city knows no bounds."

"I had no idea."

"Let me show you something, Mr. Tate." Mary stepped to a side window in the kitchen.

Tate followed. He could hear noise and voices outside. Mary drew back the drapes to reveal a long line of people. Some were old, others were younger than Yuen. They stood patiently.

"They start arriving before sunrise, each hoping for a wood bowl filled with food. Merchants around the city provide much of what we use. The food is blemished or stale, the kind of food the upper class refuses to touch." She faced Tate. "They don't mind. Some spices and a good frying can make almost anything taste good."

Tate looked at the food cooking in the skillets. The sweet smell of herbs mingled with the odor of fermenting fish oil as cubed pork sizzled. A wide pan on the big stove rocked with frothy boiling water and white rice. A woven basket resting on a wooden butcher-block table held fish heads and cut carrots ready for their turn on the stove. A woman with tiny bound feet shuffled into the room, carrying a headless, freshly plucked chicken. Tate caught himself staring at her feet and forced himself to look away.

Mary caught his gaze. "She is the victim of a nine-hundred-year-old Chinese tradition that required some families to bind the feet of girls at birth to keep their feet small. It is painful and renders the feet almost useless."

"Why would anyone do that? It makes no sense."

"The Chinese culture sees it as a sign of beauty and elevated social status. In fact, it is only a frustrating handicap. But the women willingly submit. It is a sign that a woman is of great value and does not need to work or walk far."

The bound-feet woman saw Tate, immediately turned, and hobbled back outside. Mary called after her, but she slipped through the door. Mary said something in Chinese and one of the cooks followed the woman.

"I take it something happened."

"I think a white man's presence in the kitchen frightened her."

Tate watched the strange happenings through the window but soon redirected his gaze to Mary. The sight of her, the smell of her, the sound of her in the same room made his heart feel like wax warming in the summer sun. He was smitten, he knew that now, but he feared the feelings might not be shared. Why should they be? She had refinement; he was a worn soldier, wearied by his experiences, a former farmer still rough around the edges and probably too hard to change.

"You're staring, Mr. Tate."

He felt his face warm. "Was I? My apologies."

She grinned and returned to the kitchen table.

"I don't mean to be rude, but I bet many men have stared at you." He joined her at the table and took a swallow of the strong coffee.

"It would be immodest of me to speak of such things." She softened. "I did have one man offer me money while I strolled along Dupont Street."

"Did you slap him?"

"What? Why would I . . . Oh." She blushed. "In San Francisco, men outnumber women by the hundreds, even thousands. The man was just lonely. He explained how he'd left his own family back in Ohio to find work here in the city. He had been living alone for a year."

"So?"

"So what?" Mary said.

"Did you say anything to him?"

She smiled again and the room seemed to glow. "I said, 'Isn't it a nice day, and it is also so nice to find such a gentleman on this fine morning.'"

"And the money?"

"I refused it, of course." Her gaze left Tate. "The man wept as I walked away. I felt so sorry for him. It is a horrible thing to be all alone."

"It is."

• • •

Upstairs, above the kitchen, Yuen awakened to the rattling of pots and pans and kitchen banter. His body ached, and the opium-diluted pain felt as if a thousand needles were pressing through his flesh.

He moaned and tried to force the cloudy images of the previous night from his mind.

"Lie still. You are not ready to move." The voice was young and female.

Yuen blinked several times and tried to order his thoughts, which flew in his head like moths around a campfire. A soft hand stroked his forehead, and he turned his head to see who touched him.

A Chinese woman with raven black hair, dark almond eyes, and a concerned expression looked back. The glow of the morning sun pressed through the window, casting her frame in a soft gold.

"Who . . . ?"

"Quiet please. You must rest."

"But . . . ?"

"I am Kim Lee. Dr. Ling has asked me to care for you while he rests. He did not sleep last night. He only now left."

Her touch was gentle and welcome. Yuen had not spoken to a woman in months.

"Thirsty."

Kim Lee reached for a bamboo cup, filled it from a pitcher, and held it out. Yuen reached for it but nothing happened. He tried again, but his arm wouldn't move. An explosion of realization ignited in his head. His arm did not move as it should because it was gone.

"My arm! My arm!"

"Do you not remember the surgery?"

Again he tried to order his thoughts. Many events of the past days were gone or only dim images. "My arm was broken."

"And infected. If Dr. Ling had not done surgery, you might not have lived through the night." She held out the cup again. "Take this with your other hand. I will help you rise enough to swallow."

Yuen did as she instructed. The water tasted sweet and cool, but he could only swallow a sip or two before the pain became too great.

He clenched his teeth and waited for the pain to pass—if it would pass.

It dulled.

"Who are you?" Yuen choked out the words.

"Kim Lee. Do you not remember me telling you my name?"

"I remember. I mean, who are you, Kim Lee?" He wished he could be more coherent, but the pain or the opium muddled his mind.

"You are in too much pain to hear of such unimportant matters from a girl of no consequence."

"Please tell me. I want to hear. It will help me think of other matters besides my pain."

Kim Lee spoke softly. "I have lived at the mission for several months and am being trained to be a nurse."

Yuen's arm felt on fire. He tried to ignore it. Sweat peppered his brow. Kim Lee patted his brow dry with a cool cloth.

"It is most honorable work," she said. She went on. "I came from the Pearl River. My family lived on a junk. It was only one of many in our floating village. My father was a poor fisherman and was no better off when he also tried farming in the nearby fields. The seeds he planted were cursed and refused to grow well in the sandy soil. Father told Mother that my younger brothers would starve if he did not sell her daughter. Father told her that one lame son is better than eighteen gifted daughters, so I must be sold."

Yuen opened his eyes and looked at the nurse-in-training.

She lowered her head. "When Mother heard this, she could say nothing and only bowed her head and let her hair fall over her face to hide her tears." Kim Lee wiped tears from her own eyes. "I said nothing of his decision. It was not my place."

Yuen winced, then closed his eyes again. "I have heard of poor families who sold daughters into slavery. In my village, the girls are called *mui tsai*."

"Yes, that is true. I am a *mui tsai*, just as you say."

Yuen listened, knowing his pain was less than what Kim Lee had known. He had seen the treatment *mui tsai* received.

She continued. "The next day Father took me to a ferryboat moored along the mouth of the river. He left me standing on the deck of the ship while he negotiated my sale with the captain. I could see several pieces of silver dropped into my father's open hand. He left. He never looked back. I arrived in San Francisco months later and was bought by a man named Cheong Moon."

"I know the name. He is the man who met us when my ship arrived from China."

"He took me from the ship. I tried to pull away. I screamed. I called for help. I said I was being kidnapped. No one paid attention. No one helped."

"The whites do not know our language. And our countrymen are too afraid to act."

Kim Lee rose, stepped to a bowl of water and rinsed the cloth, returned to Yuen and placed the cool rag on his forehead. It felt soothing. "No one pays attention to a Chinese girl. Not even . . ." She stopped.

"What?"

"It is nothing."

"It is something. What happened?"

"Cheong Moon lifted the back of his hand to slap me, but he stopped. He said, 'A ripe pear is worth more at market if not bruised.' He then frowned. 'I paid two hundred dollars for you, so now you are mine. I own you. Own you until tomorrow, when I sell you at auction.'"

Yuen asked, "Why would he sell you?"

"You are new to this land."

"I arrived some months ago. I worked on the rail-road line."

Kim Lee nodded. "There are many evil people here. They care only for money and pleasure. Cheong Moon wanted to sell me for a profit. I was frightened. My buyer might have been a man of wealth seeking a house servant, but if the buyer turned out to be a miner, or a man of evil intent, I could be treated like a dog, and even locked up in a room and used—" She bit her lip, failing to finish the sentence. "I have heard of many *mui tsai* being treated that way."

Yuen forced a smile. "Good fortune has brought you to a big home like this. You live under a sign of great luck."

"It was not luck that brought me here. It was God." She took a faint breath, as if telling the story winded her. "At my auction, many men walked by and looked at me, touched me, and then bid on me. None were rich men needing a domestic servant, as I had hoped. They wanted another kind of slave. All were filthy, bearded men who shouted numbers and held up fists of money. I was so frightened." She took a deep breath. "But a woman with red hair stepped forward, a woman with a kind face but also an expression of steel. She bought me with the highest offer. Her name is Mary Connor, but everyone here calls her the White Angel because she has saved many girls such as me from a life of slavery to the whites. The Tong hatc her."

"Red hair." Yuen struggled to drag a memory forward. "Last night a woman spoke to me. She had hair red as fire. She spoke Cantonese and read from a black book. She prayed to her God for me."

"That is the woman. She lives here at the mission. She is the woman who came to help me. She knows the man who brought you here. They traveled on a long sea journey on the same boat. This is not of luck that they know each other. This is by design of God."

A loud noise jarred Yuen. Kim Lee leapt to her feet.

The pounding returned. Someone was at the front door, banging . . . banging . . . banging . . .

chapter **23**

MARY'S HEART STUTTERED and her body tensed. She smoothed her hair back and walked to the front door, her head high and her face a mask of composure. A movement at the top of the stairs caught her attention. Kim Lee stood on the upper landing trembling, her hands over her lips. As Mary approached the door, she saw Tate slip into the hall behind her, staying out of sight, as if he were scouting an enemy's movements. His presence gave her more strength.

Taking hold of the door handle, she slowly pulled open the slab of wood, which rode easily on oiled hinges.

She saw more than she had feared.

A Chinese man with an ugly scar on his face stood on her porch, arms crossed. Seeing a Chinaman at her door was not unusual, but this man was no ordinary Chinese. Mary had seen him before and the sight of the Tong member chilled her.

The Tong had a shaved forehead and a long, braided pigtail hanging to his waist. He rattled on in rapid Cantonese. He curled his lips as if disgusted to be on Mary's porch. Chinese men like him considered it a disgrace to speak to a simple woman.

Mary stood in silence as the man spewed venomous and threatening words. Saliva flew with each sentence of his tirade and Mary had to fight the urge to back away. Instead, she stood fast and nodded. She then said something in Chinese and clutched the door until her knuckles turned white. When finished, the Tong turned and stormed away. Several menacing Chinese men met him in the street. Slowly Mary removed her hand from the door and tried to hide her trembling. Before she could close the door, one of the men in the street pulled something from a flour sack and tossed it on the porch, near Mary's feet.

Her heart rattled in her rib cage. Every bone within her seemed to dissolve. The door latched in place and Mary locked it. She leaned on the door as if it were the only thing holding her up.

Tate stepped from the hall and placed his large hands on her shoulders. "Who was that?"

She turned, saddened when he removed his touch. "I . . . I need to sit. In the parlor. Please."

Tate escorted her to the side parlor and eased her onto a padded chair. She raised a hand to her mouth and stared at the floorboards, straining to hold back tears that threatened to breech the dam of her eyes. A minute passed before she could look at Tate.

"He is a powerful man in San Francisco. He is part of a criminal element of Chinese known as the Tong. They are men without caring or pity."

"What does he want with you?" Tate asked. He pulled a chair close and sat.

"He knows Yuen is here and that you are the one who brought him. He wants the boy back. He said his leader, Cheong Moon, paid for his travel to America from China and that the boy is his property. He wants the boy to be returned or the money paid back. He said he has lost face with the man named Blue Mike and that if he is not given the boy or the money, then he will cause much harm to this house."

Tate's face reddened and he started to speak but Mary lifted her hand. She whispered behind a sob, "I told him that boy had his arm amputated and that he can no longer work. I told him I would never return the boy whom he said you stole from the railroad camp. He said you caused this bad thing to happen to us."

"That's ridiculous. The boy was going to die if I didn't help him."

"It doesn't matter to them. They don't see things the way we do. He demands five hundred dollars for all this bad luck you have brought to Cheong Moon."

"Well, he ain't getting it."

"He said he'd have you killed if the money is not paid. He also said . . ."

"What, Mary? What did he say?"

"He promised he'd kill me, too, but I told him I would not return the boy." She put her hands together in a sign of prayer. "To die is gain in the Kingdom work of our Lord."

Tate rose, unable to sit still. "It's a bunch of loose talk. That's what it is. Nothing but a bluff."

Mary shook her head. "He . . . he . . ." She couldn't say the words. The most she could muster was a finger pointing at the open door of the parlor, to the front door. "He threw the poor creature on the front porch as a sign."

Tate moved from the parlor to the front door and swung it open without hesitation. The head of a cat, its vacant eyes staring back at Tate, rested a few feet away. He slammed the door, rattling loose windowpanes, and returned to Mary.

"It's a sign," she said. "A message to prove his intent." She shuddered. "We have one week to get the money to him."

"Don't you fret. It's nothing but a try at scaring us. I will deal with this my way."

"No, Mr. Tate, it is anything but a scare tactic. He means to follow through on his threat. He will lose face with his men if he does not get what he wants. His kind does not bluff."

"Then we'll go to the police. Things like this are their responsibility."

Again she shook her head. "Cheong Moon pays the police and the judges, anyone who can protect him. Those who will not take bribes are threatened. Some have been killed. He is a wealthy man, and wealthy men can buy their way past police, past anybody who may stop them. It is the way here in Chinatown, the way we have to live. He will keep selling yellow-skinned slave labor and opium, and we cannot stop him."

Tate's face darkened and his jaw set tight. "I will take care of it." He hissed the words, then spun and started for the stairs. Mary followed.

They passed Kim Lee sitting on the lowest step, her arms tightly grasping raised knees. As they passed, she bowed her head but said nothing. To Mary, the young woman's face said enough.

Mary followed Tate into his room. Before she could speak, he was riffling through his canvas bag. "Mr. Tate, you must not be rash. Your anger is getting the better of you."

"I have dealt with an enemy before, and I learned to never give in to them. Give them what they want and they'll take more. The only way to stop them is to meet them head-on with this." He pulled a well-worn Colt Dragoon revolver from the bag.

Mary saw it glint in the sunlight that poured through the window. The sight of it stoked the fire of fear blazing in her. "I had to be strong at the door while talking to the Tong, but I know that the only way to stop Cheong Moon is to give him what he wants."

"No, ma'am. I have different ways." He spun the pistol's cylinder on his forearm.

Mary stepped closer and begged him, "Promise me you will not do anything that is not of the Lord, only what is good and right. God is on our side. He will be on our side only if we do not fight evil with evil. The man who lives by the sword dies by the sword."

"I have been in many a fight and I was always the one standing when it was over. I was still standing because I used my sword better than they did." He turned to her. "I never had the Lord with me in battle. I never saw Him do any fighting. During the war, just as many men in gray uniforms prayed as those in blue, and I am sure the Lord didn't see the need to fight for both sides. Maybe He lets us take care of our own wars. I'm sure God would want this evil stopped, and I am more than obliged to spare Him the effort of helping. He hasn't seemed to come a-running when I called Him before."

"Evil only begets evil." Mary pointed to his Bible, visible in the open sack on the table.

"That's church talk." Tate paced the room like a caged animal. "This ain't a church situation; it's a fighting one. You have an enemy that just came to your door and all you can say is evil begets evil. I know little of church and too much of dealing with an enemy who says he's a-coming. When he says that, you better be ready and not have your eyes closed in any prayer meeting."

Mary pleaded, "It is not what I ask, it is what God commands. Promise me you will not do anything that is not born of peace."

Tate stopped his pacing to look at Mary. "Your hands shake. Your eyes are full of fear. Why? Because of me. I brought Yuen to this house, to this place where you live and work."

"This is no fault of yours."

"It is every bit my fault, and I must deal with it."

She felt so fragile, like a frightened child. "No, you're wrong. This is not your fault. You have done good by me and by Yuen. You did what was right and what was honorable. Because of you, Yuen still lives. If you had not acted, he would be dead and his poor body would probably be used to help fill a ravine." She paused to draw a breath. "You must not do wrong now. You must listen to me and do as I say. Promise me you will. Promise."

Tate frowned and spoke slowly. "I will do as you wish, but I do not have five hundred dollars to pay that man even if I wanted to. When I sold my farm after the war, I took only enough money to get me to San Francisco and sent the rest to the mother of the boy I shot. I sent her a letter and told her to buy a piece of land and make a park for the town in the boy's name. But even if I had every cent of that back, I would not give a penny of it to that man."

Mary stepped forward and cupped his hands in hers. She rubbed the white scars that bleached his skin, the scars that he'd received saving the young girl on the ship. She looked into his darkening eyes. "Behold what God can do if we just ask Him." She bowed her head and prayed, "I know, dear Lord, that You parted the Red Sea and made a way for the fleeing Israelites; that You led the way in the wilderness with a pillar of cloud by day and a pillar of fire by night; that You gave water to drink from a rock and rained manna from Heaven. I now ask You to help us in our hour of want and need, amen."

Before lifting her head, she heard Tate whisper, "Amen." She wondered about his sincerity.

Mary took Tate's Bible in hand and held it up.

"This is the sword of God; it is a flaming sword of truth. I want you to let me use this book and you will see the power of God's ways."

Tate frowned, then nodded.

chapter 24

JULY 2, 1980
SAN FRANCISCO, CALIFORNIA

GARY SLOWLY CRUISED down Sacramento Street, passing a hardware store, several boutiques, and an office-supply house in a redbrick building. The building wore its bronze historical marker like a badge. He eased his motorcycle to the side of the road so he could read the plaque. It read:

> MISSION OF MERCY.
> ON THIS SITE FROM 1863 TO 1894
> STOOD THE FIRST CHINESE HOSPITAL
> IN SAN FRANCISCO.
> HERE MANY CHINESE RECEIVED FOOD
> AND MEDICAL HELP FROM MISSIONARIES.

Yvonne had checked all the death records for women named Mary Connor, the woman who had recorded Tate's death in the back of the Bible. She had listed the date and place in San Francisco, so the search proved easier than expected. Most of the city's records had been destroyed in the 1906

185

earthquake and subsequent fires. The newspaper archives of the *Alta Times* had been spared and provided a wealth of information, because Mary Connor was always causing stories of interest. Yvonne had gleaned a lot of details she didn't mind sharing with Gary. After another collect phone call earlier that day, Gary learned just how fast and passionately Yvonne could talk. At least she was becoming comfortable with him.

"She was a crusader for the freedom of the women in the yellow slave trade, which started during the Gold Rush and lasted unofficially in San Francisco into the 1920s. Did you know the life expectancy of a prostitute at that time was only six years? Six years!"

"No. I didn't—"

"Slavery may have been abolished after the Civil War, but a sad and virtually unknown dirty secret remained: slaves of all kinds were kept as prostitutes for many years after the final shots of the Civil War had been fired. They kept most of these women in cages or locked in basements. It is unimaginable that paid-off politicians and police allowed this to go on in a country that called itself the land of the free, but it happened. Some of these girls—and I mean girls, since most never lived long enough to be called women—were never allowed to go outside. Occasionally, they might be allowed out on Chinese New Year, but that's it. If they disobeyed, they were lashed or burned with hot irons to make them submissive. Mary Connor committed her life to abolishing such an unjust and inhumane situation—she was a crusader to free those in slavery. She is my new hero."

"Easy, Yvonne. You're taking this personally."

"*You* take it easy. Of course it's personal. I'm a woman. Everyone should care."

"I'm not diminishing the crime, Yvonne, I'm just trying to save my eardrums."

"Oh. Sorry. I tend to get loud when I get excited."

"No problem. I can take it. Go on."

"Mary Connor was a remarkable woman. The more research I do on her, the more heroic she becomes. I think all the riddles you're trying to solve are tied up in her. I have an address for you."

"An address?"

"For the Mission of Mercy that Mary founded. It's on Sacramento Street." She had recited the address and Gary had committed it to memory.

Now Gary stood in front of the building that had once housed Mary Connor and her mission. Perhaps the answers would be found somewhere in the old redbrick building.

Gary walked to the window of the old mission house. A red and white plastic sign in the window read CLOSED, but a light was coming from an office behind a service desk. Gary cupped his hands around his eyes and peered inside. The place was old but had been refurbished sometime in the recent past. He tapped his motorcycle key against the glass and waited. Nothing. He tapped louder.

A Chinese man in a white dress shirt and loosened black tie appeared. He pointed at the sign and mouthed the words, *We're closed.*

Gary put his palms together in a pleading gesture. The man lowered his head, took an exaggerated breath, and walked to the glass door. He spoke loudly to be heard through the glass. "We are closed for the night. Sorry." He started to walk away.

"Wait." Gary felt foolish trying to carry on a conversation through a glass door. "Let me show you something." He pulled the Bible from his backpack, opened it to the inscription about Mary, and held it up for the man to see. "Mary Connor ran a mission here. Her name is in this Bible and dated 1866. I'm doing research on her."

The man studied the page for a minute, cocked his head in surprise, then reached into his pocket and removed a key ring. He opened the door a crack but no more. "Who are you?"

"My name is Gary Brandon. I came up from Phoenix. I'm trying to research some of the people in this old Bible. This used to be Mary Connor's mission, right? I mean, that's what it says on the plaque."

"This was her home and mission, but that was a long time ago."

"Do you know the story of Mary Connor? Do you know anything that will help me?"

"I know she helped the Chinese in this area. It was after the time of the Civil War. They called her the White Angel." He studied the Bible. "Where did you get that?"

"It was given to me by a family member. I'm trying to learn more about the people mentioned in it."

"I know about Mary Connor. She saved my great-great-grandfather's life."

"May I ask how?"

"He was one of the many who came from China looking for a better life. Instead, he badly injured his arm in a railroad construction accident. The amputation took place in this very building."

Gary lowered the Bible. "Please tell me about him."

"He studied to be a doctor and saved many lives—just as his life was saved by an old Chinese doctor. He and his wife, Kim Lee, did a great deal of good work in Chinatown. They died only weeks apart, in 1888."

He gazed at the Bible again. "My family tells the story often, passing it down through the generations. We own this building and have for over a century." He pointed at the Bible. "That is the Bible of the Bell Messenger. I've heard the story many times."

The words stunned Gary.

"You know about this Bible? This *very* Bible?"

"Yes. My whole family does. I think you had better come inside." Gary followed him in. "What did you say your name was?"

"Gary Brandon."

The man nodded. "My name is Steve." He held out his hand. "Steve Yuen."

chapter **25**

DECEMBER 14, 1865
JACKSON STREET, SAN FRANCISCO, CALIFORNIA

MARY WALKED DOWN a narrow alley off Jackson Street, a dingy, fifteen-foot-wide sliver of walkway between brick buildings. She wore her best, knowing Chinese men would view her as a mere woman. She had on a long blue skirt, a frilled white blouse, and chinchilla-collared short coat. Her flower-strewn, blue-ribboned, laced hat was pulled tight on her swirled red pompadour. A wide veil was tied around her slender throat, and hands in white cotton gloves tightly held Tate's Bible.

She had told no one about the meeting, not even Tate. *He would never be able to control his anger if confronted.* She had asked for a meeting with Cheong Moon and was told that he would never meet with a woman, that if she had the money owed, she could meet with Afong Moy, the woman who ran the brothel.

One of Cheong's men led Mary to her meeting.

He wore black silks and a black-brimmed hat. He kept his hand in his coat the whole time.

Men, mostly white, with a few Chinese, lined the alley. The Chinese stood in front of old wooden doors with a small opening covered with cagelike bars. Mary had heard what lay behind the barred doors. Young women called sing-song girls, dressed in blue silks with green banding, waited behind curtains. From time to time, one would appear at a window and sing, "Chinese girl nice." Chinamen standing by the doors clutched at passersby and chirped in high-pitched broken English, "One bit look."

Everyone noticed Mary as she strolled by. The white men milling about the doors of the prostitutes turned and looked away, trying to hide their faces and the shame of their intentions. The Chinese men gawked at the long bustled dress. One of the Chinese girls at the mission had told her that they could not understand why a woman would wear a dress so long it touched the ground and dragged behind her on the dirty streets.

The man escorting Mary stopped at a red-painted doorway, knocked three times, waited a second, then rapped two more times. The door opened with a slight creak. He motioned for Mary to enter. Once inside, Mary was told to take a seat on a straight-backed chair positioned at a black wood table and across from a large upholstered chair.

"You wait here," the escort said, then disappeared

through an interior door. Mary waited alone. The more time that passed, the more apprehensive she became. Perhaps she should have told Tate. She pushed the thought from her mind. *His warrior ways would do harm at this sensitive moment.* She prayed silently, *Oh dear Lord, protect me now.* She prayed this phrase again and again until she lost count.

A paper lantern with a flickering candle lit the room from above. Minutes slogged by, and finally a woman clutching a dark bottle entered the room and sat in the chair on the other side of the table. An undersize black robe barely covered her round, large belly. Her long black hair sat on her head in loose coils and her face was ghost white from a thick coating of rice powder. She smelled of alcohol.

"I am Afong Moy." She slurred her words. "I am told to meet you to get the money you owe Cheong Moon. Do you have the money that Cheong Moon asks from you?"

Mary opened the Bible and removed eighty dollars, laying the bills on the table one by one and smoothing them flat. "I will get the remainder of the money he asks for, but I will need some time."

The woman looked concerned. "No time. Cheong Moon not wait."

Mary kept her voice steady, slow, and calm. "I ask for his forgiveness and time in this matter. You will be paid, but I cannot get such a large amount of money in such a short time."

"Cheong Moon will not discuss with a woman. He will not talk with you. It is below his honor to have a woman meet with him and not pay as he asks. He will get payment soon or there be big problems for you, I think."

"I will trust that God will help me in my hour of need."

Afong Moy stood. "It does not matter if God or you pays, it only matters that Cheong Moon gets his money. You keep this." She pushed the bills back to Mary. "It is no good. It is insult for Cheong Moon that you offer so little. He will be angry if I take it."

Mary tried a different approach. "Why do you work in such a place as this?"

Afong Moy looked puzzled. "I am of no interest to you. I am of no interest to anyone."

"Please," Mary said. "I would like to hear why you work in such a place."

She frowned. "I will tell you but only so that you may understand the man you cheat. Maybe then you will bring the money you owe." She turned her eyes away. "I am old now and as fat as a milk cow. I am desired by only the old men. Cheong Moon lets me live because I take care of the young girls; I give them perfume for the palms of their hands, red wine stain for their lips. I make them look, talk, and walk in desirable ways. But in time all the girls start to lose the look of youth or, like me, get the disease. When this happens, I take them to the room of no windows."

Mary felt ill.

Afong took another sip from the bottle.

"What is the room of no windows?" Mary asked the question even though she didn't want to know.

"Room is in basement. It is a place the girls are taken when they are of little use for men, when the blush leaves young faces and skin is no longer like polished marble, but a cobbled stone from the streets.

"I have seen women taken to this room many times. It is bad place. On one side is a shelf off the dirty floor. On top of the shelf is a rice mat. No furniture, not even a chair . . . only a dark room with stale air from the breath of the unfortunate last woman to be there."

"That's horrible." Mary saw the pain in Afong's eyes.

"One who is no longer young and needed is given opium by a Chinese attendant. He tells her that she has a new duty—to die fast. He gives her a knife. A last cup of water and a last bowl of rice are set at her side. A lamp is lit, the oil is only a thimbleful, and by the time it is eaten by the flame the woman is expected to have done her duty and ended the ordeal in private. When there is no spark of flame, the attendant returns to the room and unbars the door. If they find a corpse, it is over, but if the woman is found alive, it makes no difference, for in minutes her life will be ended. No one ever leaves the room with no windows alive."

The revelation stunned Mary. She searched for words but came up empty.

Afong gazed at her. "I do not want to go to the room with no windows." She lifted her head, as if proud. "I am smart woman. I make myself valuable to the Tongs. I do what I can to be useful so that I can live long time. You white women have men tip their hats when you walk by, but Chinese woman never receive such respect. We are a possession only and no more."

Mary asked, "What do you do here to live so long, Afong?"

"I make sure girls are healthy. I tend to the hot water for their daily baths and shave their bodies." She stopped her talk, as if realizing her loose tongue had said too much. She lowered her voice. "Cheong Moon will accept nothing less than five hundred dollars. This is the way of the man's business; I have nothing to say that will change that."

The woman stepped to the interior door, then stopped and turned. "I hope you find the luck needed to pay money owed."

Mary stood. "Do you know of God?"

"I know of many gods."

Mary spoke again, now with steel in her voice. "Do you know about Jesus our Lord and the one true God?"

"There are many lords and many gods. We should not be so blasphemous toward other gods in whom one has no faith for fear of offending them.

This will surely bring bad luck, so better to pay homage to many gods."

"I thank you for your warning, but I fear no man because I have a God who will protect me in this life and usher me into the next Celestial Kingdom called Heaven. It is a wonderful place where no one can ever hurt or disgrace you—not me or you."

Afong walked back to Mary. "I have heard of such a place from another woman who said such words. One girl has read to me from a book she called Bible. She was given book by missionaries in Canton and she followed the ways of the wise man Jesus. She told me things about Him, things I had not heard before. She called herself a Christian. You are Christian woman?"

"I am." Mary smiled warmly.

"I think of her often. She frequently spoke of Jesus but always with tears. At night she would cry because of the work she was forced to do." Sadness filled Afong's face. "I liked that girl very much. She died after being taken to the room with no windows. She had the disease from a man." Her voice softened to a whisper. "She gave me Bible to read, but I cannot read words. Women from my family not allowed to read. We only work."

"Tell me, Afong, how did you come to be here?"

She lowered her head. Mary sensed that something inside the woman had ripped open an old wound. "Many years ago my father sold me to a man in Hong Kong. He sent me across the big sea to America. Miners treated me as an animal. I was in a cage on a wagon and taken from one gold-mining camp to another. I was used in ways I will not speak of. I think I will hate all men forever . . . except for this Jesus man. I think I will not hate Him."

"The Bible says that Jesus loves us. He loves you, Afong."

"I am beyond love."

"No one is beyond His love, Afong. Not me. Not you."

She turned her gaze to Tate's Bible. "Can you read the words of the book in Chinese?"

Mary smiled and fought back rising tears. "Yes, I can."

Afong looked over her shoulder, as if someone else were in the room. Mary wondered at the horrible life the woman must have lived to be so frightened. "Read to me now from this book. I would like to know more about the man Jesus. He good man, I think." She returned to the table and sat.

Mary read from the Gospels, stopping occasionally to offer a comment or answer a question. Every fifteen minutes the man in the black skullcap walked by the room's door and watched as Mary read. He frowned with each inspection. The scowl on his face made Mary uneasy.

Two hours passed. Afong Moy listened intently, at times weeping. As she listened, she'd pause and swig something from a whiskey bottle. After a final sip, she indicated that the bottle had gone empty. "Is this the word of the one true God?"

"Yes, it is."

Afong Moy asked the same question over and over and Mary patiently answered the same way.

The man returned to the door and gazed in. Eyeing the Bible, he entered the room, the door crashing against the wall. Before Mary could speak, the man clamped his hands on her shoulders and yanked her from her chair. The Bible tumbled to the floor. Cheong Moon's man spit on the book.

Afong Moy leapt to her feet and slurred in drunken Chinese, "This place of devil I think."

The man sent a firm backhand across Afong's face, then seized Mary's arm again. Afong's large body crumpled to the floor. Mary resisted, but the man was too strong and too angry. He pulled her from the room and back into the alley. Mustering all her strength, Mary pulled free and raced back into the room, reclaiming the Bible from the floor. She wiped the spittle off her dress and turned on the man. "You blasphemer!"

Before Mary could speak again, her assailant grabbed her, and dragged her back to the door. This time he shoved her through the opening. She landed hard, the Bible still in her hand. She heard the door slam. To Mary it sounded like a gunshot.

She rose and ran to the door, banging on it with her gloved hand. "Afong? Afong!"

A woman's scream came from inside the room—Afong's scream. Mary heard other noises she couldn't identify. Something slammed against the inside of the door. She backed away.

Muddled shouts and screams in Chinese came from the building. Mary looked around. "Help! He's going to kill her."

No one moved.

Mary ran to three white men waiting in line by one of the brothel doors. They were dressed like sailors. "Please. He will kill the poor woman. She needs help. You must help."

"Sorry, ma'am, it ain't none of our business," one of them said.

"She'll be killed without help."

"Go home, ma'am. A woman like you don't belong on a street like this."

She moved to a line of Chinese men and begged for help in Cantonese. They refused to meet her eyes or to speak to her. Mary raced back to the door and tried turning the locked knob. It was hot to the touch. She pounded on the door again.

"Fire!" someone shouted.

Mary smelled it first, then noticed the black smoke seeping through the cracks around the doors and windows of the building. Doors burst open and half-dressed prostitutes and men poured into the alley. The piercing voice of Afong Moy followed. "You are free now. Jesus sets you free. Run."

Mary had no idea how the fire had started. Maybe one of the many paper lamps ignited. Maybe the Tong thug had started it. Perhaps Afong, drugged by opium and whiskey and maddened by years of harsh slavery, had set it.

A window above shattered, and an orange flame propelled shards of glass onto the street and onto frantically fleeing people.

The crowded alley erupted into chaos. Many fled. Others brought buckets of water from a nearby horse trough. Still others carried bamboo tubes filled with water, and some even thought bottles of beer would help.

"Free. You are all free." Afong's words mixed with the snapping and popping of burning wood and the voices of panicked people. The Tong escort who had manhandled her minutes before stumbled into the street coughing and struggling to find his breath. There were bleeding scratches on his face.

The fire grew rapidly, consuming furniture, wood floors, and paneling. Two years before, Mary had seen a house burn and the speed at which the flame spread surprised her. This building was older and little more than tinder for the ravenous flames.

"Free. You are—"

A crash drowned out the words.

"The second floor has caved in," someone shouted. "The building is all gone for sure."

Mary heard the sharp clanging of bells coming

down the street. She turned to see a horse-drawn fire wagon turn up the alley, the fire chief shouting from the side step, "Get out of the way," through a brass trumpet-megaphone. Mary sprinted to the door through which Cheong Moon's man had just emerged and started in. Hot, thick smoke pushed her back. She tried again but could not step across the threshold.

"Mary!"

She felt a strong hand on her arm. She started to pull away, expecting another battle with the Tong member. Instead, she saw the worried eyes of Jeremiah Tate.

"We're leaving," he said firmly.

"But the woman—"

"Ain't nothing you can do for anyone in that building now. It's best we leave."

"I have to try!"

"Mary, it is too late. You're coming with me."

She let him pull her along.

chapter 26

"YOU COULD HAVE been killed," Tate shouted as the front door to the mission slammed behind him.

"But I wasn't. God has watched over me, just like I told you He would."

"It wasn't God who went to get you in that alley. It was me."

"And how did you know where to find me?"

"Kim Lee told me."

"Mr. Tate, you are not my father."

Tate stormed up the stairs.

A half hour later the front door rattled, pummeled by a strong fist. Mary approached the door just as a new round of pounding began. Tate arrived at the bottom of the stairs and positioned himself to the side, out of sight of any visitor. Mary took a deep breath and opened the door.

A tall and wide man stood at the doorway. He held a hog's-leg shotgun. Five men were with him. Each wore a badge.

"Jeremiah Tate here?" His voice was husky and honed with a sharp edge.

"May I ask who is—"

The officer pushed his way over the threshold.

Mary felt faint.

Tate emerged from the stairs. "I'm Tate."

The broad man in the long coat took one step into the house. On his breast he wore a shield-shaped badge engraved with a multipointed star and the word DETECTIVE. The other officers wore similar gray uniforms that reminded Tate of Confederate garb. Their star-shaped badges glistened in the sun. The detective twitched his nose and the thick mustache beneath it leapt with the movement. The mustache ran from lip to ear and showed gray hairs. Below his policeman's cap were steady, cold, intelligent eyes.

"I have a man here who says you and a woman killed three white men in a fire. He also says you killed a Chinaman named Cheong Moon and a Chinese woman. That's five people. Who knows? The fire department may find more bodies."

"We didn't start any fire." Tate spoke firmly and steadily.

"There's not much worry about the Orientals," the detective said with a slight brogue, "but the three white men, well, that's a bit different, isn't it?"

"Like I said, we had nothing to do with any fire."

The detective stroked the shotgun, turned, and motioned for someone to come forward.

Blue Mike emerged from behind the officers. "That's the woman I saw start the fire, Detective.

That's her for sure. And that's the man that ran out of the building after she started it all. That fire killed three of my men—men who were only having a bit of rest and recreation." Blue Mike fought off a grin as he said, "I don't care none about those Chinese burning up, but those three white men are going to be hard to replace."

Mary's head moved from side to side. "You lying devil."

Blue Mike started forward. An officer placed a hand on his shoulder, stopping him in midstep, but it didn't keep him quiet. "You both started that fire to get out of paying a debt owed to Cheong Moon. That's what you did all right. I seen it."

The detective let his gaze run over Mary. "Connor, isn't it? Mary Connor?"

"Yes. I'm Mary Connor."

"That what happened, Mrs. Connor?"

"No, sir, I assure you it is not, and it is Miss Connor."

"Well, Miss Connor, I have several men who saw you go in the brothel, and this man said you started the fire. That makes you a murderer, and that means you may hang for this."

Mike pointed a long, dirty finger at Tate and Mary. "I'll swear out a statement, Detective. I'll do it right now if you want. I know what I saw, and I'll go to any court and speak it again. That's the woman and that's the man. It is justice we're after here. Nothing more, nothing less."

"Miss, you've got to understand," the detective said, " I have men who put you on the scene and a witness who saw you fleeing the building before the fire gutted everything and killed three white men. It looks like you'll be going with me. Never arrested the likes of a proper woman before, but has to be done just the same."

The sheriff came toward Mary; she backed away and shuddered. Tate stepped between them and held out his hands to accept the cold steel cuffs. The sheriff seemed confused. "What's this 'bout, anyway?"

Tate said, "I am afraid you are arresting the wrong person. I set that fire. It was me who put the torch to that building, and me alone. The woman had nothing at all to do with it—nothing at all."

"Explain yourself real fast, Mr. Tate."

"That Chinaman Moon swindled me with one of those girls down there, and I just got angry." He looked at Mary. Her skin had gone pale. "Seems a man sometimes does a thing that goes beyond any reason."

"The story I hear is that it was both of you."

"Think about it, Detective. What would a woman like her be doing down there among the prostitutes and their men? She's a missionary. Mary just went looking for me. She's been trying to get me some religion. You know how it is."

"Aye, that I do."

"Tate—," Mary began.

"You just stay out of this, woman. No need to waste your time explaining the deed of a Christian like you trying to save the soul of a tired, worthless soldier like me. Lying don't suit you, even if it is to help me out. No, I done wrong and I need a reckoning with the law."

"But—"

The detective looked at Blue Mike. "This man says he did the crime. Says he did it alone. What do you say to that?"

Blue Mike rubbed his chin. "Well, there was a lot of people running about, and I had a couple of whiskies in me, not that I was drunk. I know what I saw."

"So you saw the woman leave the building?" The detective appeared annoyed.

Mike eyed Tate up and down. "I seem to remember a little better now that I ponder on it some. Seems it was this here man alone. Yes, it surely was him. I am certain of it all now. Maybe the woman was just in the alley looking about for him like he says. But I know what I saw, and this man fled out of that building with a burning torch in his hand. He was laughing to boot. Now that I have time to settle it all in my mind, it's come back to me real clear."

The steel cuffs felt cold on Tate's wrists. "I just ask one minute here to tell the woman something before you take me away."

"Don't go trying anything stupid. This shotgun leaves a real big hole."

"You'll get no trouble from me." Tate leaned to Mary and whispered in her ear, "I want to give the Bible to Yuen. See to it that he gets the Good Book. If there is a God, then He brought the boy into my life for a good reason. The way I figure it, he is to be the Messenger now."

Mary began to cry. "Tate . . . I . . ."

"That's enough now, Tate." The detective prodded him in the ribs with the shotgun barrel. Tate didn't look back as the armed men pushed him to a waiting wagon.

Blue Mike grinned at Mary. "He is all I really wanted to hang anyway."

chapter 27

STEVE YUEN LED Gary up Euclid Street. Gary had taken half an hour to tell Steve all he knew about the Bible. Steve agreed to share what he knew, but not in the office-supply store that had once been a mission. "My house will be more comfortable," he said. "Besides, there's something I want to show you. I'll call ahead to let my wife know I'm bringing a guest."

Steve drove his dated Impala and Gary trailed

behind on his Triumph. The drive was short, and minutes later, Gary, with backpack in hand, followed Steve up the steps to his three-story home. Like others in the area, the house was narrow, with the first floor being the garage and the two upper levels living space. It looked well cared for, with fresh white paint on the wood trim and a putty color coat on the exterior walls. Gary guessed it had been remodeled several times over the years.

Steve opened the door and his wife, Lim, met him immediately. Like Steve, she was Asian, with dark almond eyes, smooth olive skin, and a quick smile. She was lovely. After greeting them with a slight bow and exchanging pleasantries, she directed Gary to a large book with a worn red-cloth cover resting on an ornate, hand-carved teak book stand. "It is the family register, a diary of sorts. On the phone, my husband told me this book would be of interest to you."

"Looks interesting," Gary said.

Lim continued, "It is written by hand, with over a hundred pages penned in Chinese symbols. It has been in his family for generations." She looked at Steve, who smiled. Gary could see the affection he felt for Lim.

"Can you read this?" Gary asked Steve.

"No. I never learned Chinese, but Lim can if you like. She came over from China as a child. Me? My parents didn't speak Chinese in the home."

Lim stepped forward. "I would be pleased to

read the words, but it is long and most of the writings will be of little interest to you."

"I would like to know if there is anything about a man named Tate or a woman named Mary Connor."

"Yes, there is. I know these names. They are in the register. Please sit. I will find the passages for you."

Gary took a seat on a narrow, jade green sofa. Steve plopped down in his leather easy chair. Lim moved to a side chair and set the large book on her lap. She opened it and scanned the yellowed pages. From his place on the sofa, Gary could see that the edges of the paper bore the stains of countless hands.

"I remember a man named Tate in the book." She turned pages until she found the passage she sought. She smiled shyly. "I have read this book many times. My husband's family is of great interest to me. Tate is known as 'the one who gives life.' It is recorded that he died in prison, convicted of murder, and was sentenced to be hanged."

"Murder?"

"Yes. It is said that he killed five people, but was only charged with three because two were Chinese." She returned her eyes to the book and ran a finger down a column of characters. "It says that he was innocent of the crime. It is also written that he was not hanged, but died in prison two days before his execution and then was buried in the

Chinese section of the cemetery." She read aloud, " *'God spared him the pain and dishonor of hanging till dead. Instead he got the smallpox and died; a gift from God.' "*

"I've never heard smallpox called a gift from God," Gary said.

"It doesn't make any sense at all, but it is what the book says." She turned pages. "It is written on other pages in the registry that Tate saved my husband's great-great-grandfather Yuen's life, but the book does not say how or why.

"My husband's great-great-grandmother Kim Lee, the wife of Dr. Yuen," she continued, "writes in this book that the funeral was carried out the very day Tate died. It says everyone wanted to burn the body because of the disease it carried, but a man named Dr. Ling protested and said he would see to it that the body was buried by day's end. Tate was laid to rest by the Chinese community because no whites wanted to be near the corpse that carried the smallpox sickness. Dr. Ling was given the body by . . ." She returned her gaze to the pages. ". . . Judge Stiles for burial. Chinese men put the body into a wooden coffin, which rested on a cart. On the way, mourners dressed in white wept and tossed brown paper into the air."

Gary said, "Brown paper?"

Steve explained. "The strips of paper represent money. By tossing them into the air, they believed they were helping Tate on his way to Heaven."

"It was the custom of the day," Lim said, "to place a canopy over the cemetery entrance. Also, there would be a stack of bricks resting on sand. Messages, paper money, and paper servant dolls were burned on the altar so the smoke would rise into the air, taking it to the afterworld." Again, Lim read silently. "The wooden box holding Mr. Tate rested under an American flag. The coffin was buried, and Dr. Yuen became the Messenger and remained so for many years."

Lim looked at Gary. "There is a very interesting comment here at the end of the story. Kim Lee writes it was later found that though Tate died, he somehow came back to life years later. That is odd, I know, but that is what the book says and anyone writing in a family register would not lie. After our honorable ancestor Dr. Yuen died, a woman named Ruth was given the famous Bible. She became the Messenger in 1888.

"Dr. Yuen learned to read English from the Bible and it was from that book he gained his belief in God Almighty. He saved many lives—so many that only God knows the number."

Lim closed the big family history but did not look up. "We are now a family of little means. We live in a humble home in a wonderful city, but it takes all our money to pay the bills. We are trying to repair the old mission house to help the many homeless in San Francisco, to once again feed the indigent as they did long ago, to give basic medical care for those with no hope. The orphans, the widows . . ." She began to cry. "I am sorry, but reading the family register has reminded me that our dream of reopening the old mission house may never happen . . . that is, unless there is a miracle."

"I believe God excels at miracles," Gary said and opened his backpack. He removed the Bible. "Thank you for sharing the family history with me. Let me show you something that may encourage you." He held out the Bible. "This is the same Bible owned by Elijah Bell, then Jeremiah Tate, then your great-great-grandfather Dr. Yuen. It's the Bible mentioned in your family book."

Lim took the book and held it as if holding precious jewels.

Gary smiled. "This Bible came to me in a very unusual way—in a miraculous way. Your dream of restarting the mission will be realized when you least expect it."

chapter 28

OCTOBER 6, 1888
SAN FRANCISCO, CALIFORNIA

THE FUNERAL OF Yuen was a simple affair, just as he had wished. Mary knew he would be happy with the way things were handled. His disease had progressively weakened him, until he could no longer work, no longer stand. There were no customary funeral fires lifting burnt offerings to the gods. Yuen had become a Christian after reading Tate's Bible.

The day Tate was arrested he had told Mary: "Whoever has this book will save life and give life." The Bible was given to Yuen, who became a doctor, a minister, and a friend to all who met him.

The funeral mourners left when Dr. Ling asked if those closest to Yuen could have a private moment. Kim Lee stood by the grave of her husband, holding the chipped white teacup Yuen's mother had given him. He, in turn, had given it to his wife.

Dr. Ling sat behind her in a spindle chair and Mary stood behind him with her hands on his shoulders. He had always been the strong one in a crisis, but he was now too old and feeble to stand for more than a minute or two. He would surely be the next to go. Ruth stood next to him. The years had changed her from a frolicking child on a long-distance steamship into a woman of poise. Mary didn't know why Ling had sent for her and asked that she attend the funeral. She was not family, but seeing her again eased some of the pain.

Yuen's gravestone was a simple white marble monument, a testament to a large, extraordinary life. The grave had been dug next to Tate's, which had long been grown over with tall, slender grass. The weathered grave marker bore the mossy face of twenty years in the ocean breeze.

Yuen had slipped from this world only two days

earlier. Though his illness was painful, he never complained. In the last days, however, every movement made him wince, something Mary knew indicated the end was near. The cancer that had systematically eroded his body and strength would win. And it did. It could not, however, take his faith or dignity.

Again, Mary read the simple grave marker:

DR. YUEN
BORN 1848 DIED 1888.
HE SAVED LIFE AND GAVE LIFE.

Mary held the Bible tight in her hands. It, too, had grown old, its edges worn and still bearing the smudges of a boy slain in a cornfield two decades before. To complete Tate's request that the Bible be passed on to Yuen, Mary had to teach Yuen the wisdom contained in its pages, so that he could take courage from its stories of faith, honor, and devotion. In time, Yuen would learn to read English from the holy book. First from Mary, then from the Bible itself, he learned about God, about Jesus, and about the latter's sacrifice so others might live.

Mary stared at Tate's headstone. At the bottom were chiseled the words: THOUGH HE DIES, HE LIVES.

When she raised her eyes, she noticed a tall man with gray hair standing silently at the cemetery gate. He looked like a stone statue except for a slight stoop. He held three yellow long-stemmed roses in hands marred with white scars.

Mary's heart squeezed, and she raised a hand to her mouth. The man approached and offered the roses. A ghost? Was she gazing at the specter of a man long dead? A man over whom she had shed countless tears?

The man smiled, then turned to the others. "I am sorry to be late for the service. I came as soon as I got Dr. Ling's telegram."

Ling's smile was toothless but genuine, and his eyes sparkled. "So many years, my old friend." His voice quavered with joy.

"Too many years, too many miles." The man paused.

Mary tried to speak, making several attempts before succeeding. Her stomach tumbled, and her breath came in ragged inhalations. "Tate? Jeremiah Tate?"

Kim Lee turned from the grave, stared at the stranger's hands, then gasped.

"Yes, Mary. It's me. Ol' Jeremiah Tate."

Mary began to shake.

Ruth stepped to Mary and put her arm around her. Mary leaned on Ruth for support. Ruth gazed at the injured hands that had protected her as a child, that at the very least had saved her from permanent disfigurement and blindness, and most likely had saved her life.

Tate looked worn and tired. His hair had grayed, as had the whiskers on his chin and cheeks. The blanched scars remained the same. Mary watched as Ruth pulled down her collar and fingered the ragged scars on her neck.

Mary found her voice again. "You . . . died in prison. You . . . we buried you right there. That's your grave."

"No, ma'am, even though I'm sure Heaven is a real nice place, I'm happy to say I'm not there—not just yet. I'm happy right here looking at you, Mary."

He looked to Ling, who pulled up from the chair and steadied himself on a cane. The old man nodded, as if approving of the gathering. "Mr. Tate is no ghost. He is alive because he escaped jail after the guards thought him dead. We planned the whole thing." He glanced at Ruth. "Your father, Judge Stiles, came up with the plan. It was so impossible that I considered it a fool's scheme, but it worked nonetheless."

"I don't understand," Mary said. "This can't be."

"Believe your eyes," Ling said. "Mr. Tate was awaiting execution in jail when I went to see him one night. In his dark cell, I told him that Jesus had come back from the dead and so could he if he did exactly as I said." Ling's voice was paper thin. "I asked if he would like to rise from the dead. I'm afraid I confused him with my words. I spoke more plainly, saying, 'Do what I ask of you and you will live; if you do not you will surely die.' He agreed and I left a pail of food for his evening meal. Only a doctor or a minister is allowed to visit a condemned man in prison and bring any food. Since I was both a doctor and a minister, they did not refuse me.

Ling smiled. "The guards looked in the pail of food and saw it contained leeches and what we from China call peach blossom fish. Some sailors call the sea creatures jellyfish. I told the guards it was a Chinese delicacy." He chuckled. "I even offered them some to eat. They said no. I suppose it was disgusting for them to even think of eating the slimy creatures, but they let Tate have the meal. I told Tate what to do and that night he rubbed the poison from the purple tentacles of the jellyfish over his face and arms as I had asked. That must have been a painful thing to do."

Tate cleared his throat, seeing the old Chinaman tire from standing. "You should sit, my old friend." Tate waited while Ling eased back into the chair. He continued the story. "It was painful. It felt as if a thousand stinging needles met my skin all at once. I put the leeches on me and left them to suck my blood—that was the most difficult part, but we had to convince them I had the pox. When I peeled the leeches off, I had a rash of red welts the size of silver dollars all over me. It looked like I had smallpox for sure. I knew well what the illness looked like because my wife and young boy were taken by it in 1860. I looked close enough to having the sickness all right, especially being in the dark cell. When the guard lifted his lantern and saw me all red and swollen, he almost fell over, dead of fright." Tate's smile disappeared. "The very sickness that took the ones I loved the most became the tool that saved my life."

Mary asked, "But how did you get out of the prison?"

"Dr. Ling came to visit me the next night and I pretended to be dead. I lay there like a shot deer. Ling shouted for the guards and said I was dead from the pox. They had seen me all rashy and sick looking earlier that morning when they brought me my breakfast and I'd told them then I was bad sick. Nonetheless, old Dr. Ling here told them to burn everything in sight, that a decomposing body was even more contagious. He told them it was a smallpox infection that I had and the body needed removing as fast as could be done.

"The guards ran to get the prison chief to verify that I was dead so they could get my carcass out of there. They could not release the body for burial until a death certificate was officially signed. Well, the prison chief was drunk at the local bar with a judge named Stiles."

Ruth spoke up. "My father wouldn't—my father did not frequent bars."

"It happened just this way. Dr. Ling filled in the parts I didn't see. Your father came into the cell and said, 'Dead as a man can get.' He sent the guards running for a stretcher, telling them to get some Chinese to carry the body. Turns out, four Chinese men just happened to be outside the prison with a wagon waiting—Chinese well known to Dr. Ling."

Tate took a breath. "Once the guards were out of earshot, the good judge bent down and whispered, 'Thank you, my friend, for saving the most precious thing in the world to me—my little Ruth. I shall always be in your debt for your bravery on that ship.'"

Tate chuckled; to Mary it was music.

"Tell the rest of it, Mr. Tate," Ling said.

"Yes, sir. Judge Stiles instructed Dr. Ling to get me out of there before I stunk up the place and infected the whole jail. The guards didn't argue a bit and left us alone. Dr. Ling wrapped me in a dirty prison blanket and four Chinese men carried me out. They had a chore of it with me being so tall, but I was soon bouncing along in the back of a carriage. They took me to a Chinese mortuary. A coffin was got quick and bags of sand put in so that those that buried me would think they was actually burying a heavy body. It's an odd thing to see preparations for your own funeral. I was given a horse and was never seen hereabouts ever again."

Ruth narrowed her eyes. "My father really did this." She shook her head. "It's too difficult for me to imagine."

Tate smiled. "I'm grateful he did. Don't think harshly of him. He knew well and good that I was innocent. He also knew I was the one who saved you when you were just a girl on that ship. I guess he felt beholden to me for that. I had been falsely accused and a jury had come to the verdict based on a lie by a man named Blue Mike. Your father was not the presiding judge at the trial, but after I was sentenced and just two days before I was to be hung, he came to visit the mission and met with Dr. Ling. He told Dr. Ling just what to do."

Ruth shook her head. "My father always adhered to the law. The law was the most important thing in the world to him. Even in his old age, he speaks of the cases he tried."

Dr. Ling said, "No, his family was the most important thing to him. It was not to break the law that he did this, it was to uphold the fact that a man was wrongfully condemned by a corrupt system. To save an only begotten child is the greatest gift anyone can give to another; it is a debt that is hard to repay, but your father did just that. Sometimes a man seems duty bound to reconcile such a great debt of gratitude. To lose you would have been the greatest of all losses to your father. That kind of loss can kill a man; your father knew this and was spared that enormous grief because of Mr. Tate."

Tate walked to Mary and lifted the Bible from her fingers. He turned and showed the Bible to Ruth. "It was not me who saved you that day, it was this Bible that I hold now, the same Bible that I was holding back then on the day of that storm when a wagon busted free and broke a steam pipe. I held this Bible in my hands. The boy in the cornfield said all who have this Bible will save lives and give life." He faced the others. "They buried my coffin that day, but not me. Just old rice bags stuffed with beach sand."

Mary pulled away from the others. "All these years I thought you were dead." She looked at Ling. "You kept this from me year after year. You let me mourn his death." She began to weep.

Tate stepped to her. His words were soft. "I couldn't tell you. I could never take you away from your work here, and I certainly could never appear in public around this city. We couldn't take the chance. If word got out, it would destroy Judge Stiles and Dr. Ling. It might even endanger you and your work. Don't forget, I confessed to murder and arson. We had to keep it secret."

"It is so unfair. I'm the one who grieved."

"You're right about it being unfair. But you are not the only one who grieved."

"But where have you been?"

"I went to Monterey and worked in a hardware store using the name Elijah Bell. After years of hard work, I came to buy the business. All the while, I kept in contact with Dr. Ling and sent him money now and again so Yuen could learn doctoring. I thought, what better way to save and give life than to help someone become a doctor?"

He took a deep breath. "Dr. Ling sent me many letters telling me about how hard Yuen worked, and how many people he helped." He turned to Kim Lee. "I also heard what a good husband Yuen was."

Tate took the book and looked it over as if seeing an old acquaintance after a long separation. "Hello, old friend." Tears welled in Tate's eyes.

"I am not any kind of a prophet. I am only a man who has been given many new chances to live again." He gazed at Mary and added softly, "And to love again."

Tate asked Ruth, "Did you know Dr. Yuen?"

"No. I am here because Dr. Ling sent for me." She paused. "I am pleased that I came. I have seen my father's love for me in a new way. He was not the kind of man to say I love you, but I guess he did not have to. I can see that now. He has shown me his deep love by what he did for you, Mr. Tate."

Tate handed Ruth the Bible. "The man buried today was saved by a story I read in this sacred book—a story about Moses, who once kept a slave from being beaten to death. That is why I helped Yuen. It was from that message in this book, this very Bible, that saved you during a storm on a ship when you were a young girl. I don't even know if you remember that day."

"I do. It is an unforgettable day." She pulled at her collar again and felt the raised scar. "I remember, it was a frightening storm that sent no rain—only dark wind that rocked the big ship. I remember falling and seeing you with blood coming out of your head as you lay on the deck, and my father shouting. I remember that much."

"Do you remember the Bible?" Tate asked as he opened its water-stained and curled pages—pages that had endured the onslaught of steam from a broken pipe. "I held this Bible and it saved you. You would have been bad scarred or worse."

He told her of Elijah Bell, his death and his words. "I thought he had died, so I left him lying in that field. It wasn't long after that when I was given a letter that told me to be the Messenger and take the Bible and that if I did, it would save lives. It saved Yuen as it saved you. I don't know these things, but it seems the Bible came to you; it sought you as it sought Yuen. I think it's only fitting that you have it now."

Tate lifted the book. "Take the Bible and be the Messenger."

Ruth stammered. "I-I don't want it."

"Your life will be as a dry rain if you don't take it."

"You're trying to frighten me." The words came slowly. She struggled to be respectful.

"What's in this book saved me and somehow it will save you. I can't explain the mystery of it all, but one day you will know why you have it and what purpose God has for you."

"Please know I hear your sincerity, but I am not of a religious nature. I have no interest in being a Messenger. I only wish to travel far away and see the world; I want to have a family." She faced Mary. "Some are just not cut out to be feeding the poor and all that. I commend you for giving a good and caring service to the less fortunate, but please know this is not a venture that appeals to me in the least."

Mary smiled. "You will come to see how God will use you in ways you cannot guess." She took the book from Tate and handed it to Ruth. "Take the book and be the Messenger."

Ruth hesitated, then took it.

Tate turned away, walked to the grave, and knelt, setting the roses to the side. He placed his palms on the sand and looked up at a clear blue sky. "Lord, I thank You for following me." He then slowly stood and lifted the three yellow roses to Mary's smiling face. She breathed in deeply, then took them in her hand. This wasn't a dream at the end of a long night. It was a new beginning.

Mary, Tate, Dr. Ling, and Kim Lee walked from the cemetery, leaving Ruth standing in silence, staring at the open Bible resting in her palms. The autumn breeze flipped the frail pages to a note tucked inside. She unfolded the letter and read. Her eyes found the last words inscribed by the dead Confederate boy.

Ruth listened to rising wind sprinting through the tufts of grass. She tasted the briny sea air, looked far away, and for the first time thought about everlasting life.

chapter **29**

A S STEVE AND Gary looked on, Lim carefully copied relevant passages from the family register into English.

Gary scanned the list of deaths recorded in the back of the Bible and found Tate's name written next to Mary Connor's. Next on the list of the deceased was *Paul Cooper.* There was no *Ruth.* Gary felt sure that Paul Cooper was connected to the dying R.C. Cooper and his mysterious note to Emily in White.

It was time to say good-bye. He thanked Steve and Lim for their courtesy and time, then asked, "Can you tell me how to get to the county courthouse?"

A short time later, Gary was immersed in county records.

Although he doubted Judge Stiles had any connection to the Bible, Gary felt inclined to research the man. He was in the right place to do it and would hate to find out later that he'd been wrong. Stiles's name was listed among circuit court judges who had presided in the San Francisco second district from 1865 to 1881.

Gary borrowed a phone book from a clerk and started searching. He discovered twenty entries with the last name of Stiles. Finding a pay phone, he began dialing phone numbers. After eleven calls he connected with Monty Stiles.

"I'm sorry to bother you. My name is Gary Brandon and I'm looking for relatives of Judge William Stiles. He lived in the mid-1800s."

"You've called the right place. William Stiles is a great-great-uncle on my father's side." The voice was male and friendly. "He's the hero of the family. Not only was he a distinguished judge but he served two terms in Congress. We're pretty proud of that."

"Really? I was beginning to think I was wasting my time. I've called nearly a dozen people."

"Persistence pays off in these matters. I've been researching my ancestors for years. It's a bit of an addiction for people like me."

"I'm trying to track down information on other people from that time period. Maybe you've heard of them: a woman named Ruth and a man named Paul Cooper."

"You seem to know an awful lot about the skeletons in our family closet. Since you're going to this much effort, I assume we're related?"

"No," Gary admitted. "I'm afraid not. I have a different motivation."

The phone went silent. "Maybe you should tell me why you're so interested in my family."

Gary explained about the Bible and gave a little information about Tate. "Judge Stiles may have saved Tate's life."

There was a long pause, then, "We need to talk."

RUTH AND EDMOND

chapter 30

THE WESTERN COAST of Alexandria, Egypt, radiated heat from a hot stretch of sun-seared sand.
Crumbling mud-brick buildings crouching below a
smattering of spiked Muslim minarets stretched
under a cloudless sky. Edmond Donahue had hated
it before they ever landed at this parched land.
Ruth could tell by his expression and cranky
responses. Ruth, on the other hand, had scarcely
been able to speak of anything else. She'd loved
this place before they'd set sail.

They passed the ruins of the Tower of Abuser
and slowly navigated unseen reefs and shoals.
Tumbled stone blocks from ancient ruins peppered the brackish green water of the harbor. To
the right of town stood a Corinthian stone
column called Pompey's Pillar; on the eastern
shore stood a broken obelisk. Between the land-
marks rested a bustling waterfront city. Skiffs
rowed endlessly to and from the larger schooners
and side-wheeler craft anchored a short distance
offshore.

Ruth and Edmond disembarked from a skiff that
had ferried them to the dock area. Ruth smelled the
stench of death wafting from a shore littered with

thick piles of rubbish and decaying animal carcasses.

"The whole city reeks," Edmond said.

Ruth removed a lace handkerchief from her
purse and a tiny bottle of perfume. She sprinkled
some of the liquid on the cloth and handed it to
Edmond. "This should help."

He held it to his nose. "Doesn't the smell bother
you?"

"No, not at all. I find it exhilarating."

He snorted. "And I, my dear, find it all repulsive.
I didn't know I was marrying an adventurer."

"It's been almost six months. Weary of me
already?" She took his arm as they walked from
the landing.

"Not of you, just of strange places, strange food,
and . . ." He waved the handkerchief. ". . . strange
smells."

"I have dreamed of this day: a chance to be away
from the confining refinement of San Francisco
and Europe. This is adventure, Edmond—pure,
raw adventure. I have wanted to visit this land
since I was a child. Thank you for making my
dream come true."

"You're welcome. You've been enamored of
Egypt ever since you read that childish book."

"*The Arabian Nights* is not childish. It is exqui-
site literature full of action and adventure. It swept
me away then, and now here we are. It's all too, too
exciting."

They had been married for less than six months, but this was turning out to be not much of a honeymoon—Edmond was romantically arthritic, stoic, and quiet. But Ruth had accepted that fact and tried to make the best of the already staling relationship.

Edmond's proposal a year ago had come across more like a business transaction than a request for marriage. Ruth scanned the words of his letter of intent for affection and hardly felt wooed, but she was beyond thirty and felt she lacked the kind of features to attract a man.

No one else had asked for her hand in matrimony. She attributed that to her capriciousness and her tendency to appear uninterested in suitors. She weighed the offer carefully. Edmond was not a handsome man. He was skinny and unfamiliar with the ways of obtaining a woman's notice. But he was also pragmatic, loyal, predictable, and from a wealthy family.

Ruth remembered the day she had read Edmond's letter of proposal aloud while standing under a buckeye tree in front of her house.

I do not love you at present, but in time I am sure that love will emerge in a favorable manner. My assumption is that we feel a mutual inclination toward the process of marriage, as I wish in the most profound way to have several sons. If I am errant in my

*assessment, then please disregard this letter.
If, however, you are favorable to this
endeavor, then we should consider this as a
course of planning. I await your answer to
my intimate inquiry.*

Ruth thought it anything but intimate, but
decided then and there to accept the proposal—
oddly delivered though it was.

Edmond and Ruth had not kissed till they arrived
at the wedding altar, and then it was only a light
peck, as required by the occasion. They had met a
year earlier at one of the many social events to
which her father had taken her. Her elderly father
knew his daughter had limited marital opportunities and feared others would soon take to calling
her an old maid. He had told her so. He thought it
was just as easy for Ruth to fall in love with a rich
man as a poor one. The parents on both sides
encouraged Ruth and Edmond to marry as soon as
plans permitted. The deal was complete.

Ruth knew full well that her common looks had
not enticed any serious suitors in her social class
and probably never would. In time, she thought,
almost anyone could build a marriage and make it
a successful venture if given enough effort. She
felt no physical attraction to Edmond, but the marriage was a well-strategized coupling that might
just work . . . given time, of course. She was from
the family of a judge and congressman; Edmond

was from a family of wealth, his father having amassed a fortune in the real estate market. A union with Edmond would give Ruth a lifetime of financial security. Besides, she had many friends who had been entwined in adolescent feelings and superficial flirtation and had married for love. After several years of marriage, most of those acquaintances showed little signs of love. In the end, they had no love and no money. She was already ahead of the game.

The ceremony was lavish, the social event of the season. Ruth insisted on three yellow roses in her bouquet. The newlyweds then took a train to New York for a yearlong, world-sightseeing honeymoon. While still in California, Ruth enjoyed the travel by rails that snaked up from Sacramento toward the green forests in the High Sierra.

From the steep, rocky Cape Horn mountain she looked down the valley, awed at the deep abyss over a thousand feet below carved out by the surging, foaming waters of the American River. A thousand Chinese laborers had chiseled and clawed the rail bed from the difficult rock; their work had made it possible for her to now travel in speed and ease. Just beyond a sheer-walled bend, the train passed an aging, decaying workers' camp that had once housed a man named Tate, a boy named Yuen, and their line boss, Blue Mike. Her father had told her the story, so she knew of the place. In one of those cabins, on a freezing morning, Blue Mike was found dead. Over time, word had circulated to San Francisco, and newspapers reported that Blue Mike had drunk himself to sleep and someone had poured water down his stovepipe, dousing the flame in his potbellied stove. Workmen found him dead from the cold and as hard as a dried carp. No one knew who committed the crime. Her father had said that no one cared enough to look into it.

Then she saw the strange, unique trees that looked out of place in this land of spruce and pine. The trees, about twenty in all, lined the tracks, their purple budding blossoms shimmering in the springtime sun. A fellow traveler, an elderly Chinese man, overheard Ruth question her husband about the trees and explained that she was seeing the paulownia, from China, a tree whose blossoms gave off a sweet jasmine scent.

"What are they doing here?" Ruth had asked.

The elderly Chinaman shrugged. "Perhaps one of the workers brought seeds from China. The tree is of royal heritage."

Emerging from the mountains on the eastern slope, they rode steel rails through Omaha and across the great plains, forging mile after mile until they reached the populated cities of the East and arrived in New York. It took seven days, a lot less than the four months aboard a steamer she had spent as a child.

They then boarded a paddled steamer and

crossed the Atlantic to England. After a week in England, they continued on to France and Italy. Ruth's long-held desire to travel the world, to visit distant, exotic lands, was being fulfilled. She never tired of it. Edmond grew less talkative, and seemed bored with it all. Damp European air aggravated his respiratory problems. He complained often.

The only part of the trip Edmond enjoyed was playing cards with the men in the main parlor. He seemed to spend more time there than with his bride. Not that she minded. Silence was preferable to hours of complaint. She busied herself in friendly conversation with fellow travelers and enjoyed the scenery.

They sailed from Venice to Sicily and then to Malta. From there they traveled to Alexandria, Egypt—the place Ruth most wanted to see. At last, the land of the pharaohs, of amazing ruins, of adventure. Her heart skipped just thinking of what awaited her. Sailing from the grand harbor of Valetta on the schooner *Bonnono* they arrived in Alexandria in good time, with no storms and no other mishaps. Many who made this trip traveled on creaking side-wheel paddle boats or on the newer, propeller-driven ships, but traveling under full canvas was more exciting and added new thrills to the adventure. She liked the sailing ship for another reason: it had no steam pipes to burst and wound little children. The *Bonnono* cut the blue waters of the Mediterranean and was more than capable of outrunning the pirates that plied the North African coast.

The passengers onboard were a unique mixture of entrepreneurs, adventurers, and bureaucrats from various countries. Some, however, came hoping to liberate buried riches that hibernated in ancient sands. Other well-traveled passengers warned Ruth about such efforts. "There are many unscrupulous locals willing to sell useless maps to greedy, gullible fortune seekers. They find nothing. Some die in the desert."

Ruth drank in the sights as the carriage she and Edmond had hired moved slowly through the crowded streets. In her mind, cities like Alexandria were grand, glinting with beauty in the Egyptian sun. What she saw proved the opposite. Beggars worked the streets, buildings were worn and scarred. She found it difficult to imagine that the city had once held the greatest library the world had ever known. The library at Alexandria had at one time held so many documents that they could not be counted. A fire had consumed the lot, reducing the combined writings of thousands to an ashy memory.

The horse-drawn carriage clattered to a stop in front of a set of structures, an enclosure of several two-story houses with a shared courtyard and gate. They were to wait there for two days in quarantine before officials would allow them to sail on to Cairo.

For those two days, their room and the courtyard would be all the city they would see. A restaurant provided meals in the courtyard for the travelers.

Once in her room on the second floor, Ruth flung open the wooden blinds and looked across the rooftops from a stone-arched window. Two palm trees, still laden with a cluster of last season's maroon-and-amber-colored dates, provided cooling shade. She wiped her face and neck of perspiration with a moist towel that she had dipped into water in a clay pot. Edmond was already napping on the sagging, squeaky bed.

As Ruth pulled the soothing towel across her brow, her eyes caught the graceful movement of a woman walking across a terraced roof beyond the courtyard garden. The woman wore many golden rings coiled about her arms and a long red robe. A sheer, white veil screened her dark face and wafted gracefully behind her in the currents of a faint desert breeze.

The sight of the Egyptian woman was momentarily lost in a rising cloud of pigeons frightened into flight. When the tightly packed birds banked to the west in a synchronized glide, the woman was gone. To Ruth, it was as if the flock had somehow lifted the woman from the rooftop and carried her into the cloudless sky.

That night Ruth walked down a curved stairway to dinner with Edmond, cradling her arm in his. She was dressed in a lacy white cotton dress—a plain cut, but she noticed several women taking notice of it. They walked to a lush garden restaurant in a thatch-roofed courtyard. The roof was made of long, slender palm rafters and irregularly spaced reed matting that allowed shafts of light from the full moon to fall upon the patrons.

They sat next to a man smoking a cigar and drinking brandy from a snifter.

"Lovely night," the man said.

"A very nice night," Ruth answered.

The man smiled; Edmond did not.

"The name is Paul Cooper, from England." He lowered his head as if bowing. Ruth returned the gesture, noting the man's handsome appearance, with his curly blond hair and closely trimmed beard. She guessed his age to be twenty-five or twenty-six.

"What brings you to Egypt, Mr. Cooper?" Edmond asked. Despite the question, Ruth knew Edmond didn't care.

"I'm a linguist. The British Museum has sent me here to report on a dig."

"A dig?" Ruth said.

"Yes, ma'am. An archeological dig is what I mean, of course. The scientists are removing an obelisk in Luxor. The museum has not received a dispatch in several months."

"And you're here to find out why?" Ruth was intrigued.

"Precisely."

"Well, I hope everything is all right with your people."

Edmond grunted. "I'm sure they're fine, dear. Nothing to worry your head about."

Edmond furrowed his brow when the meal was brought to Cooper. It arrived on a large silver tray mounded with savory-smelling flame-roasted mutton, rice laced with raisins, and cucumbers stuffed with a spiced meat.

"That looks sumptuous," Ruth said.

Edmond sniffed. "It might even be appetizing if it weren't for the horrible smell."

"Sheep skin," Cooper answered without looking up from the meal. "The kitchen staff just tossed it outside. I saw it. They do it all the time. Thing will be covered with flies before you know it."

"I didn't need to know that." Edmond closed his eyes.

"My husband is sensitive about such things."

Edmond gave Ruth a hard look. "I should think that every gentleman would feel the same way."

"I wouldn't know, sir," Cooper said. "I have never claimed to be a gentleman nor sensitive." He winked at Ruth.

From his hand, the waiter dropped large green peppercorns on Cooper's plate, the dry seeds hitting the metal tray like an erratic drumbeat. He then plopped two white onions on the tray with his other hand. They rolled around the rim like billiard balls.

Edmond ignored the presentation, choosing instead to swat at flies. A camel tied just outside the courtyard released its bladder in a yellow stream of splashing liquid. Edmond gagged. "The filth of this place! This must be the most backward corner of the world."

"I'm sorry you're uncomfortable, Edmond, but I find it all very exciting. At long last, I am here." She looked again at Cooper's meal. "I'm famished."

Edmond said, "I am sorry, Ruth, but I am no longer hungry." He swatted at another pair of flies swirling about his face.

"Maybe your appetite will return when they bring the food." She stole a glimpse of Cooper as he speared a bit of mutton and saffron-dusted rice. "Let's order."

A tall man with a puckered smile, wearing a crimson fez and tasseled vest, came by the table toting a large wooden box camera with a tin cup covering the lens. "Can I take your picture?" the man asked with a bow. "I can have it for you the day after tomorrow, before the boats go to Cairo, before the—"

Edmond cut the man off. "We are not interested in your incessant talk or your photograph."

Ruth looked at the man and said kindly, "We would love to have a keepsake of our travels to your wonderful country; it will be our treasured memory for many years."

Edmond narrowed his eyes.

Ruth placed her hand on Edmond's arm. "Happiness is not something you experience; it is something that you remember."

"Very well, take the picture."

The cameraman set up and aimed his camera. Just as the powder flash went off, Ruth caught something from the corner of her eye. Cooper had leaned in to the shot and smiled.

chapter 31

MAY 25, 1892
NORTH COAST OF EGYPT

THE GOVERNMENT-ORDERED QUARANTINE of foreign travelers kept Ruth and Edmond in the little upstairs apartment and its surrounding courtyard for two nights. The photograph was delivered as promised, and Ruth carefully noted her remarks on the back of the picture. It showed Ruth sitting at the table, raising a glass of red wine in a celebratory toast, Cooper smiling mischievously in the background and Edmond with his hand blurred, the result of waving at a fly as the shutter opened.

They took the carriage back to the docks and boarded a shallow draft, flat-bottomed boat called a *dahabeeyah*. For Edmond it had been two days too long in Alexandria. The wailing of Muslim prayers that wafted across the city from spiked minarets, the constant shouting in the street mingled with a maddening cacophony of animal noises was more than he could bear, and he took great pains to make sure Ruth understood his discomfort.

Ruth had no idea what kind of ship they would use to travel up the Nile, but Edmond had spent the last two days negotiating for just the right craft. Edmond finally found the most expensive, cleanest, and most finely appointed boat.

The ship sported the British Union Jack and sailed low in the water, her bow three feet above the surface. Her design was perfect for the Nile. If caught on a sandbar, it could be poled free. The broad canopy over the cabins would shield them from the sun. The boat was forty feet long and no more than twelve feet at its widest point. It had one tall spire mast at the forward bow and one smaller mast middeck, a crew of four, and had four cabins and a drawing room in the aft that sported fine wood tables and chairs with crimson-and-orange cushions.

Edmond chartered the boat to take them to Cairo and told Ruth there would be only one other passenger. "It's still summer and too hot for normal humans. The tourist season is a month away."

"Do you still wish we were going by train?"

"Of course, but it won't be running until they fix the rails where the last train derailed. At least, that's what they tell me."

"The boat will be more enjoyable, I'm sure," Ruth said.

"Ever the optimist. I suppose I should admire that." His words carried no admiration.

Edmond led Ruth onboard the *dahabeeyah*. "Quite tidy, isn't it? Most of the other boats were filthy. You would have been uncomfortable."

"I would have managed, Edmond. I'm not a china doll."

The captain, a short man, bowed and said, "Salaam," then handed Ruth a moist towel. Edmond took it. The captain snapped his fingers and barked an order. A deckhand appeared with another towel.

He led them to the parlor and Ruth felt surprised to see a well-stocked library and a maple piano with the lid opened. Along the walls were mounted vases with flowers arrayed to best show their many colors. Ruth hoped Edmond would relax and enjoy the trip, but she saw him frown when they heard a faint cacophony of cackling through the parlor walls.

"What is that?" Ruth asked.

"Geese. Geese in cages strapped to the deck. I insisted that the geese be left behind, but the captain refused."

"Geese?"

"And chickens. And pigeons." He shuddered.

Ruth fought a smile. "This is all divine."

"Not divine, dear. Just expensive."

A conversation outside caught Ruth's attention. Apparently, the only other passenger had arrived and they stepped outside the parlor to greet the other traveler. They were met by a familiar grin. At exactly 1:00 P.M., Cooper trotted up the gangplank.

"Mr. Cooper," Ruth said. "This is a surprise."

"Your husband didn't tell you that I would be traveling with you?"

"I just hadn't gotten to it, that's all," Edmond said. "Since Mr. Cooper was traveling in the same direction and since he knows more about these parts than we do, I invited him along. Of course, he's paying his share."

"Of course," Cooper said.

A short time later a small swivel cannon blasted from the bow, signaling the beginning of the voyage. The boat slipped from the dock, pushed along by a slender young barefoot crew dressed in light blue robes. The sails unfurled and flapped erratically, then billowed full, gulping the wind sweeping along the Nile.

Cooper served as tour guide, lecturing like a professor in some East Coast university. "Unless I miss my guess, that is el-Rachid." He pointed to a community along the shore of the Nile. "In July 1799, just north of the town, French soldiers garrisoned there were removing rubble and debris from around the fort. Thousands of Ottoman invaders had landed nearby in Abukir and were headed their way. The fort had pitiful fortification, with decaying earthen walls that had been built in the fifteenth century by Sultan Qaitbay. The soldier had few materials, except for some scattered debris from the aged fort and some nearby boulders that were discarded ballast from ships."

"How horrible," Ruth said.

"While gathering some of these boulders," Cooper continued, "for the coastal fortifications, a man named d'Hautpoul noticed a strange block of stone and alerted a young lieutenant named Bouchard. The Rosetta stone, one of the most important finds in all history, was chiseled in 196 BC in three languages and for the first time unlocked the mystery to our understanding of the lost and forgotten languages of the pharaohs. For a linguist like me, it was a monumental discovery."

"I have read of it," Ruth said. "It is no longer in Egypt, is it?"

"No. It's in the British Museum. It's been there since 1802. I have seen it many times."

While they sailed, Ruth read from the Bible, as she had done since the start of the trip in San Francisco. She had come to enjoy the stories, especially those of Exodus, knowing that this was the land she was about to see. She could barely believe she was now looking at the same horizon Moses had seen. Or that the sands along the shore may have been where Mary and the young child Jesus walked while in exile from Herod's reign. This was the land that emerged from the pages of the

Bible, so she eagerly read the black book she had inherited from Jeremiah Tate.

After the long sail on the meandering Nile, Edmond and Ruth arrived in the ancient river port of Boolak in Cairo—a port of three hundred bobbing boats at anchor with tall, slender masts. The many other boats were for hire and their captains were willing to take a steady stream of English, American, Belgian, German, and French tourists up the wide, green vein of water that coursed through the harsh desert. What they would see were mostly ruins, dusty cities, and empty tombs long since robbed of their treasure.

They were met on the dock by several beggars with outstretched hands. Edmond screamed, "Back away. Get away from us."

Ruth took his arm. "They are just trying to feed themselves."

Edmond frowned. "They can work and make money like everyone else in the world. These are common beggars unwilling to toil; thus they are, in all regards, just human parasites."

A familiar sadness ached within her. "Please try and be a little more compassionate."

Cooper quickly summoned a carriage to transport the Americans' luggage to the hotel. Edmond smiled, but the expression evaporated as a crowd of men surrounded him. *"Baksheesh, baksheesh."* They extended empty hands toward him. Edmond waved his hand at the men as if they were irritating flies.

Edmond shouted to Cooper, waving him over to help push the beggars aside.

It was clear that Edmond wanted out of the disgusting place, but Ruth loved the wonder of it all. Not far from the dock, a veiled woman sold slippers in a tiny stall. She sat silently in front of stacks of red and yellow morocco slippers with turned-up toes for young girls, small scarlet bluchers with red tassels for little boys, and velvet slippers embroidered with fine gold strands and seed pearls for the women in wealthy harems. Next to her, another woman sold bags of red hard candy. Ruth bought a bag while workers loaded the luggage on the wagon.

The wagon was soon loaded with several steamer trunks and, with the snap of a whip from the driver, the three passengers moved slowly through the press of children who had watched Ruth buy the candy. They held out hands, hoping for a piece. Ruth happily handed out pieces from the carriage.

Edmond pushed Ruth's arms down, stopping her from creating a further ruckus. "You are only exacerbating the situation."

"They are only children. I doubt they get many treats." She gently pulled her arm free and tossed the remaining candy into the street, which in an instant was crowded with a gaggle of children wrestling for one of the sweets.

She turned her head and watched the children

frantically groping in the pile of candy that lay scattered in the dusty lane. It reminded Ruth of when she was a child and had fed the seagulls by throwing scraps of bread over the side of the ship. As she turned around in the carriage, she remembered Tate. In her mind's eye she could see his tall, handsome frame holding out a thick slice of bread in one hand and a black book in the other. She reached down into her carpetbag and felt for the book.

The only thing that Ruth disliked was seeing the many mothers who stood in the doorways of their simple mud homes as she passed by. They seemed to stare at her from empty eyes as they held crying babies straddling their cocked hips. All the babies seemed to have black flies crawling across their cherubic faces, feasting on mucus dripping from brown, shiny noses. The babies' hands were lifted, as if in a plea for help, but their pleas were ignored by their stoic mothers, who did nothing but stare.

"Most of the children in Egypt have eyes infected with fly larvae." Cooper sighed. "It's a hard thing to see."

Ruth saw one child no older than five with an empty eye socket. Only a pink, fleshy lump remained where once an eyeball had been. It broke her heart to see such poverty. She looked to Edmond, who seemed inconvenienced by the squalor. No doubt to him, the child was less than human, a dirty creature who had every pore, every fold of skin, every follicle of black hair coated in vermin.

Edmond's lack of enthusiasm had clearly reached rock bottom. He rode in silence, scowling at everything that moved. Ruth knew he had promised her they would see Egypt, but she also knew he'd never promised to be in an accommodating mood while they did it.

Cooper and Ruth ignored Edmond's dark mood. They cheerfully pointed out the unfolding panorama of fascinating scenery. They traveled the labyrinth of dirty streets lined with shops laden with hanging copper pots; ornate, brightly colored rugs; and silk scarves. Sacks of pungent spices sat open under shanks of hanging lamb's quarters peppered with crawling flies. Tanned, swarthy-faced men, lips mantled with thick black mustaches, seemed uninterested as they sat sucking the draping tubes from their tall, elaborately colored bubble pipes. Women with large almond eyes peered from behind delicate veils as the strangely dressed Westerners rode past.

Narrow paths gave way to a wide boulevard lined with merchants and craftsmen at work. Ruth gazed at the evolving scenery with wonder. She craned her neck to see as much as possible: saddle merchants hammering, stitching, punching, and riveting away; a tobacco salesman squatting in the dark recess of his shop, his face lit by the soft red glow of the cigarette between his lips. Then there were the narrow, dark alleys crammed with robed men sitting on piles of multicolored, handmade, vegetable-dyed rugs. The carriage driver told them the rugs came from Persia, Morocco, and Libya.

The most interesting of all the merchants were those who displayed mummies wrapped in brown, crumbling cloth.

"Driver? Are those really mummies?" Ruth asked.

"Yes, missus. Mummies are good business. Grave robbers dig them up by the wagonful. Since long time it has been believed that mummies possess strong medicine."

Cooper had something to add. "In Scotland during the 1600s, the market value of a mummy was about twelve shillings a pound. The dried corpses were purchased with such an insatiable greed that the lucrative trade became a taxed enterprise. In Cairo, it was easy to find open markets and bazaars with a completely wrapped mummy for sale standing in a merchant's stall in full view of all. The merchant might even unravel some of the decaying bandages wrapped around the corpse and allow a glimpse at the blackened face."

"That's fascinating, Mr. Cooper."

Cooper added, "All across Egypt, farmers made more money selling dug-up mummies than they could ever make digging their own crops."

"What did people do with the mummies?"

"Are you sure you want to know?"

"Yes," Ruth said.

"No," Edmond snapped.

"Tell us, Mr. Cooper."

"Most people would grind parts of the mummy to powder and eat the dried granules."

"I did not need to hear that," Edmond grumbled under his breath.

Cooper continued. "People all over Europe did just that. King Francis the First of France was known to carry a bag of mummy dust just in case he needed a little swallow for emergency medicinal treatment. Many leaving Egypt hauled several mummies back to England and sold them at such a profit they could pay for the entire trip."

Ruth thought of the hearts that had once beat below those now leather-stiff chests. *These men once had children who climbed upon their knees and placed a loving kiss upon a cheek that was now cracked and dried brown.* The thought saddened her.

She turned to Edmond. "I hope you can endure this."

Edmond smiled at her words. "I will be fine once we get to the hotel." He put a handkerchief to his face to fend off the brown spray of dust from the spinning carriage wheels.

After a few moments of silence, Cooper said, "I will be returning to the docks tomorrow to arrange for a boat to Luxor."

Ruth gave Edmond's arm a squeeze. He finally

got the hint. "Why don't you wait two more days? We will visit the pyramids and be done with this wretched city. After that we plan to sail the Nile for two weeks. You can join us if you like. We will sail to Luxor and give you companionship while you conduct your business."

"Thank you, but this is your newlywed holiday. I would only be intruding on your honeymoon."

"Nonsense," said Edmond. "You have already been of great help to us. As you might have noticed, I am not an experienced traveler. If you voyage with us down the Nile, then you can see most of the country in clean air and with an ease of travel on a *good* boat."

Ruth turned to Cooper. "You have been most informative. I would like to learn as much as I can. We can see the many wonders of an ancient world and you can teach us what you know. Then we stop off at Luxor and see your obelisk. It should prove to be a grand adventure."

"We would consider it an honor." Edmond almost sounded genuine. It made Ruth smile.

"If you're certain I will not be in the way, then I accept your offer. Traveling alone isn't nearly as enjoyable as having the presence of new friends."

"Fine," Edmond said. "It is all agreed. We shall journey down the Nile together."

Ruth let her eyes meet the young Mr. Cooper's.

chapter **32**

JULY 2, 1980
SAN FRANCISCO, CALIFORNIA

THE HOUSE—A NARROW, two-story structure that shared walls with its neighbors and sat on a very steep street—was set in a fashionable part of the city. Gary parked his motorcycle and made his way up the walk and front steps. A few moments later, he was looking at a man with a full head of white hair and bright blue eyes. Gary decided the man was eighty-five if he was a day. He wore casual trousers and a golf shirt. The smell of rich coffee wafted out the open door.

"I appreciate your seeing me, Mr. Stiles." Gary shook the elderly man's hand, a hand that had a slight tremor.

"It's not every day I get a call about a relative who died over a century ago. Come in, take off your coat. You drink coffee?"

"I've been known to take a cup or two."

"Fine. I've just brewed a nice Ethiopian blend. It might be a little strong."

"Fine with me. Coffee should be strong. Just so long as it doesn't walk and talk."

Stiles chuckled. "You should see what they made us drink in the navy. What wasn't consumed was used to strip paint."

Gary slipped off his backpack and coat and followed Stiles through a surprisingly modern living room, past a dining room, and into the kitchen. Everything in the kitchen seemed new, polished, and bright. After first seeing Stiles, Gary had assumed the home would be packed with antiques.

Stiles poured coffee into plain white, wide mugs. "Do you need to doctor yours? I have fresh cream."

"Just a touch will be fine."

Stiles added just enough cream to lighten the brew. "Take these to the dining table, will you? I have something to show you." He walked from the kitchen. Gary slipped into the dining room, set down his backpack, hung his coat on the back of a chair, and returned to retrieve the coffee. A minute later, Stiles returned with a large book.

"I've kept a family album," he said as he sat down. He sipped his coffee, then opened the book. "I have pictures going back to the early days of photography."

"That's amazing."

"Not so amazing. My family tended to be socially involved. Having their picture taken was all part of the process. Fortunately I had an old aunt who collected everything she could find. She passed it down to me."

He turned a page or two. "Here. This is Congressman Stiles seated behind his desk in Washington." The image showed a stately, serious man with a grave expression. "And this—this is my great-great-aunt Ruth on her honeymoon. She traveled the world over and mailed several of these photos to family here in San Francisco. This photo was returned to the family after her death. It shows the newlyweds in 1892 sitting in a restaurant in Alexandria." He removed it from the plastic sleeve and handed it to Gary, who took it delicately.

The photo was cracked and faded; the black tones had paled to sepia. When Gary turned it over, he saw a smeared and faded inked notation: *Edmond and I having a meal in Alexandria with the Englishman named Paul Cooper.*

"And here's a photo of—"

"Wait." Gary's heart galloped and his mouth went dry. He pulled the old Bible from his backpack and opened its blood-smeared pages to the words he had studied so many times before.

"Is that the Bible you mentioned on the phone?"

"Yes." Gary read aloud: *" 'Killed here with Frederick—found it all—Emily in White—R.C. Cooper, 1921.' "*

"R.C. Cooper, you say?"

"Yes. Do you know an R.C. Cooper?"

He shook his head. "I have no knowledge of Paul Cooper or R.C. Cooper. How does that have anything to do with Judge Stiles?"

"I don't know, but I think it's important."

"I don't know about that. Should I go on?"

"Of course. I'm sorry."

"She married Edmond Donahue, a well-to-do man. As the family story goes, they were pushed into marrying by the parents on both sides. In those days, marriage was often for a consolidation of wealth. Kind of like a business merger today."

"What happened to Ruth and Edmond?"

"Well, they went on a round-the-world honeymoon and never returned."

"Never returned?"

"That's right. Ruth was widowed over there and never came home."

"That's odd."

"Yes, the woman just walked away from all her wealth and stayed in Egypt. The last we heard was that she got religion and worked at an orphanage in Cairo till the day she died. There aren't many of her letters still intact."

"That's all you know about her?"

"That's all I know."

Gary nodded.

chapter **33**

MAY 27, 1892
BOOLAK, EGYPT

THEY STAYED FOR two nights at the famed Shepherd Hotel in Cairo. Edmond complained that it was overpriced for such a dank and small room. The huge dining hall, however, served good food, and the milling crowd of Americans and Europeans made it more palatable for Edmond. He stayed up most of the night smoking cigars and listening to other men talk of business opportunities in the burgeoning city of Cairo, adolescent as it was in the ways of the Westerners.

They traveled back to Boolak in a rickety carriage even worse for wear than the one they had used upon their arrival. It was pulled by an old, thin, ginger mare with a gray-haired snout and mane. They had seen the great pyramids and, in spite of the usual throng of beggars and merchants milling about with outstretched hands, it was an amazing sight that even impressed Edmond. But like Alexandria, the city of Cairo was noisy, dusty, and inhospitable, and they were eager for the river passage into clean desert.

They drank Oriental green tea while waiting for the luggage to be hauled aboard. Once mooring ropes were untied, one of the crew, dressed only in a loincloth, slid over the side of the gunwales and stood waist deep in river water. He was a tall man, bronzed and muscular, and had no problem shouldering the heavy wooden hull into the swifter currents while another crew member stood on deck moving the boat with a long pole.

Once the dripping man had crawled back on deck, the captain maneuvered the boat into the rippling currents and expertly tillered it into position. The sail distended tightly, like a bloated wineskin, as it took in the warm wind and bowed the tall, thin mast.

They glided past a line of ugly mud warehouses, then old mansions that were peeled to their raw wood by gnawing sun and blowing desert sand. They sailed on, marveling at the lush green gardens of Roda and picturesque clusters of old, crumbling, Coptic churches. The great pyramids of Giza were the last reminders of Cairo, and they soon sank below the horizon.

Cooper sat alone on the aft cabin lid furiously sketching the passing scenery and taking notes. Ruth and Edmond were at the bow. She was wearing a wide-brimmed robin's-egg-blue hat and, to Ruth's surprise, Edmond wore a sweat-stained turban that he bought from one of the crew. He stood regally, with one foot propped on the bowsprit as he breathed in the desert air that rolled across the water.

"This is better," Edmond said. "This dry air is magnificent. Nothing like the damp air of San Francisco."

"Yes," Ruth said, "it is fabulous."

Ruth pointed out the fascinating scenery like a child at her first state fair. Sinewy men laboring in the fields of maize were chopping weeds with wooden hoes. To the starboard, a plodding water buffalo walked in circles as a little girl whipped its rump with a lanyard of leather tied to a stick. The beast turned a huge wooden waterwheel with wide-mouthed clay jars tied with hemp on the rim. Scoop after scoop of water was cupped from the Nile and then drained into dusty furrows above. The liquid fed thirsty sprouts of cotton and maize.

The Nile made its serpentine way through the desert, and around each bend new delights awaited them. First, young boys jumping from the backs of docile water buffalo that stood submerged to their necks in the ancient waters. Then a line of ten women, dressed in flowing *galabiyas*, walking in a grove of palms. They stepped from the bulrushes and up onto the edge of the embankment carrying heavy, red, baked jars filled with water on their heads. Their hands were stained a brown-orange from the crude adornment. Their faces reflected the burden upon their heads. Ruth had no idea how they could carry something so heavy that way.

Ruth grew reflective. For Edmond and her, it was an unfolding, fascinating world, but it was an arduous place for those trying to live another day in a hard land with no mercy.

Edmond seemed a changed man. Ruth had never seen him smile more broadly. At long last, he seemed content. Edmond took her hand and squeezed. Ruth blushed from the rare gesture of affection. "Are you happy, dear?"

"Yes, I believe I am happy." He paused, then asked, "Why did you decide to marry such a bore? Was it for the money?"

She thought a moment. "In times such as these, a woman needs security more than love."

"Then it was for money." He nodded, showing his approval of her honesty.

Still, she sensed that her answer had saddened him. "I will come to love you, Edmond. As you said in your proposal, our arrangement would take time, but that we would someday fall in love."

Edmond looked to the rough planking on the deck and then into her eyes. "Seeing you with the red burn of the sun on your cheeks, with the wind pulling your hair about your face, I fear that I shall never be as fond of you as I am right now."

The words took Ruth aback. This was not the man she thought she knew.

"I have married well, that is what I am told, this is what I know, yet I have not treated you well in return." He faced the passing river. "I am not one to enjoy life. I am a man who works for his father and shall never be the man he is. I suppose that's why I am so melancholy. I am an accountant who does nothing more than count the money my father earns. All I can do for you as a husband is wait for my father to die and inherit his money. All I can do is count the days and hope to earn your love."

"I will love you someday, I pray. Time will bring it. If I said anything else, it would be a lie, and I know you would not love me under any false notion." She, too, turned to the coursing water.

"I will wait, but I will also pray for a swift notification of your love."

"I have never heard you speak of love or prayer."

"Maybe a little prayer is what we both need."

Ruth took his hand in hers and scanned the desert shadows of the dying day.

They sailed from dusk till dawn for the next three days and soon fell into the rhythm of ship life. Edmond continued to grow more talkative and Ruth decided she enjoyed this new side of her husband.

The crew were all Egyptian except for one young boy. He was a desert Bedouin, about fourteen, and different in many ways. One evening, the passengers passed the time listening to his story while Cooper translated.

He was from Al Bad, in northern Arabia, and had come to Egypt after his father disowned him for becoming a Christian. The father had killed the traveling missionary who converted the boy, hanging him in the sun, leaving the preacher's body to the birds. The father then ordered his only child to leave the village because he had disgraced his father. Faris was an outcast, unwelcome in his own home and unwanted in his town. He had been forced to cross the desert, into Egypt. In one way he felt fortunate. Most fathers would have killed their sons for choosing Christianity over their

Muslim faith. What his father could not bring himself to do directly, though, he did indirectly by sending his son to die in the desert.

The day he left, his mother, not allowed a single word of protest, brought a camel, water skins, and some food for her son. She kissed him good-bye and turned away. A few steps later she collapsed, to her knees, wailing, and threw sand into the air. Faris knew what she would do next. He had seen it once with another. His mother would cut her hair off with a knife. She would never be allowed to speak of the event.

Faris traveled in mountain wadis, going north, then west, passing the Gulf of Aqaba. As he crossed the northern Sinai, he ran short of water. Uncertain of the distance he would need to travel, he had consumed his water too quickly. When he came to a well or an oasis, he found the water undrinkable, always bitter or salty. Drinking would only make him sick or enhance his thirst. He did not drink, but the camel did.

Soon his tongue began to swell. After two days with no water, he feared he would not make it across the desert alive. His hearing was hollow; he wondered if his brain was melting with the rising heat of the cloudless day. That night he slept out a sandstorm in fitful dreams, curled next to the camel. In the morning, he awoke delirious.

In desperation he slit the camel's throat and cut open the camel's stomach to get what little moisture remained. He was found later that day, unconscious, with dried blood caked on his face. The people who found him were part of a large spice caravan from Yemen. They took Faris with them to Cairo.

Days later, the captain of the boat heard of the boy's story as it circulated in the bazaar, and he took pity on Faris. He hired him as the boat boy for his vessel and soon came to love Faris as his own.

Ruth was taken by the boy as well. His toothy smile and short bow when he brought her tea and sliced melon were most charming. Ruth soon began teaching the boy English. He showed a talent for languages. Cooper aided in the teaching. Faris's favorite phrase was, "Yes, indeed."

During the next five days, the land they passed changed very little. It looked like it had a thousand years earlier, Ruth supposed. Just beyond the fertile banks lay the dry death of the desert, harsh, stark, and strikingly beautiful with a wide bed of white sands that melted into chalky cliffs.

The only thing that changed was the temperature. It grew hotter with each mile. The evenings, however, were mild, and the travelers sat on the foredeck, guessing what time the sun would touch the horizon. Edmond always won. Ruth and Cooper didn't much care, but Edmond would watch the horizon and grimace if a hill or a cliff came into view—the only things that would upset his calculations.

Ruth loved the evenings. She would stare into the purple dusk, watching the swallows and bats in their aerial ballet as they swooped low across the dark river searching for insects. It was possibly the most tranquil place on earth.

The sounds of water massaging the hull, the squeaky rub of the tiller against the stern, Faris singing a childhood song from Arabia as he cheerfully brought her a bowl of dates and a steaming cup of tea—all these gave her joy.

Every minute had been pleasant—until ten o'clock one morning. Somewhere far away in the vast desert of Libya, the hot sun had sucked wind over the endless dunes, carrying countless tons of sand. The storm raced unabated toward them, darkening the skies and pushing the agitated water into a navy of whitecaps.

The first sign that anything was wrong was when grains of sand started to pepper the windowpanes of the main cabin. The boat was nudged sideways in the gathering wind and was soon listing toward the opposite shore. To Ruth, it seemed as if an invisible hand pushed with all its might against the boat. The captain ordered the crew to reef the sails. Ruth's heart began to pound when the roaring wind hurtled larger stones, breaking several windows. Her mind flew to another boat and another sea battered by a storm off the coast of central Mexico in 1865. She saw it all again: the wagon breaking loose from its deck ties; felt the big hand of Tate covering her face; felt the sting of steam upon her neck as it erupted from the severed pipe. The nightmare seemed to be coming back to life.

Ruth stood on the deck, sheltered from flying sand and pebbles by the main cabin. Edmond pleaded with her to go below and close the hatch. Cooper tried to coax her inside.

The sky was a gurgling, dark brown that frothed high on the horizon. Because the sandstorm had come across the desert, inhaling strength as it came, these were no clouds of rain that would bring a drop of moisture. These were chapped, dry, choking clouds engorged with a thousand tons of sand. The captain wrapped a cloth over his face and shouted above the howling wind, "Bedouins call this a dry rain." Ripping air currents hurled large grains of sand against the ship, sounding like a thick cut of bacon sizzling in a skillet.

Ruth was too terrified to move. A tug on her arm moved her a foot, then she felt herself being dragged into the protective shelter of the cabin. Edmond pulled her below as Cooper buttoned down the hatch.

Ruth said, "Did you hear the captain?"

"Why wouldn't you come in?" Edmond's voice bore the fear he felt.

"The captain said that the storm is called a dry rain." She ran into her cabin and foraged for the Bible.

Edmond followed. "What are you doing?"

"A dry rain. You heard him say that, didn't you?"

"So what if he did?"

"I've heard it before. It was something that Jeremiah Tate said when he gave me this Bible." She riffled through the pages and found the note she was looking for—a letter from a boy soldier. "The day he gave me the Bible he mentioned a dry rain." She flipped the pages hurriedly and found the letter written by a boy named Bell. She read it aloud. *"'But if anyone who has this book and does not follow the Lord, then I fear a dry rain cometh.'"*

"What's that supposed to mean?"

Ruth read the note a second time. The sky dimmed. Ruth moved to the window and repeated the words as desert sand seeped beneath the door. "Where are the others?"

"Most are in the parlor."

Ruth brushed past her husband and moved into the parlor. As soon as she stepped into the room, the ship hit something with a jarring thud. The impact broke another window, and brown wind swirled into the space.

Cooper looked out the windows port and starboard. "We're still in the river. We must have gotten hung up on a sandbar."

Passengers and crew reached for support where they could find it. Ruth clamped her eyes shut and tried to choke down her fear. Visions of the ocean storm she'd endured as a child mingled with the present danger, churning in her mind. Her knees grew weak. She felt Edmond take hold of her shoulders.

The ship began to lean to the port side from the weight of the mounting dirt on the deck.

"She's going to capsize!" Cooper shouted. "Get ready to swim."

"I . . . I can't swim," Edmond said.

The words terrified her more than the biting, stinging sandstorm. Ruth dropped to her knees and held the Bible tight against her chest. "Lord, I will return to you. Please find it in Your will to spare us. Please end this dry rain."

She trembled. The unwanted vision of Edmond struggling in the water made her ill. She repeated the prayer again, then again. Edmond lifted her from the deck and wrapped his arms around her. He tightened his hold, and she realized that he was attempting to shield her from the abrasive sand being blown in through the shattered windows.

The boat tilted more.

"Stay with me," Ruth said. "I can swim some. I'll help you."

"No, you won't," Edmond said, his mouth an inch from her ear. "You will make straight for the riverbank."

"No—"

"Yes, you will. You will do as I say. I'll be fine."

"But you can't swim."

"I'll stay with the boat. Cooper will help you."

"I'm not leaving you. You're my husband."

"You will do as I say."

He moved toward the door, Ruth still in his arms.

"We wait until the last second," Cooper shouted. He had stepped close to the couple. "Make for the riverbank. The river will move you downstream some but keep swimming for land."

"Stay with Ruth," Edmond said. "She'll need your help."

"We all stay together."

The boat tilted several more degrees. Ruth continued to mutter her prayer, her face buried in Edmond's chest.

"Now?" Edmond asked.

Cooper shook his head. "No. Wait until you see the crew abandon ship, then jump."

"Edmond?"

"Shush. It's all going to be fine."

They waited, Edmond and Ruth supporting themselves against the tilted wall of the parlor. Sand continued to flow in through the open windows and gather at their feet.

Minutes later, the wind began to slow. Ruth waited, clinging to Edmond, whose arms had not budged since encircling her. With each minute that passed, the wind diminished. Twenty minutes later, the crew began to clear the deck of sand.

Finally Edmond released his hold and stepped back. He leaned forward and kissed her on the lips. The impropriety of it didn't matter to Ruth. She returned the kiss, then wrapped her arms around him again, the Bible still in one hand.

"I feared I was going to lose you, Ruth. I never want to feel that again."

She began to weep. "I kept seeing you struggling in the water. If you drowned, I . . . I don't know what I would do."

"Thank God none of that happened. We're safe now."

"Yes, thank God. My prayer was answered. I prayed for deliverance, and God granted it."

"Maybe there's something to that old Bible after all." Edmond began to laugh. The sudden release of tension had made him giddy. Ruth's laughter replaced her tears.

Cooper, who had been checking on damages, stepped to the couple and slapped Edmond on the back. "How's that for adventure, old man?"

The captain didn't seem angered by the damage. He calmly led the crew in cleaning away the debris and sand, explaining that it was the will of Allah. Everyone helped. Ruth swept the parlor, Edmond and Cooper used flat boards from the broken chicken coops to scrape away the dirt. Most of the chicken and geese had survived the assault. Crewmen tossed those that hadn't overboard.

After several hours, the boat was ready. The craft, now lighter without the unwanted load of sand, and with the backbreaking use of long poles, was freed from the sandbar and they were off again.

That afternoon, Ruth held the Bible and read until dusk. Faris, as usual, brought some tea, then pointed to the Bible. Ruth felt confused. He bowed his head and clasped his hands as if in prayer.

"You pray, Faris?" she said.

He smiled. "Yes, indeed."

chapter **34**

THE MORNING WAS hot and an ovenlike wind rolled in from distant, ghostly mountains. Ruth stood at the bow, watching the boat split the waters of the Nile. Faris brought her tea as she read from the Bible. She thanked him and turned her gaze upriver.

"*Neharrak.*" It was the captain, and his Egyptian greeting drew Ruth's attention. He pointed over the bow. "We at Luxor."

In the distance, Ruth could see the desert give way to a city. This was the farthest Ruth and Edmond would go. Ruth felt she had reached the end of the world. She had promised Edmond that they would return home after Luxor, home to San Francisco, to a life of prominence; to servants; and to staid, boring social events.

Stately palm groves lined the bank to her left; to the right a crude patchwork of cultivated fields spread into a craggy ridge of gray limestone cliffs. The flat, green river widened as they neared the city. Cut-rock tombs appeared out of the dusty haze. The sight of them bewildered Ruth. A short distance ahead, a forest of masts appeared along the bank, evidence that they were arriving in the tiny port that was situated beside a grove of sycamore trees.

"This is the port to the grandest ruins in the world."

The voice startled Ruth. "Oh, Mr. Cooper. I didn't hear you approach."

"You seemed lost in the scenery."

"I was. It's easy to do."

Cooper looked around. "I don't see your husband."

"He slept a little late this morning. I expect him soon."

The crew assembled on the aft deck, above the pilot's cabin, and began singing loudly and tying brightly colored flags to a line heralding their arrival. As he tied the last flag, the captain shouted to Ruth, "*Kharûf, Luxor*—all right, Luxor!"

Ruth smiled back. "Thank you, Captain."

Luxor was a congested, dirty city with a mosque at one end, a brothel at the other, and, in between, drab, whitewashed, windowless homes. But there was no mistaking that this was a special place of the past. Rising from the humble mud hamlet were magnificent granite columns and huge stone statues.

Cooper couldn't wait and said he would walk into town, hoping to find camels that would take them to the archeological site. Edmond was beginning to show signs of adventure; he put on his turban and went along to help. A row of four kneeling camels had been tied to a rail near the dock.

Ruth refused to be outdone. She took a pair of Edmond's pants from the steamer trunk and folded up the legs to just above her laced, black, ankle-high shoes. She had never worn pants before but liked the feel of them. No corset, no frilly long dress to drag in the dirt. She was determined to ride a camel.

By the time she joined Edmond and Cooper, they were in deep negotiations with the family that owned the camels. It didn't take long for Ruth to realize that camel rental was the family's business. European tourists and scientists arrived at this same port and needed transportation. The family provided it for a price. Cooper promised a good payment if they could leave soon. The deal was done.

The herder stood by the kneeling camels. He was a scruffy-looking Arab, with a thin nose. He wore a sun-faded *galabiya* that appeared to have never been washed and was permanently stained with grease and dried sheep's blood.

Ruth and the others mounted their respective animals with the help of the Arab owncr, who tapped a stick on each camel's round rump and made a clicking sound with his throat. The animals would lean forward sharply, unfold gangly legs, and then lurch back. One almost sent Edmond tumbling off and onto the hard-packed sand. It took time for Ruth to settle herself; sitting on her camel made her dizzy.

The four were soon swaying on wood saddles draped with black woven carpets fringed with red tassels.

At first they headed along the bank of the Nile, weaving through the sycamores. They passed mud-brick shops peppered among temple ruins. Huge walls etched with the pageantry of the long-dead pharaoh and massive stone facades over-shadowed prowling dogs, robed men, veiled women riding donkeys, vagrant water buffalo, camels, and dozens of scabby cats probing trash heaps. A gaggle of women squatted shoulder to shoulder by the river's edge, washing pots, pans, and clothes, then piling them on top of their heads. When done, they walked packed dirt paths that had been pedestrian thoroughfares for thousands of years.

Men labored in fields under a cloudless sky, repeating a never-ending cycle of tilling parched land with crude wooden hoes. Others filled bucket after bucket by hand from the river, then poured the water into furrows. It was a lifestyle repeated generation after generation, dating back to biblical times.

The camel herder turned to Cooper and said something. Cooper nodded as he listened.

"What did he say?" Edmond asked.

"He said his wife is with child. The day draws near when a son will be born."

"How does he know it will be a son?" Ruth struggled to find a more comfortable spot on the saddle. She doubted she would.

"He seems an optimistic man," Cooper said with a grin.

The bellowing beasts turned toward the russet cliffs that lay beyond patches of farmland choked with meager brown-bearded corn and barley. As they passed each field, men dropped their hoes and ran alongside the caravan shouting, "*Anteek, mister.*"

"What's this all about?" Edmond asked.

Cooper spoke to the camel herder, then said, "They're saying, 'Antique, mister.' He says everyone has an ancient scarab or stone statue of some kind to sell. It seems they make a little extra money this way."

"They look desperate," Ruth said.

"It is a hard life," Cooper said. "I imagine they do what they have to do."

The workers followed far longer than Ruth thought they would, but they finally gave up and returned to their waiting tools.

The early morning cool was soon gone, and the hills surrendered their taupe hues to the sun's unrelenting blaze. Luxor slipped from sight.

"Just how far is this dig of yours, Cooper?" Edmond asked.

"Not far. Just eight miles. Soon we will see where the obelisk lay."

"*Just* eight miles," Edmond grunted. "I'm already saddle sore, and we've just begun."

"I'm eager to get there," Cooper said. "But it is foolish to rush. The obelisk has been waiting three thousand years. I suppose we can be patient."

"Patience, my friend, is not my strong suit."

"My husband speaks the truth." Ruth laughed. "Speaking of the truth, please tell us about your family. You have never mentioned them."

Cooper's smile turned sad. "I have a son, but he is living with my sister, Emily, on the Isle of Wight, in England. My wife died some time back. I can't see my son's face without seeing hers, without feeling the pain of losing her. Besides, what life would it be for my son traipsing around in the desert like this?"

Ruth could see the man's pain. "The boy needs a father, Mr. Cooper. More than that, you need to mend your heart."

Paul Cooper turned in his saddle. "How could you possibly know what I need to do?"

Ruth sighed. "I do not know how to be a father, that is true, or how to be a son, for that matter. But

I do know that the love given by anyone is always returned. Maybe not how we expect, but it returns, I assure you of that. If you pursue that love, you will be blessed beyond what a heart can possibly carry."

His tone softened. "I suppose you are right. Thank you for the kind words."

"They are not my words, but come from an old book I have recently started to read."

A little more than an hour later, they arrived at the worksite of the stone obelisk. The camels came to a stop.

"This doesn't look right," Cooper said.

No one was working. A weathered and wind-beaten canvas tent stood alone, its flaps snapping in the breeze. Next to the tent was a half-unearthed obelisk still in the grip of the sand. A lone camel kneeled nearby.

"It looks abandoned," Edmond said. "Should there be some of your people around here?"

"Yes." Cooper looked dazed. "Yes, there should be." He stared at the tent. "Not completely abandoned."

Cooper spoke to the camel herder, who used his long pole to tap the front legs of his camel. The beast kneeled. Soon everyone was on foot again. Cooper stepped to the tent, Ruth and Edmond close behind.

Inside, an old man with a frayed turban and wearing a worn and stained robe sat near a mud-brick oven cooking flat bread. The side of the tent had been cut open to allow the fire to breathe. He was using mummy bones and rags for fuel. The man sat with an empty stare. Gray stubble covered his sun-scarred mahogany face. He jumped when Cooper and the others approached, then rose on wobbly legs and bowed. He stepped outside the tent.

Cooper spoke in Arabic, then said, "I asked him his name and what happened to the project."

The man looked at Ruth and smiled with ribbed black gums that resembled the spine of a Nile crocodile. He spoke, then nodded at Ruth.

"Did I do something wrong?" Ruth asked.

Cooper said, "No. He wonders why a white woman would be in the desert and why you are wearing pants."

"Tell him it's all the rage."

Edmond frowned.

Cooper spoke to the man again, and to Ruth's ear it sounded very much like what he had said moments before.

The man shifted his gaze from Ruth to Cooper and began to speak quickly. He flung out his arms as he spoke.

"His name is Salim. He says Blair did not wake up one morning. He had been ill with dysentery. Many days of cramps and fever."

"Blair is one of yours?" Edmond said.

Cooper nodded. "Yes."

"He's dead?" Ruth gasped.

"Apparently." Cooper showed no emotion.

Salim rattled on again and Cooper translated. "Most Franks have such sickness when they come to this land. Many fall ill. Some die."

The old man lowered his head as if in great remorse.

"When did he die?" Cooper caught himself and repeated the question in Arabic.

"He was so sick he could eat little more than cheese, soured curds, and some dates for many days. He grew weaker and weaker. The desert loves to kill those who come from afar and try to take from it. He died two months ago." The man pointed with his ruddy stump of a finger in the direction of a nearby hill. "I buried him there."

Ruth looked in the direction the man indicated and saw a mound of rocks.

Again, Cooper translated. "I buried him deep, so the jackals would not dig him up, but they dug him up anyway the first night, so I buried what was left of him deeper and threw sticks and more rocks on him to stop the jackals. They did not come here again."

"How horrible," Ruth said.

"Ask him about the other workers," Edmond said.

Cooper did.

"All the workers stopped work that day. There was no more money when the white boss from

England died. The only money we have gotten since that time was after a camel caravan of Moors had passed in the night and the workers went to rob them. I am old, and they did not share anything with me. So I wait here, knowing that the English from the museum will come and bring more money. The English—they always bring money to us. I pray you see the value in my tending to your obelisk."

Cooper nodded as he finished this translation.

The man lowered his head. "I buried him myself. The others . . . they left Mr. Blair to the sun, but I buried him." Salim pointed to his fire, which was now burning his bread black, and spoke.

"He says he would not be a good Bedouin if he didn't offer us tea and bread."

"It might be a good way to get the rest of the story," Edmond said.

The old man stepped back into the tent and reemerged with two wooden chairs. He set one down and motioned for Ruth to sit. Edmond took the other. Again the man disappeared through the tent flap and reappeared with a saddle. He set it on the ground for Cooper.

Cooper slapped the dust from his clothes and sat. Salim then unfurled a scrap of woven wool, vegetable-dyed carpet for himself and the camel herder. Ruth thought the carpet too expensive for the man who sat on it and assumed it belonged to Blair. Within minutes, tea was poured into three silver cups taken from a knit bag. Salim took a long-stemmed pot and trickled out the amber brew. Ruth sipped the tea, swished the liquid in her mouth, then spit out the trapped desert granules embedded between her teeth.

Cooper held up the teacup and asked Salim something. He responded and shrugged. "I asked if the cups and teapot belong to Blair. He said, 'Not anymore. The dead have no need of such things.' "

"Crass but accurate, I suppose," Edmond said.

Cooper tried to pull more information from Salim, but there was little to get. "He says he knows nothing more. He worked at the camp for a month, overseeing the younger workers. Blair fell ill and died. The workers left and he alone stayed."

A noise rolled over the sand. Ruth lifted her head to see a soft cloud of dust rising from the ground. She heard a camel's bellowing. From the lip of a ridge came a line of travelers. It was as if the Theban hills had yawned and a caravan suddenly appeared, loaded with rugs, bedding, mats, and crates holding squawking chickens. As they drew closer, she could see two women with babies walking in front of the caravan, presumably to avoid the choking dust kicked up by the animals. They nursed the infants under the shade of sun-faded robes pulled over their tiny forms. Their heads were wrapped with white gauze dangling with coins as ornaments. Five younger men fol-lowed the caravan with long sticks and mercilessly whacked the bony rumps of dusty gray donkeys and bleating sheep. Salim waved to the group, shouting, "*Chi, chi.*"

When the band of Bedouins neared, Salim rose and raced to a man in a yellow turban. He fell at the man's feet, then kissed the man's hands. He rose and kissed the newcomer on each cheek. "*Salaam aleikum. Salaam aleikum.*"

The man in the yellow turban received the adulation like someone used to such things.

chapter **35**

MAY 28, 1892
EIGHT MILES OUTSIDE LUXOR, EGYPT

TRADERS," COOPER SAID. "Bedouin traders."

"Are they dangerous?" Edmond asked.

"I doubt it, but it's clear the man in the yellow turban carries some weight in these parts."

"Fascinating," Ruth said.

The caravan animals were led to shade in the cleft of the rocks and the attendants unrolled a long strand of hemp rope attached at one end around a camel's stomach. A bag at the other end of the rope was lowered into a well rimmed with rocks. The animals were soon lapping water poured into the shallow depression of a wind-smoothed rock. One of the women dumped out a bag of donkey dung and lit a fire.

Salim led the man in the yellow turban to the others, who stood to show respect. The man's eyes widened when Cooper spoke to him in Arabic. Cooper made introductions. The man introduced only himself.

"His name is Machmed," Cooper said.

Salim surrendered his seat on the carpet, as did the camel herder. Cooper spoke to Machmed again, and the man laughed loudly, then uttered something under his breath.

"He thinks my Arabic is amusing. He's never heard a European speak his language," Cooper said, smiling as he went on translating.

Machmed put his right hand to his chest and lowered his eyes. "I do not speak to many infidels. I only know the ways of the desert and follow the ways of Allah and his prophet Muhammad, peace be upon his name." He then looked at Ruth. "I see you have two husbands. I did not know it was the way of Christian women to have two husbands."

Ruth smiled, lifted her hand, and pointed to Cooper. "This man is Paul Cooper. He is not my husband." She turned to Edmond. "This man is my husband. He is Edmond."

Salim looked away, and Machmed's face hardened. "It is not proper for Muslim woman to introduce the man as husband or even call him by name." He looked at Edmond. "He would be called the father of your firstborn son's name. If you do not have a son, then he would be called the father of your firstborn daughter's name."

Ruth looked to Cooper for a translation. She sensed she had done something wrong. "We have no children . . . but we want a boy." She smiled at Edmond.

Machmed nodded, then said to Cooper in Arabic, "The only reason a white would be in the desert is to find treasure. How is your search?"

"The search has gone poorly. The man whom I came to help in this place has died, and all is lost in our venture to remove the obelisk. I will be leaving soon to return to England, and Ruth and Edmond will return to America."

Machmed said, "I do not know why a large stone is of value. It has been here a long time; the Bedouin have no want of it. Why do you British want to take such a worthless object? We have many things in the desert that offer much more than a stone carved by our long-dead ancestors." He lifted his head and looked about, as if sniffing the hot wind for answers. "Where is this land, America?"

"It is far beyond the great sea," Cooper said.

Machmed nodded as if he understood, then rose and shouted to one of the boys attending the camels. The boy brought a large leather pouch, cracked and blistered from the sun, to him. Machmed opened the pouch. A second later he dumped on the carpet a single gold ring. Its band was rimmed with hieroglyphics.

"The desert is not always cruel to those seeking treasure. This is much better than an obelisk, no?" Machmed said, pointing at the ring. "*Anteek*. You like *anteek* treasure?"

Ruth eyed the ring, then looked at Cooper. He seemed transfixed. Could the ring be from some pharaoh? She didn't have the training to know. This was Cooper's territory.

Machmed then slid a rolled piece of parchment from the leather pouch and unfurled the stiff leather scroll, its brittle skin crackling. Cooper, Ruth, and Edmond leaned forward. A date across the top read *1654*. That was all they could read—the words were in Greek.

"This looks like a job for a linguist." Cooper took the parchment and read the first lines.

"You can read Greek?" Edmond asked.

"I speak and read several languages. I studied Greek before college. It's one of the things that made me interested in ancient languages and people." He glanced over the document again. "The writing is hurried, indistinct in places. Whoever wrote it did so in a rush."

Ruth leaned in closer to look at the document. "What are the brown splatters? It resembles—"

"Blood?" Cooper ventured. "I agree."

"Come on, man," Edmond said, "what does it say? Don't keep us in suspense."

Cooper's eyes raced across the document. "It's a sheepskin parchment written in formal Greek."

"We already know that much," Edmond said.

"Patience, dear. Let the man do his work." Ruth smiled so as not to give Machmed a reason to believe she was correcting her husband.

"I can read much of it—"

The roll disappeared from Cooper's hand. Machmed had snatched it away.

"I pray Allah gives you the wisdom to know its value." Machmed handed the document to the waiting boy, who slipped it back into the large pouch.

"What does it say?" Edmond was growing exasperated.

Cooper gazed into the distance. "It speaks of a treasure buried long ago."

"What kind of treasure?" Ruth asked softly.

Machmed laughed. "I believe I can get many piasters for such a prize in Cairo."

Ruth turned to Cooper with an imploring stare.

Cooper spoke just above a whisper. "The parchment is from a Greek monk, who told where a great treasure is buried in the sands of Arabia."

"How great a treasure?" Edmond snapped.

Ruth sat in silence, surprised by her husband's impatience.

Cooper gazed into the undulating waves of heat radiating off the baked sand. "The parchment mentions the gold of Moses."

Machmed stood and asked kindly, "Do you want

this map? It is either sold to you now or at market in Cairo. It is of no difference to me."

Cooper translated, then asked, "How much?"

"Four hundred piasters."

Cooper said, "I do not have such a large amount."

"What? What's going on?" Edmond said.

"He wants a large sum of money. Four hundred piasters."

With no hesitation Edmond pulled a leather pouch from under his shirt and removed a wad of local money. Salim stuttered with surprise.

Machmed waved a finger at Edmond and spoke.

"He says there is an old desert saying, 'The sooner a fool shows his wealth to a stranger, the sooner it will make him regretfully dead.'"

"Is he threatening me?" Edmond said.

"I don't think so," Ruth said. "I think he's warning you, and properly so."

Edmond handed four hundred piasters to Cooper in a wad of crumpled bills. Cooper then handed it to Machmed. Without counting the money, Machmed handed over the parchment. He looked approvingly at Ruth, then said to Edmond, "I pray to Allah that you will have the wisdom to know the true treasure you already have before you seek to find another."

After Cooper translated, Ruth felt her face blush.

Machmed looked at his sons and nothing further needed to be said. The camels were prodded into standing with long sticks and throat clicks from the men and women. Within minutes the caravan trekked into the desert. Machmed rode a camel with silver coins hanging from the beast's ears and brisket. He waved good-bye and the caravan melted into translucent, shimmering, distant heat waves.

Salim sat down on the carpet again and sipped his tea. Only Ruth seemed to notice him.

She took Edmond by the arm. "Give the old man some money."

"He is not my concern."

Ruth squeezed his arm. "We are supposed to be Christians. Everyone is our concern."

Edmond sighed, pulled out the leather pouch, and removed a paltry sum. Ruth's darting fingers removed twenty times as much and quickly placed the money into the lap of the old man's tattered robe. The man lifted the money and then looked around as he removed his turban and secretively plopped it inside before crowning his greasy, gray hair with it once again. He looked at Ruth and smiled broadly, revealing his shiny gums and three yellow teeth.

chapter **36**

MAY 28, 1892
EIGHT MILES OUTSIDE LUXOR, EGYPT

THAT EVENING THE boat was made ready to return to Cairo. The crew was swift and efficient. The boat slipped from the teetering wood dock and merged again with the Nile. This time they were floating with the currents and the sails were not needed.

Ruth, Edmond, and Cooper were together in the parlor talking over each other in excited bursts of conversation. On the table lay the old, faded parchment, its hastily penned Greek letters visible in the lamplight. Faris brought tea.

Cooper read slowly, using a magnifying glass Ruth had brought on the trip to help her thread needles should any mending be needed. Cooper would read a phrase in Greek, then translate. The work was deliberate and slow.

" *'I am Petro, a Greek monk of simple mind and means but rich in the knowledge of the Lord. I write these words knowing that I have transgressed against the traditions of the Church and know my days in this mortal body are soon to be ended. What I have done is such an egregious and blasphemous act that I am surely to be punished for it. I will die by man's hand or God's wrath. I live in a*

290

church built in the sixth century by Justinian. It is my duty to write this truth in hopes that there will be eyes that will find these words. It will matter nothing to me after I am dead, but it matters greatly to my obligation to God to speak the truth while I am alive.' "

"He sounds frightened," Ruth said.

"Hush, Ruth. Let the man read."

Cooper continued his translating.

" *'This is the story I must tell. This is the story that must be heard. An old Bedouin man was left at the monastery door by a passing camel caravan. The man was unable to travel and near death because of sickness. I have never seen such an illness. His face was twisted and yellow and his black eyes were tinted red, as if he had just gazed upon the devil himself.*

" *'The other monks told me that the sick Bedouin was filled with demons and that I should leave him to die. I, and I alone, tended to the man, who told me a tale of great interest. With his last words he told me of his caravan that had crossed the desert mountains of Arabia. They camped at the base of a tall mountain, with a strange blackened summit that the Bedouins call Jabal Musa. It was there that they found several gold pieces of jewelry from the time of the great pharaohs; many rings with beautiful markings of the gods of old and heavy necklaces with large jewels.' "*

"This is amazing," Edmond said. "I can hardly believe what I'm hearing."

"Now who is interrupting?" Ruth said.

"Sorry. Carry on."

Cooper did.

" *'The man told me that the Bedouins in that area believe that this is the mountain where Moses escaped pharaoh with the Hebrews and that the place is the Mount Sinai of the Koran and of the Bible.*

" *'I wanted to go to this mountain and see its many treasures and asked the bishop of Saint Catherine's monastery if I could go on a religious pilgrimage into the desert to fast and to pray for three days, just as Moses had asked pharaoh. I told him this because he would disapprove of my carnal ways in seeking such an earthly prize. I was in turmoil myself at the want of gold; it is not the pious trail I have chosen for myself. But the lure was so much, I was intoxicated with the thought of it all and I went on the forbidden journey of greed into the land of Arabia. I fear I am now to be killed for this as punishment from God.*

" *'I went to find the bounty hidden in the sands, which cannot be counted by man. It is the gold from the Exodus of the Hebrews of Moses. It is the gold taken by the slaves as mentioned in the Holy Book, the gold plundered from the Egyptians and carried off in the Exodus.*

" *'I found some gold in the sands below the*

mountain called Musa, many fine pieces of gold and jewels, jewels fat as summer dates. I buried all that treasure I found in a cave in the red canyon by the wells of bitter black water. The gold is under the place of the stone candles of the menorah.' "

"Amazing," Cooper whispered.

"That's the whole thing?" Edmond asked.

Cooper shook his head. "There's more." He began translating again.

" 'This is the mountain of God mentioned in the Bible, the holy spot where God gave Moses the Ten Commandments, where the Ark of the Covenant was built. Saint Catherine's Monastery in Egypt is not the Mountain of God. The mountain is an . . .' "

Cooper tilted his head to the side.

"What?" Edmond demanded.

"Give me a second . . . imposter. The mountain is an imposter." Cooper read the next lines.

" 'The mountain in Arabia is where the real Mountain of God lies. It is described in the Holy Scriptures in the book of Galatians and this is where the true mountain has been waiting silently to be discovered.

" 'My brethren at Saint Catherine's Monastery would be most disturbed at my writing this because I go against their tradition; this is hearsay they will say, an act punishable by death. I am hiding this letter in case I meet my demise, and maybe, if God wills, it shall be found.' "

Cooper looked up from the manuscript. "May I

trouble you for your Bible, please? We will see if the monk is correct."

Ruth hurriedly retrieved the Bible from her cabin and returned to the parlor. "The manuscript said Galatians, correct?"

"Yes," Cooper said.

Ruth glanced over the pages, then stopped. "I believe I have it." She read from the Scriptures. " 'Now this Horeb is Mount Sinai in Arabia.' "

"Let me see," Edmond said, reaching for the Bible. Ruth relinquished it. " 'Mount Sinai in Arabia. That's what it says.' "

Cooper spoke softly, as if conversing with himself. "Mount Sinai is in Arabia and not in Egypt."

Edmond returned the Bible to Ruth, who immediately turned to the front of the book. "I was reading the story of the Exodus the other day." She flipped pages and found what she was looking for. "The Bible says Moses was tending his father-in-law Jethro's flocks in the land of Midian. It was in Midian that he met God at the burning bush." She paused, then, "Where is Midian?"

"I don't know," Cooper said.

"Well, I certainly don't know," Edmond admitted. "This is my first time abroad."

"I . . . know." Faris stood with a silver teapot in his hand.

"Faris, you know where Midian is?" Ruth felt surprise and pride. He had learned a few words and phrases in English under her and Cooper's tute-lage, but conversation was still beyond him.

"Yes, indeed."

Cooper spoke to the boy in Arabic, translating the conversation as he went. "Do you know this Midian?"

Faris nodded. "It is my homeland. It is now called Arabia, but we once called it Midian."

Motioning the boy to come closer, Cooper said, "This old manuscript mentions a mountain called Jabal Musa. Do you know it?"

"Yes, indeed. It is near my home."

"You grew up near the mountain?" Ruth asked and Cooper translated.

"Yes. It is near the town of Al Bad beyond Tabuk. It is a great and holy mountain. All Bedouin call it the Mountain of Moses. That is what Jabal Musa means—Mountain of Moses."

"Well, what do you know?" Edmond said.

Faris had more to say and he struggled not to hurry his words. "There is a legend that a great treasure can be found there. It is said to be buried somewhere in the mountains. My people call it the treasure of Musa. It is unknown, but the legends of this place are spoken of often in the tents of Bedouins. My father told me it has been so for hundreds of years."

Cooper asked, "Can you take us to this place? Can you find the Mountain of Musa?"

"Yes. It is not far from my home—no more than

two or three days' walk by camel from where I was born. But for me to go there would be death. I am a Christian, and my father or his brothers would kill me as an infidel. I am as a dead man; they never will speak of me again. But if I return, they will kill me."

Cooper looked at Edmond. Edmond turned to Ruth. "Gold, my dear, gold for the finding." He raised his arms. "I have never been more alive than right now. Will you allow me to go with Cooper to this place? Will you please afford me this one indulgence of impetuous greed?"

Ruth didn't know what to say. Part of her feared for Edmond; part of her wanted to join the expedition. She dismissed the last thought. A Western woman traveling very far beyond the tourist trails could endanger everyone.

"I have lived so long in the dark shadow of my father," Edmond continued. "I suspect I will make nothing of my own life aside from hanging on to his success, which will never be my own. I long to be successful based on my own efforts. It is a shameful pride, I know, but I need to go . . . no, I *must* go."

Seconds slipped by. Finally Ruth said, "I want a man who will follow his dreams and not drown in the regrets of yesteryear, nor live the rest of his life in the fears of tomorrow. Yes, you may go."

Edmond seized her in a hug with surprising force. Ruth did not care; she had found more than a treasure, she hoped.

RICHARD COOPER

chapter **37**

AUGUST 18, 1917
WESTERN FRONT, BELGIUM

A DULL, MISERABLE RAIN. Days of constant
soaking. Days of waiting. The only cook still
alive carried the last of the soggy bread and cheese
to the shivering soldiers. They would have preferred whiskey in hot tea. "Take it, lads," the cook
insisted. "Better to die with a full stomach."

Richard Cooper did not want to die. His father,
Paul Cooper, an archeologist, had died young in
the desert of Arabia . . . so young that his son never
had a chance to know him.

Richard feared his own premature death now. He
had not slept that night. Explosion after shrieking
shrapnel-laced explosion had made his lungs grunt
with each thunderous impact. At 1:00 A.M. he gave
up any hope of sleep and spent the rest of the long
night checking and rechecking his equipment—
field dressings, two packs of Abdullah Egyptian
cigarettes, ammunition, message maps, spare boot
laces, pencils, scissors, canteen, gas mask in
satchel, and metal disks to identify his body when
found.

Richard looked over at Sergeant-Major Niles,
whose stout frame cast a commanding presence
against the meek dawn. He stood still and sure,

field glasses pressed against his eyes as he scanned the dreary, rain-soaked wasteland. After a minute of silence, he said, "What time is it, Cooper?"

Richard pulled back his oiled rain slicker. "Five-ten, Sergeant-Major."

The beating rain came faster now, harder, and louder. The descending drops fell like a hail of lead pellets, filling trenches and shell holes. The mud trenches and shell craters were barely enough for a man to hide inside when dry, but with rising water they became muddy swamps. Many wounded had died in the night from drowning, their bodies so torn from metal fragments and bullets that they couldn't crawl out of the craters to escape the rising rainwater. *A good way to die*, Richard thought. *They had at least ended their agony in a pleasant death under the water's quieting ebb*. He thought that by staying alive all he was doing was prolonging the inevitable.

It seemed impossible, but smoke from bombs and gunfire mingled with the rain, creating a clinging fog. Mutilated wreckage, dead bodies, and disemboweled horses covered the field before them. Not even a farmhouse stood in view; there was no green foliage in the muddy expanse. The only things living were ragged trees, now limbless and splintered.

Richard watched from under his dripping helmet and saw a yellow observation balloon floating over the enemy's placements. He knew messages about their positions were rapidly being sent to the ground and transferred to the big heavies by telephone wire. He figured another round of shelling would soon ensue, but the shelling never came. Maybe it wasn't worth the gunpowder to kill such few men; maybe the Germans could see that there were only a small number of gray-rimmed helmets peering over the shell holes.

Richard had it better than most. In the night, he and the sergeant-major had crawled up the greasy slope and found a knob of earth, cratered from a shell impact, without much water inside. They dug out a mud-cupped seat and held over their heads an oilcloth rain slicker taken from a dead soldier. The drainage was good, but the conversation was non-existent. Sergeant-Major Niles just stared into the dark, never resting. He kept a constant vigil. The only sounds that came from him were the tapping beats of the rain on his metal helmet and slicker.

Just past dawn three cows came out of the gloom and sauntered through no-man's-land, their bells clanging with each step. The cows clumsily stepped around the pockmarked ground that looked like a hundred ponds. To the soldiers' surprise, a woman followed the animals, prodding them with a stick when necessary. They walked slowly up the valley between the two lines of soldiers, seemingly unconcerned with the drama of it all.

She was beautiful, Richard thought, but what woman wouldn't be? The last female he'd seen was at the café in La Poupée two months earlier. His mind drifted back to that night . . .

The café had a low ceiling and was nestled in a quaint building. It had a glass-roofed garden that had miraculously remained intact. A smiling sixteen-year-old girl served him that night and when he asked her name she naively gave it to him: Bridgette. All that night Richard drank liquor and smoked cigars. Late that night, as he left the café, an incoming shell landed not far away, tossing him to the ground and shattering the glass around the garden. Razorlike shards fell in a flesh-rending cascade. Richard struggled to his feet and raced back into the structure. He found Bridgette, a broom in hand, hard at work before the dust had even settled. Richard marveled at her pluck. Fortunately, he had been the last patron to leave and the staff had not been in the glass housing when the shell landed . . .

The woman who walked past him now with the cows was older than Bridgette. *At least thirty, maybe older.* Her long brown hair was wet and smoothed to her head. She wore a blue scarf tied loosely under her chin. He watched the feminine sway of her hips that kept pace with the swinging gait of the cows. Even under a heavy jacket and wearing tall rubber boots, she drew whistles and catcalls from men on both sides. Even more impressive to Richard was her ability to remain unflappable when a shrapnel burst lit the sky. She kept moving, not flinching at the loud concussion, passing the Germans to her right and the Tommies to her left. The woman stooped suddenly, her bulky coat snagged on a barb sticking from a coil of rusty wire. She freed herself and soon moved out of sight.

Certain he and those around him would be dead by nightfall, Richard Cooper thought this was the last thing of beauty he would see in this life. At some point, the Boches in the trenches across from him would make a charge of it. He pressed his eyes together and dredged his mind for any image from home. He thought of a warm, dry place with beds that had mattresses and sheets that were cool, crisp, and dry, and blankets that could be pulled up around his neck while he slept in the quiet dark of home with warm tea settling in his stomach.

He wanted to think of anything that would keep him from dying with fear as his last emotion. He strained his mind to picture his precious sweetheart Martha on the Isle of Wight, her female form shaped by the wind against her dress as it blew in off the Portsmouth Channel. He could see her clearly, as if he were standing on the chalky cliffs that rose from the green sea. He then thought of his aunt Emily. He could envision her frail hands with silky, aging skin . . . hands that had touched his face while at the Waterloo rail station the day he shipped out. Her expression showed no fear, but he knew it was only a mask. A quivering lip betrayed her. "Never be without the Bible, son. Keep it close, read it often, and pray every day."

Richard reached inside his tunic where he kept the Bible tucked in a pocket. He touched it as if it were the only thing to give affection to, the only thing from his family, the only thing of value he had left of home.

The Bible was situated in a pouch that his aunt Emily had lovingly sewn inside his tunic to hold the book close to his heart. In his mind's eye, he could see his aunt pulling the needle through the shirt he wore and then slipping the Bible inside the cloth cradle. Aunt Emily had reared him after his mother died when he was six. His aunt was a wonderful woman. She had never married, choosing instead to give all her life to the boy she was given to bring up as a proper English lad.

He reached in his tunic and felt the cover. He remembered the very day it had come in the post. It had arrived only a month before he shipped out to the Western front. A strange letter from a woman calling herself Sister Ruth came with the Bible:

Mr. R.C. Cooper,
I have been laboring in a devotion of love for the children at an orphanage in Cairo for over twenty years. I suppose that I will die here as well. My husband and I knew your father, Paul Cooper. We were good friends and had toured Egypt together. My husband, Edmond, and

your father died together in Arabia some years after that, or so I fear.

When your father and my husband perished in the desert, they were seeking a hopeless treasure. I will tell you this story after the war, but for now I want you to live until that day.

When your father died, I often exchanged letters with your aunt Emily as a way of comforting each other in our mutual distress. In a way, I feel I know you.

The Bible I am sending is a very special book. All Bibles are special, of course, but this Bible comes from the hands of a boy prophet who was killed in the American Civil War, and who upon his deathbed foretold that all who came to have this holy book would give life and save life. It has saved me, and it will come to save you during this horrible time of war.

I hope this war will not touch you, but if the reports I hear are true, then it most certainly will. I believe you should have this Bible. May it be a blessing to you as it has been to me.

Sister Ruth
A humble servant of God's children,
in the year of our Lord 1916
Orphanage of Mother Mary, Cairo, Egypt

The letter lay creased and embedded in the front of the Bible along with the strange Civil War letter written by a boy named Elijah Bell.

One month after the letter and Bible had arrived in the post, on August 2, 1916, Richard had shipped out on a troop train. He was excited then about the grand adventure before him and shouted wildly at the cheering crowd, many of whom waved handkerchiefs. They had all come to see some loved one off to the Great War. The other soldiers stared back at the well-wishers, each straining to force a smile, an attempt to offer one last display of comfort and encouragement. The train started to move.

His childhood sweetheart, Martha, a tawny beauty, stood next to his aunt Emily, gamely waving a handkerchief. Both women cried as they waved, but Martha could not bear the strain. She desperately wanted to touch Richard one last time before the train left for good. She elbowed free of the throng of people and ran along the rail bed with arms outstretched to touch Richard. He hung out the window reaching for her hand.

As the train gained speed, Richard leaned so far out the window that the men inside had to hold his legs to keep him from falling through the opening. Martha ran alongside the rails and through the swirling white mist of expelled steam. Just as the tips of their fingers were about to meet, Richard saw her stumble, falling to her knees on the jagged, black-stained stones lining the rail bed.

She knelt there, weeping, as the train rounded the bend. Richard slumped back into the cushioned seat, sobered by it all. Realizing that he had just left his girl, aunt, and home to go to war in France fell on him with crushing force. Maybe he would find glory over there, maybe death—or maybe he would find both. But for now he could only think of Martha kneeling on the rough rock by the tracks . . .

The clanking of a German tank churning up a swale brought Richard back to the moment. The tank stopped. A dark figure astride a horse followed the tank into position and seemed to be offering some words to a man standing in the tank's open hatch. Richard returned the Bible to its pocket.

It would be a long shot, an impossible shot, for Richard to hit the distant figures. They were four hundred—no, five hundred—yards away, but a tall man in a shell hole right below Richard leveled his rifle anyway. He adjusted the range of his rifle's iron sights atop his rifle, setting them as high as possible, then tilted his weapon even more to compensate for the impossibly long shot and cranked off a round. The bullet fell far short, splattering mud where it impacted the ground.

"Leave 'em till they are close and crawling down our throats." Sergeant-Major Niles's command was calm. "You'll have opportunity soon enough to shoot at close range."

As the morning light ripened, Richard could see rats feasting on the lifeless forms of German and

English soldiers in the no-man's-land between the opposing forces. The bodies were embedded in oozing mud, all in various states of decomposition and contortion.

Richard took aim at one of the hairy rodents only fifty yards away. *Hideous creatures.* The big rat was poking his pointed nose under the helmet of a dead German soldier. The rat exploded into a pink mist after Richard touched off a round. A German soldier from across the open field shouted a hooray at the keen marksmanship. Soon several soldiers from both sides started shooting at the rats that were scurrying about in no-man's-land. The rodents became mutual symbols of evil that, for a time, united both sides in a display of crossfire.

Sergeant-Major Niles looked at Cooper. "Brilliant shot, old man." He cupped his hands around his mouth and shouted up and down the line for his troops to save bullets. The impromptu barrage from both sides ceased almost as soon as it had begun and the eerie silence returned, punctuated only by the droning rain and the rumbling bombs far off in the murky dark.

Niles looked at Cooper and said, "Just make sure the next rat you shoot is wearing a bleeding German helmet."

Richard's teeth clattered in the cold. He pressed his lips tight so the sergeant-major wouldn't notice, but he knew he had.

The bells from a church in the nearby village pealed. Richard imagined a priest had set about his liturgical duties, pulling the ropes dangling in the bell tower to set the large bronze bell in the belfry swinging. Even though a war was raging, it was a call to Mass—a call no one would respond to. Nonetheless, the faithful priest rang the bell. The tower was the only thing left of the bombed sanctuary and the loud ringing comforted the soldiers. To Richard, its ringing was a soothing divine voice.

Richard squinted through the rain and saw several dark-helmeted figures moving back and forth across the enemy line. He wondered what the activity meant. What could be going on in the German trenches? Were they praying? Were they laughing? Were they dedicated to the cause—a cause that would take the lives of so many of their young men? Did they complain, like most of the soldiers on his side? Surely they grumbled. With all this miserable wet and the cold, they had to be complaining; they had to be as frightened and as despairing as he.

Niles reached to his side, found his bayonet under his oilcloth raincoat, and unsheathed it. He raised it, affixing it to the end of his rifle, and with a twist it snapped into place with a metallic click. Richard and the others did the same. Niles then reached in his jacket pocket and removed a metal flask; he unscrewed its cap, took a chug, then handed the flask to Richard. As Richard took it, he was surprised to see the sergeant-major close his eyes and silently mouth a prayer. He had never seen the man pray. It made Richard's heart thump against his rib cage even faster.

We are going to die.

It was the time when they all would soon be ushered into the distant unknown.

The sizzling round from the tank sliced the air and impacted in the mud right in front of Richard, knocking him back. A liquid wave of mud covered him.

Niles pulled his half-buried body from the earthen gruel and shouted a command. "We fight for England and the loves we left behind, boys. So fight hard and die brave."

Germans spilled from the trench across the way. They came in too many numbers to count, bent forward, determined faces tilted up.

Richard crawled up the slimy slope with his rifle cocked. His mouth was dry. He flopped forward to plant his elbows in the mud for a braced shot, but his rifle accidentally discharged in his terrified grip before he could sight on his foe. He fumbled with the bolt action and clumsily chambered another round.

A bullet had hit the ground right in front of him, spraying stinging mud into his eyes. The splattered muck blinded him and he clumsily wiped at his face. He strained to see but could make out only an opaque brown nothingness of shadowy figures. Shots rang out, piercing his ears. The screams of the wounded and dying rattled in his mind. Plaintive and frantic cries mingled in the droning rain.

"Got the bugger!" Niles screamed.

Richard could hear the man's rifle fire, then fire again. He wiped frantically at his eyes, trying to clear his vision. Frightened nearly to madness, he groped for his canteen and, with hands that shook uncontrollably, unscrewed the top. Tilting back his head, he poured water over his eyes and blinked rapidly. The water cleansed his fluttering lids. He splashed more liquid onto his eyeballs and could once again see.

As his eyes cleared, he took in his surroundings. He saw a form—a crumpled, familiar shape in the mud next to him. Niles lay unmoving, his steel hat off, and his temple shot away with gray brain matter pushing out from the place where his ear had been.

Movement on the side made Richard whirl his rifle to meet the charging men, but a German soldier already towered above him. The enemy soldier leapt upon Richard. The German's boot came down hard against Richard's rifle. The German pulled his bayonet-tipped rifle back, ready to thrust it deep into Richard's chest. Richard raised his hands to ward off the plunging cold steel that was sure to split his rib cage and still his thundering heart. The Bible he had sewn into his shirt was exposed from the gap in his tunic and the German saw it.

The bayonet never came.

With eyes closed, Richard waited. He felt no pain. Was this the way of death? No pain preceding it? Was he already dead? Where was the searing feel of the bayonet's wrath as it entered his organs?

He slowly opened his eyes and saw the German with the shining dagger still angling down from the end of his rifle. The man stooped but did not follow through with the death blow.

The German put his boot on Richard's rifle, stomping it deeper into the mud, then placed his other boot on Richard's throat. Around him, Richard could hear the grunts, the shrieks of fury, the cries of pain as hand-to-hand fighting raged. The sharp crack of gunfire pierced the air.

The German removed his foot from Richard's throat and then reached into Richard's shirt with his free hand and took the Bible.

"Christian man?" The words came from a flushed face streaked with muddy rivulets.

Richard felt nodding was the best course. The man returned the Bible to Richard, who tucked it back in his pocket.

The German stared at Cooper, then in an almost emotional collapse, held up his rifle and shook his head while pointing to the gun, then to Richard again, and then to the Bible.

He held out his hand and pulled Richard from the mud. He was a strong man who smelled of schnapps, urine, and death. Richard was numb and confused. The event was too surreal to believe.

The two crouched in the shell hole. Gunfire continued around them.

"My name is Frederick. I, too, am a Christian." His words were weighted with a heavy accent. "I went to university to learn about God. I learned English. Do you understand me now?"

Richard nodded but said nothing. The soldier gave a smile that did nothing to hide his own fear.

The gunfire ceased and several men shouted in German. To Richard, they sounded happy and relieved. The battle was over, minutes after it had started. Frederick frowned and stood. He motioned sharply for Richard to raise his hands and lace his fingers behind his head. Richard complied and Frederick led him out of the hole and to the east. Every few steps Richard felt the sharp nudge from the German's bayonet.

The Bible bounced against his chest.

chapter 38

FREDERICK MARCHED RICHARD across no-man's-land to German HQ. German soldiers spit on him as he walked with his hands behind his head.

Frederick shouted at the men. "Fools! He is not your enemy. The politicians that started all this madness are your enemy."

An officer with a pointed helmet, pointed beard, and greased, narrow mustache stepped from behind the tank and stopped Frederick with a raised hand. "Why is this man still alive?"

"He is my prisoner."

The officer's face reddened. "That is against my orders to shoot all the English swine!"

"Perhaps, but to shoot a prisoner is against the higher authority I serve."

"There is no higher authority than me."

"I am answerable to God first and you second."

"In war and in this army, I am the only God you need to know. You will obey me. I want this man shot now." The officer removed his pistol from a leather side holster and aimed it at Richard's temple.

Frederick watched Richard clamp his eyes shut and wait. Frederick moved quickly, interposing himself between the officer's pistol and his prisoner. "I will not kill him, nor will I allow anyone to murder him. He is a prisoner now. I will take the man to the rear encampment."

"All war is murder." The officer pointed the weapon at Frederick's head.

"This is not my war," said Frederick.

"I will put you on report for this." The officer's face had darkened and globs of spittle flew as he shouted.

"It will not matter. I will be dead long before the report is even seen."

"I suppose you would like to have some good deed to tell God in Heaven when you die."

"Yes. It will be a more favorable greeting than you will have."

The officer holstered the weapon. "Go, but be back within the hour. We need every man. The British are sure to counterattack."

Frederick nodded, then poked Richard again with his bayonet, prodding him down a bombed, muddy lane.

The scene was hideous: a green swamp blanketed with smoke from burning carcasses; a tank sunk in the mud to its turret. Men, covered with blood-soaked bandages, staggered past with vacant stares. A limping, reeling lot of half-dead men, going to who knew where, and looking like they had just climbed out of a tunnel from hell. Shell holes filled with yellow water and the blood of those who had died there pockmarked the ground.

Bodies with blue faces and black lips huddled together half submerged in the rancid water. They had not been able to pull their masks from their satchels in time during a surprise gas attack. It was pitiful to see their entwined bodies contorted in their death throes.

Richard could not imagine this place had once been a serene countryside with fields of wildflowers and meandering, gurgling brooks. War had made it a scab on the earth, wounded by mustard gas and bombs raining on desperate men in trenches positioned across from each other. Those who survived the bombings and mustard gas attacks would rise to charge the battle line, and kill or be killed.

Frederick looked at Richard. "If I save you, English, maybe God may smile on me once again."

Richard said nothing.

From the sky came the loud, whining scream of an incoming shell. It hit nearby with an ear-crushing blast and the ground trembled with its force. It was as if the whole world shook beneath the feet of the two men.

Something hot stung Frederick's leg.

Richard was thrown twenty feet by the concussive force of the explosion. Dazed, he sat up. His ears rang and blood ran from his mouth. He ran a finger between his lips. Two teeth were missing.

He shook his head, as if doing so would quiet his ears and shake off the shock.

Something warm and sticky splattered his face. He touched it. Blood. He looked at his arms, hands, legs, and torso, desperately trying to find the source of bleeding. He found nothing. His uniform showed no entrance holes caused by shrapnel. If not him, then . . .

Frederick lay in the mud. A chunk of twisted shrapnel was embedded behind his knee. Blood shot from the wound in spurts that matched Frederick's heartbeat. The red liquid spurted from the man's leg so fast that Richard knew he would bleed to death in minutes.

Richard had been in enough battles to have seen men die of similar wounds. Frederick lay unconscious, his face planted in the mud. His helmet lay nearby. Across the road a man screamed that his foot was missing. Richard saw it—still laced in its boot—resting not far from Frederick. A horse ran by, its guts trailing. It tripped in its dangling entrails, then slid to its knees and flopped to its side, legs flailing.

Richard turned Frederick over and stared into his gray, mud-smeared face. His eyes blinked open but showed no fear; it was if he expected to die this way. He grimaced in pain but made no complaint.

Richard seized Frederick's collar and pulled him

to the remains of a stone wall. It was a church. The big bell that had once called parishioners to worship lay nearby. A portion of the bell tower rested on its side, several feet from the wall. The bell tower offered a crude shelter.

Frederick was soaked in his blood. Cooper untied his belt and cinched it around Frederick's leg two inches above the mangled knee. The bleeding slowed.

Another shell whistled close by, its sound ear-splitting, but the makeshift bunker warded off the shrapnel as another wave of syrupy mud shot skyward. Sulfurous yellow fumes choked the air.

From his position, Richard could see a German run by. He had a white band around his arm with a red cross painted on it. The medic sprinted to the footless man, pulled out a needle, and jabbed it into the man's chest. He then lowered an ear over his ribs and listened. He shook his head, rose, and ran down the road to find other wounded.

The road outside turned silent. All the soldiers had retreated, gone beyond the ridge into other muddy trenches. The big heavies from the French pounded away with more 4.2 mortar fire. The bell tower became a womb of protection for the two men. Still, Richard wondered if it would become their coffin. The loose stones from the tower fell on the bell, creating an ear-numbing bong.

Minutes passed as hours but the shelling finally stopped. Richard wiped the blood from Frederick's eyes as the man slipped in and out of consciousness. "I am sorry. I do not know who holds whom captive now, but I won't let you die today."

Frederick could barely whisper, and when he did finally speak, he was delirious and spoke only in German. Instinctively Richard reached for his canteen. It was gone. He had last used it while hunkered down in the shell hole. That was before the German rush. It must still be there. He probed Frederick for a canteen but found nothing.

Frederick's tongue circled his chapped, dry lips, and he moaned in pain.

"I need to get some water. I'll be back."

Richard slipped from their hiding place and saw an empty world of smoke, broken wagons, splintered wood, gnarled and twisted metal, and bomb-cratered mud. Across the road there was a concrete pillbox that must have taken a direct hit from artillery. Two corpses lay outside the pillbox, arms around each other, like children cowering in the dark. They were so burned that Richard had trouble recognizing them as human. He walked to the charred forms and looked for their battalion markings, but the fire had scorched the uniforms too much.

He slipped inside the pillbox. A machine gun lay on its side, the barrel bent from a bomb's impact. On the floor sat a closed iron container. He jiggled it and heard water. The German soldiers used the water to cool the barrel of the machine gun. He lifted the blackened pot, smelled the water, and ran back to Frederick.

The German murmured as his head rolled back and forth in delirious pain. Richard dropped to his knees and lifted the pot of water to Frederick's face. The water trickled into his open mouth; he coughed but swallowed the liquid. Richard let him breathe, then gave him more. The water seemed to help. After several swallows, Frederick nodded with appreciation.

He was pale, shaking in waves of shock. The man would die if he didn't get medical help. Richard walked to the edge of the road and found an ambulance cart harnessed to two mules, one dead and one alive. He untied the dead mule and walked the cart to Frederick. Ten minutes later he had Frederick on the cart. He looked up and down the road but saw only scores of black smoke spires curling into the air. He had no idea where the troops were, where the ebb and flow of battle had redefined the front lines. He decided to move down the valley. The incline would be easier on the animal, which had to pull the cart without the help of its companion. Frederick grimaced with each bump or jostle. Richard watched the suffering man clench his teeth. He knew if he stopped, the man would certainly die.

For thirty minutes, they moved along the road, until they came to a large, water-filled bomb crater in the middle of the road. The lane was too sloped for them to pass on either side. There was no way to go on; they were stuck.

Richard heard the clatter of a tank coming; it chugged and churned as it struggled to get through the mud. It was coming their way. Seeing two German bodies floating facedown in the shell hole, he waded into the crater to get to the bodies, pushing past a fractured wagon wheel. He pulled one of the soldiers out of the pit by his coat collar and removed the man's long coat. It was an officer's garment. He put it over his own uniform and also took a black cross from around the officer's neck and looped it around his. He then put on the German's low-brimmed helmet.

The tank rounded a bend in the road behind them and pulled alongside the cart. Five German soldiers hopped off, saw Richard's officer's garb, and saluted. Richard did not salute, did not make eye contact.

The soldiers pulled the two stranded men aboard the tank, and they huddled under the big barrel that stuck out of the tank turret like a steel finger.

As the tank started forward, steering around the shell hole and pressing through the mud, one of the men asked Richard, "How goes it at the front?"

Frederick forced an answer. "This officer is in shock." Frederick coughed. "He does not speak.

His hearing is damaged because of a bomb. He is lucky to be alive. He saved me from bleeding to death, but he has not said a word."

Richard made eye contact but gave no indication that he had heard the conversation. He wondered at the man's ability to remain conscious and to speak.

Frederick pulled a cigarette from his coat pocket and received a light from a sergeant. He inhaled the smoke. "Where can a medical group be found?"

"No medical group is nearby," the weary, old sergeant said as he flung the extinguished match to the mud. He pointed a dirty finger at the western hills. "There is a medical field tent there. We will drop you off."

The rain returned in torrents as the tank muscled its clawing treads through the thick mire. Within the hour, they arrived at a lone medical station, 4-R. It was nothing more than a tent. The only medical doctor still alive was a tall man in his fifties who coughed in fits. He was bent over a stretcher.

The soldiers on the tank carried Frederick into the tent and laid him on the ground. A short time later they crawled back on the tank and, with black smoke spewing from the exhaust, rumbled off to the front.

Richard removed his Bible from under the jacket and placed it on Frederick's chest for comfort. Frederick laid a hand on the leather cover.

A soldier with a stretcher approached and set the

stretcher on the ground next to Frederick. "Help me lift this man."

Frederick saw Richard mime that he was deaf. The soldier seemed confused and spoke louder. "Help me lift this man onto the stretcher."

Again Richard feigned deafness.

The soldier looked at the Bible on Frederick's chest. He cocked his head. "Why do you have an English Bible?"

Frederick spoke through the pain. "It is a family keepsake and my mother told me that it would bring me luck. God speaks English as well as German, you know. Now take me to the doctor."

With Richard's help the soldier loaded Frederick on the stretcher and carried him to one of the empty cots.

"The doctor will get to you when he can." The soldier shot a glance toward the physician. "He is not well, and our only nurses were killed by shelling."

When the doctor finally made it to Frederick's cot, he saw Richard in the officer's long coat and saluted. Richard gave a short salute in return. The doctor examined Frederick's wound. He paused to cough again, then studied the belt. "This is . . . a British belt. Where did you get it?"

Without hesitation Frederick said, "From a dead British soldier, of course. There were many dead Tommies to choose from."

"Not as many as I would like." The doctor

wheezed, then cut the pants leg and gently pulled it away from the wound. He frowned. "You have lost a great deal of blood. The shrapnel has nicked the artery. You are lucky to live this long."

"What are you going to do?" Frederick asked.

"I will sew you up, but you are weak and if you lose any more blood, you will certainly die. You need a transfusion, but we have no blood. Too many wounded." The doctor looked up at Richard. "What is your blood type?"

Richard stared but said nothing.

The doctor reached under Richard's throat and grabbed his identification disks and looked at the blood type. "O negative, universal donor—these tags are in English." He whispered the words. The doctor released his grip and turned to Frederick, who had again begun to shake in waves of shock.

"Please . . . Doctor . . . say nothing. He saved my life and risked his own to bring me here."

The doctor turned to Richard. "You will be a good donor. Blood is blood, no matter your nationality."

Frederick spoke softly to Richard in English. "You must leave now. You are no longer a prisoner of war . . . you are in a German officer's uniform. This makes you a spy and now you will be shot within minutes of anyone finding out who you are."

"What did the doctor say?"

"I need a transfusion, but that is no concern of yours. You must leave."

Richard rolled up his sleeve, exposing his arm.

324

• • •

The doctor shouted to the soldier who had helped move Frederick to a cot. The aide set another cot next to Frederick's. Richard lay down and stared at the canvas ceiling that dripped with rain.

The German physician prepared for the transfusion, pausing only long enough to cover Richard with a blanket. Minutes later, blood from Richard's arm coursed through a rubber tube strung between the men and into Frederick's vein. Within minutes Frederick's blood pressure had risen, his heartbeat had grown stronger, his pale lips blushed.

When the transfusion ended, Richard rolled to his side to watch the doctor work. The aide held a red rag doused with chloroform on Frederick's face. His eyes closed and his body slackened. As the drug took effect, Frederick whispered in English, "It is blood that saves life." He tapped the Bible on his chest. "The book speaks of the blood of a lamb that saves us all . . ."

Richard kept his voice low. "I have heard that before."

"It is true. We will see each other again because . . . of that blood . . . because of this book . . ." Frederick slipped into unconsciousness.

The surgery took a surprisingly short time. Richard couldn't see much, but he could tell the doctor removed the shrapnel, cleaned the wound, and spent long minutes suturing inside and outside the leg between coughing fits. Finally he slowly released the belt tourniquet, waited, then smiled. "If he can avoid infection, he will be fine." He dismissed the aide and stepped to Richard. "My English is not so good. Rest for a few hours, then you go."

Richard nodded. Three hours later, the doctor looked around to see if anyone was watching and motioned for Richard to rise. "It is time." He escorted him outside the medical tent and pointed to the eastern horizon. "English army."

He felt weak. Giving blood had taken a large portion of what strength he had left, but staying was impossible. Richard heard the bombs hissing in the distance and felt the tremors under his feet. He saw a line of five Germans marching down the road toward the medical camp. It was now or never. He took a deep breath, put a hand on the physician's blood-spattered shoulder, and staggered slowly into the dark.

He followed the pink flaring of the howitzers and the rolling of their thunder. The sights and sounds would be his guide. A half mile away, he stopped. "The Bible, I forgot to get the Bible." He patted his coat three more times, as if it would somehow appear. It was gone, left on the German's chest at the field hospital. He had no time to think of the book now. He needed to keep moving.

chapter **39**

MARTHA BROUGHT RICHARD some soup. It was his second cup. He loved her creamy potato-and-ham soup with crusty bread. It was early spring, the day was crisp and the sky clear. He sat looking out his cliff-side cottage window. In the distance, fishing boats went in and out of the churning whitecaps of Portsmouth harbor. He gazed across the wide, marshy, black sand glistening in a low tide. Several old men with pitchforks were digging for clams.

Richard did not think often of the war, but at times nightmares of horrid things would creep in, and then would be kept unspoken while he was awake.

He had been married to Martha for three months; it had been a simple wedding, not much of a crowd—too many of his comrades were buried in forgotten potters' fields across the Channel. Everyone said it was the war to end all wars. But Richard doubted that.

Martha sat next to him while he ate. She said little when he became quiet. She knew the war had not ended in his soul.

A loud thumping at the front door rumbled through the house. It was not the knock of a cautious visitor; it was a hard and intrusive banging.

Martha untied her apron, smoothed her hair, and slowly walked to the door.

On her porch stood an unshaven man smoking a cigarette that looked as if it would drop from his lips at any moment. He held a paper package and a Bible in one hand and removed his tweed cap with the other. "Is this the home of Richard Cooper?" he asked with a thick German accent. He tossed the cigarette to the ground.

"It is."

Before the man could speak again, Richard appeared from the back of the house and stood by her side. When the visitor saw Richard, he almost lost his balance. "May I come in?"

"Yes, of course," Martha said. "Where are my manners?"

The man stepped with a slight limp into the cottage.

Richard studied the man with his gaze and the visitor did the same to him. Tears flooded Richard's eyes. "Frederick? Is it really you, Frederick?"

The man nodded but didn't speak. Sobs replaced words. Richard held the man and patted his back. The two men embraced, and Frederick wept, his face pressed into Richard's shoulder. He stayed there for more than a minute, sobbing uncontrollably as Richard patted his back.

Frederick pulled away and stood erect, as if meeting an officer in the field. Regaining his composure, he turned to Martha and clicked his heels together.

"Come in, my friend." Richard felt giddy. "Have a seat."

"Please sit here," said Martha as she pointed to the big stuffed guest chair by the window. Richard pulled up a wooden slatted chair and before they sat made introductions. "Martha, this is Frederick."

"I am sorry," she said. "Should I know you?"

"I do not think so." Frederick sat, setting the Bible and paper package on his lap. "I was the man who took . . ." He looked down at her wedding ring before finishing. "I took your husband prisoner in the war."

"Prisoner of war?" Martha shot Richard a questioning glance.

Richard shrugged. "I was a prisoner, but not for very long."

Frederick laughed and Richard joined him.

"It's nothing, really. Frederick almost killed me, then saved me—all within a short minute. That madness took place in Ypres.

You remember that Bible, Martha? My aunt Emily sewed a special pocket for it so I could carry it with me in battle. She felt convinced it would save my life. Well, it has in many ways, I suppose."

Frederick lifted the Bible and handed it to his friend.

"Is that the Bible?" Martha gasped. "Richard, I assumed you lost it in the war."

"Not lost—left."

"This Bible is not mine," Frederick said. "I found it on my chest when I awoke in a field hospital. I was so weak I thought I would die, but the Bible gave me hope when there was none."

Martha stood and ran her fingers over her forehead, her hands twisting her dangling hair. "This is all very confusing. She turned to their guest. "Frederick . . . may I call you Frederick? I don't know what else to call you." She looked at Richard.

He shrugged. "We never exchanged last names."

"Von Scherling. Frederick Von Scherling of Berlin. But do call me Frederick."

"Thank you," Martha said. "I'm sorry. I should let you two talk alone." She rose and walked to the kitchen. "I will put on a kettle for tea."

Richard rubbed the old Bible, his fingers caressing the leather spine. "You have traveled all the way from Berlin just to return the Bible to me?"

"Yes. I found two letters folded inside. One is the most curious letter from another soldier who died named Elijah Bell. I believe this was an American soldier. Yes?"

"Yes," Richard said.

"The other letter is from a Sister Ruth in Egypt at the orphanage of Mother Mary. This letter was written to you, Richard, before you came to fight in Belgium. Your address was not in the letter, so I feared I could not find you. All that was mentioned was 'R.C. Cooper.' It also refers to an Emily."

"That's my aunt Emily."

Frederick nodded. "It is all I had to go on to find you, so I took a steamer to Egypt to try and locate this Ruth. I hoped she could tell me how to find you and return the Bible."

"A long steamer trip to find a woman in Egypt?" Richard asked. "All that to return an old Bible to me?"

Frederick stared at the book. "This book is a holy object. It saved your life, it saved our lives, and I think it would be bad luck forever if I did not somehow return it to you. I think it would be . . . how you say . . . a sacrilege not to do what I felt God wanted me to do, so I found the orphanage in Cairo and Sister Ruth was there as well, but she was very sick. She had been working as a common laborer at the orphanage. I was told she gave away all her wealth to the nuns who worked there. She was a woman of means at one time, but she had given away all her earthly goods. When I found her, she lay sick in bed with a picture of herself and her husband and your father, Paul, on the wall in a simple wooden frame." He paused and looked at Richard. "Your father looked like you."

"I never got to really know him. I was very young, just a boy, when he disappeared in the desert."

"That is a sad thing." He gave the solemn revelation its due, then continued, "This picture on the wall in Ruth's room—it was taken at a restaurant. Ruth was young and smiling then, but when I saw her that day, she looked sickly, with a pale, old face. She struggled for breath, but when I showed her the Bible, her face brightened. She recognized it at once. She told me how she had mailed the Bible to you to carry in the war. I told her that I was a Christian and how the Bible had saved your life and that it had saved my life as well. I also told her the story about that day in the battlefield hospital. Her eyes warmed when I told her what had happened. 'This is a book of miracles,' she said. 'It gives life and saves life.' "

Richard sat in silent awe of the story that unfolded from Frederick.

"She seemed pleased that I had come all the way from Germany to see her. I think she trusted me for that and graciously gave me your address."

"All that for a Bible?" Richard said.

"No, I have something else. Sister Ruth told me that it was her dying duty to send you something else that belonged to your father."

"My father?"

"Yes, it's a map of sorts. An old letter penned long ago on sheepskin. She called it a treasure map. She told me that she was dying and would not leave without sending you the old map your father once owned."

Frederick handed Richard the rolled-up package. It was wrapped in brown paper and tied tightly with twine. Richard opened it and found an old, cracked piece of parchment. Wrapped around the roll was a handwritten letter from Ruth. Richard read aloud:

" *'Dear Mr. Cooper,*

I pray you made it home safely from the war. I heard nothing from your aunt Emily in Wight after I sent you the Bible. I hope she is well.' "

Richard lowered the letter. "My aunt Emily died four months after I shipped out for the war. The strain of worry was too much for her heart. She passed away sitting in the chair where you sit." He lowered his eyes to the paper and read on.

" *'I give this parchment to your friend Frederick. I believe that no one would take such a long journey to find me if he did not have a soul for God and the goodness of the Lord upon him. When Frederick came to find me, he announced that he wanted to locate you and I obliged him by providing your last known address. I pray this is an agreeable arrangement.*

" *'The document I send you via Frederick speaks*

of gold and earthly treasure. *This is the kind of treasure that can make men go insane with greed. Your father and my husband, Edward, followed the parchment's lure and wandered into the desert of Arabia, never to be heard from again.*

" 'The desert seemed to swallow them whole. I waited for months for their return. They never did. The months became years, yet I still look to the eastern horizon, thinking they will appear from out of the sea of sand.

" 'The parchment tells the exact place that the treasure rests. It is in a cave very near the mountain Jabal Musa, somewhere near a town called Tabuk, in Arabia. It is not for me to tell you what to do with this information; it is now between you and God.

" 'I am dying of consumption and will not see the month out.

His servant forever,
Sister Ruth' "

Richard slowly set the letter aside and opened the paper wrapping on the ancient document. His mouth went dry.

chapter 40

JULY 3, 1980
PHOENIX, ARIZONA

GARY SPENT THE night in a budget motel just outside San Francisco, then made the long motorcycle ride back to Phoenix. He passed the hours thinking about Uncle Daniel, the Bible, and all that he had learned so far. He still had more questions than answers. Once home he ran to the phone. He called information, then called the number he was given. A woman's voice said, "Arabco Oil. Can I help you?"

Gary pressed the phone close to his ear. "I'm looking for information on a former employee. Who should I speak to?"

"That would be human resources. Please hold."

A dated instrumental version of "Blue Moon" played over the handset. Three bars into the tune, the phone began to ring again.

"Human resources, Burt Tully speaking."

"I'm looking for information on one of your former employees. You see—"

"I'm sorry, but all employee records are confidential. I'm afraid I won't be able to help you."

"Can you at least tell me if you had an employee who worked in the area of Tabuk? He would have worked on the oil rigs."

There was a pause. "Tabuk? In Saudi Arabia? We don't have oil rigs in that area. No one does. All our wells are elsewhere in the Kingdom."

"I am sorry, but there are oil wells in Tabuk. There must be some kind of mistake."

"I think we would know if we had oil work in that area. We do not have any wells there now or ever. All our wells are on the east coast of Arabia, and Tabuk is near the west coast of the Arabian Peninsula."

"I see. Do you have a record of an employee named Daniel Huff?"

"Wait a minute," Tully said. "Yup, we have a file on him. Wish we didn't, but we do."

"Why do you say that?"

"I'm sorry, but company regulations prevent me from elaborating."

"So that's all you're going to tell me?"

"I have told you too much already. Who's calling?"

Gary Brandon hung up.

chapter 41

JULY 4, 1920
CAIRO, EGYPT

A THIN LAYER OF dust coated the simple granite gravestone even though only two months had passed since gravediggers had tamped it into place. Faris, who had brought them here so Richard and Frederick could pay their respects, stood silently waiting.

The oppressive Cairo sun hovered high in a deep blue sky. Twin palms stood near the grave, providing soothing shade.

Faris stood to the side, the searing sand creeping between his sun-bronzed toes. Richard and Frederick seemed withered, their shirts soaked with sweat. It was a soul-sucking heat, a heat that men like these had never experienced.

The grave marker stood on a sandy knoll across from the orphanage playground. It bore no name, only a saying in Arabic. Richard asked what the words on the marker said. Faris didn't need to look at the tombstone; he knew what was written on the speckled brown granite. " 'I pray all who come to read this will help the abandoned little ones at the Mother Mary Orphanage—Sister Ruth.' " He spoke softly, still staring down. "Even in death she encourages people to help."

The dried remains of three roses lay on the sandy mound. The petals, once supple and bright yellow, had faded to a brittle brown. The flowers reminded Faris that everything in Egypt eventually turns to dust.

At forty-two, with gray-touched temples, Faris had aged well but had a slight bow to his back. He wore patched white pants too short for his tall frame and a white-collared shirt buttoned around his thin neck. He held three long-stemmed yellow roses in his hand.

He shuffled to the grave and knelt, easing his bony knees into the hot sand. With a sweep of his hand, Faris pushed away the decaying flower fragments. A gust of wind carried them from the grave. He gently replaced the bouquet on the mound of dirt.

Faris kept his eyes on the cemetery plot. "Before she died, Sister Ruth asked if I would once in a while put three yellow roses upon her grave. She asked nothing more of me."

Faris stood and looked at the Bible Richard held in his hand. He recognized it immediately. It bore the same scratches on its leather cover, the same tears on the spine. There were also new marks of wear. It was the same Bible Ruth had owned and loved to read.

"I hear she was a good woman," Richard commented.

Faris glanced at the empty schoolyard beyond

the fallen stone fence as if Ruth might again appear. "She was a kind woman, who possessed a spirit like a clear spring. She came from America and never left this orphanage. She could never leave the children. She called them 'the little desperate ones.' "

Faris stared at Richard's face. It was a familiar face. "I see your father in your eyes."

"I don't remember much about my father." Richard sighed. "Can you tell me about him, Faris?"

"He died a brave man. I can only tell you that I was a coward. I refused to go into Arabia with him and the American Edmond."

"Why?" Richard asked.

"My father was in the land of Arabia, and he would have killed me if I returned."

"Why would your father want to kill you?"

"I converted to Christianity, and that is enough for a Muslim father to want to kill his son."

"That's horrible."

Faris shrugged. "I weary of the story and do not wish to speak of it anymore. It is enough to say I fled across the desert and came to Cairo, where I met your father. He was with Sister Ruth and her husband, Edmond."

"You know about the parchment my father had?" Richard asked.

"I know of it. I have seen it with my own eyes."

"We have that parchment now," Richard said.

Faris looked at the hot sand. "I do not need to see it ever again, I know it well. It speaks of gold and treasure that was found by a Greek monk and that is buried in the valley of the red sand, by the wells of bitter black water, under the stone-carved candles."

"Do you know the valley of the red sand?"

"Yes, I remember the valley well."

Richard rubbed his chin. "Do you remember the well of bitter dark water?"

"Yes."

"Will you take us to that place?"

"No."

"We will pay handsomely."

Faris shook his head. "Money is not important to me. You will die if you go to this place."

Richard turned from the grave and faced Faris. "There must be something we can pay you to take us there?"

"No!" He then turned and left.

Frederick stepped to Richard. "I see we are playing a dangerous game here."

"It's not a game, Frederick. It is a chance to find gold, and that is a good thing."

"Yes, I suppose. But good things have a way of turning bad."

chapter **42**

JULY 4, 1980
PHOENIX, ARIZONA

GARY'S EYES WANDERED around the room as he waited in the detective's office. It was a sterile-looking place, white walls lined with steel filing cabinets standing on a gray vinyl floor. Except for a crooked walnut plaque the walls were bare. Gary read the plaque: PHOENIX POLICE DEPARTMENT MARKSMAN AWARD 1975. A set of eight-by-ten black-and-white photographs were strewn across a cold metal desk. The strange surroundings chilled him.

His gaze fell to the photos. They were of a man facedown in a pool of dark liquid. Gary yanked his eyes away, sickened. Seconds later his curiosity won out, and he looked at the grizzly scene.

A man's sudden entry startled him.

Detective Barry Johnson sat and leaned over the desk. "I'm Detective Barry Johnson, and I have to tell you I don't have a lot of time for this. I have a big caseload."

Gary nodded. "I am sorry to take up your time, but I needed an expert's opinion on something that is very important. And, well, they told me at the front desk that you're a handwriting expert."

"What's so important?"

341

"An old Bible."

Detective Johnson leaned back and his six-foot-two, 240-pound bulk made the chair squeak in protest. "Need a priest for that one, and I am far from being anything close to clergy."

"It's not like that. I need your opinion."

The detective laughed. "On a Bible?"

"No, on a bloody message written in the Bible. I need an opinion concerning the inscription's age and anything else you can tell me."

"Okay, I can always give an opinion if we make this short." The detective extended a hand for the Bible. "I'm just giving an opinion. I don't want some silk-tie attorney calling me tomorrow about this. Got it?"

Gary opened the Bible and handed it to the detective. He pointed to the smeared words. "There. It says 1920. That would be sixty years ago. Do you think that the blood smears are that old?"

Johnson studied the inscription and pursed his lips. His careful inspection gave Gary a measure of confidence. "The message is dated 1920, but there is no way this blood is from then."

"What?"

"First, the blood sample is not brown yet. It still has some reddish color, which means it can't be that old. Seems fairly recent to me."

"So it's not from 1920."

"Not even close. The pages from old Bibles like

this are made from acid-rich paper. That's why pages in old books yellow. In the old days, they used a lot of chemicals in the process of making paper. Those chemicals react when they come in contact with a fluid like blood, even hundreds of years later. Acid accelerates the oxidation of the hemoglobin. Hemoglobin is what gives blood its red color. So the blood on these acidic pages would turn brown and even black within a year or two at the most. Because this blood still has some red in it, I would say that it was put in the Bible only a few months ago."

Johnson snatched a magnifying glass from his cluttered desk and scanned the bloodied letters. "Another thing: based on the smear marks, I would say the writer is left-handed." He lowered the magnifying glass. "This person also had a pretty deep L-shaped scar across the tip of his finger—probably his index finger. See it there? You can see the imprint in the blood of an *L* from the scar?"

Johnson turned the Bible toward Gary. He had no trouble seeing it.

"This is a forgery, son."

"Forgery?"

"That's what my experience says. I am sure you could spend some money and have a private lab run some tests, but I can tell you straight out—it's a fake."

"I can't believe he'd do this," Gary mumbled.

chapter **43**

JULY 18, 1920
CAIRO, EGYPT

I T WAS EARLY morning when the three men set
out. Over the last two weeks, Richard had spent
his time making preparations for the trip, including
hiring a camel herder named Si. He had a reputation for being skilled in the desert and had agreed
to take them east across the Nile delta and on the
long journey east across the northern Sinai peninsula. From there they would travel around the
northern cusp of the Gulf of Aqaba, and down into
the mountainous wilderness of Arabia. Richard
kept repeating that God was with them, the Bible
was good luck, and that they would somehow find
the mysterious mountain of Jabal Musa.

Frederick hoped his friend was right.

"Riches await us," Richard assured a reluctant
Frederick, who threatened to leave the dangerous
scheme many times. But Richard was a good
friend and Frederick felt a personal obligation to
the man who had saved his life on the battlefield.
He would not abandon him now that he desperately needed Frederick's help. He could see it in
Richard's face—the obsessive gleam that grew
more intense with each hour . . . a look that went
beyond reason.

Their camel herder, Si, was a short man with a round, mischievous face. He often boasted he was a distant cousin of the governor, who would give him special travel papers to cross the desert. But Frederick soon suspected that the governor did so just to get rid of the bothersome man.

They had procured bread, meat, rice, butter, tea, eggs, and firewood for the journey. But food stocks and provisions were not enough for Si; he also bought an array of unnecessary items such as pots and rugs, which he lashed in cumbersome loads on the backs of musky-smelling camels. The animals brayed and squealed in protest. Richard made no secret of his displeasure with Si, who spent long hours trying to buy more and more to sell along the way. Waving his sword like a madman and shaking his letter from the governor, Si demanded merchants sell their goods for a paltry sum.

At the next village, the heavy loads of supplies would be sold off in the bazaars for a tidy profit and the money quickly stuffed in a leather pouch tied around the plump neck of the smiling Si. He would then go off and to the next village and again repeat the extortion.

Their progress was ponderously slow, not because of the suffocating heat or the expanse of the country crossed, but because of the time Si wasted squeezing the poor villagers at every turn.

"We should leave this wretched man, buy our own camels and head out alone," Richard complained.

"I understand," Frederick said, "but the governor's letter he carries might be of good use later. Besides, the desert is too large. What if we become lost? It is best we be patient."

The camels were mysterious creatures to the two soldiers who were accustomed to easy travel by ship, train, or truck. The desert beasts walked, erect and proud, with long, elastic strides in spite of their gangly legs. They made odd grunts and throaty bleats, depending on their mercurial moods. The beasts could move like machines all day and then suddenly stop, unwilling to budge even when Si lashed them with a whip.

That night Si explained to his charges the importance of the hairy, stubborn beasts to desert dwellers. "They are more than pack animals. Bedouin use the cow camel for milk; hair for weaving blankets; hides for water bags, sandals, and belts. As you have seen, the dung is gathered as fodder for fires. On cold desert mornings, men use the animal's urine to warm their hands. Women sometimes wash their hair and newborn babies with camel urine."

The sour expressions on their faces gave Si a reason to smile.

On the second day, Richard grew sick. He had a long, fitful night, shivering on a Persian carpet spread over the hard ground. Ophthalmia inflamed his eyes. The orbs turned red, and yellow pus oozed from his eyelids. The swelling closed his eyes so much he could barely open them. The bright light of the day became intolerable. Yet his lust for gold was never diminished. It seemed that the pain of his affliction made him more determined. Frederick wrapped a wet rag around his friend's face, leaving him to ride his camel blindfolded.

Eyes were not Richard's only problem. He contracted dysentery. They had to stop regularly so he could relieve his colon. His inner legs and buttocks grew raw from chafing. Still, to Frederick's astonishment, Richard never complained.

Frederick worried that their plans were ill conceived and might even prove fatal. Richard could eat only bread and soured curds.

By day three, they had stopped at a palm-tree-encircled city on the eastern edge of the Nile delta. The town looked like a thriving trade stop. There were shaded courtyards draped with winding vines and bazaars laden with vibrant-colored wool carpets, copper bowls, and silks. It was a garden of Oriental splendor on the edge of a vast, howling desert. Here Richard could rest, drink clean well water, and maybe regain his strength.

"This seems a pleasant place to rest," Frederick said. He and Si sat in front of Richard's tent.

"Do not let your eyes fool you. This place is ruled by Ali. He is a ruthless man. Cruel in many ways."

"How cruel?" Frederick took a long swallow of water.

"I knew a man from this town. He told me that Ali punished a thief by having his teeth knocked out. He took bits of the teeth, put them in the barrel of a gun, then shot the poor beggar."

"Maybe the man talked too much."

"Make humor, my friend, but Ali is a man who will not hesitate to make an example for his people. Beatings are common here. Sometimes Ali will hang a lawbreaker upside down and whip his feet raw. And that is for breaking the slightest of rules."

"Is that why the locals have stayed away from us?"

"We are strangers. They fear talking to us. I could not persuade any of the merchants to sell me their goods."

The next day one of Ali's guards came and ordered them to come to Ali's mud home. He called it a "palace."

When the travelers faced Ali, he was sitting in a room by a courtyard. He was a short, flabby, repulsive-looking man with a white scar and a malignant scowl across his face. He glared at the disheveled men. The guard explained that they were traveling across the desert. Si translated the whole conversation.

"To travel farther, payment must be made." He

mentioned an amount that made the camel herder blanch.

With a trembling hand, Si showed the letter he had been using to extort the merchants. "We travel with the governor's permission."

Ali laughed and slapped his thigh. "This is only a worthless paper from someone in Cairo." He lifted his outer robe and displayed two flintlocks and a sword with a white handle. "These are the only authority here."

Si rubbed his chin. "The English have magic to give you as a special gift; magic is good payment."

Ali guffawed. "I have seen all the magic there is. I need not see such things."

Si went to Richard. "Let me see the silver compass."

"What are you doing?" Frederick asked.

"Quiet. Let me do this." He held out his hand to Richard. Too sick to protest, Richard slowly removed the compass from his pocket and gave it to Si, who then passed it to Ali.

He sat in awe watching the teetering needle maintain its unwavering direction, then frowned. "This is a child's trinket. I will keep this as a gift. You may stay a night in safety and then you must return to Cairo if you choose not to pay passage."

Si looked to Richard, but he was too weak to respond. He had grown paler during the meeting. "My friend is ill."

Ali said, "You can go into the shade before your

friend dies. It is very bad luck to have a guest die in your home, even if he is an infidel." He waved dismissively. "You can have water from my wells; then maybe your minds will work better. The baksheesh for your continued travel will be paid then."

That night Si placed a damp cloth over Richard's eyes. Frederick approached and sat next to them. "How is he?"

"Not well. He grows weaker."

"But he will live, right?"

Si shrugged. "If Allah wills."

Frederick feared for his friend's life.

Outside, and a short distance from their tent, three men gathered around the fire in front of a large spun-wool tent. They had long rifles cradled in their arms. They shouted at each other.

"What are they arguing about?" Frederick asked.

"They do not argue. They speak as they always do, of feuds, of fights over grazing land, family inheritances, and the latest assassinations. It is always the same: they shout but nothing is ever settled and no one is offended."

"It sounds like they are a fighting bunch," Frederick said.

"This is a hard land populated by hard people. There are men in this area who would kill a man as easily as they would slide a blade across the throat of a sheep. But in the clan, they are like family and no one is in peril—except for strangers like us."

"I will try to remember that." Frederick lay down on a rug and used folded blankets for a pillow. He slipped his hand under the blankets—a hand holding a six-shot pistol.

A noise made Frederick open his eyes. Out of the darkness a young girl appeared at their tent flap and motioned for Frederick to follow her. He sat up. "What's all this?"

The girl whispered something and pointed away from the tent. Through the open flap he saw a veiled woman with kind but pained eyes. "Who is that?"

"The woman is Ali's principal wife. Come with me."

Frederick and Si walked to her. Her dark eyes glistened and tears streaked her cheeks. At her feet lay her five-year-old son, limp, wheezing for air, his beautiful, pale face moist with sweat. The woman spoke to Si.

"She says her son has been sick for some time," Si translated. "She fears he will die. She has heard that Franks always carry medicine."

"What's wrong with the boy?"

"Malaria. She says he became ill after herding sheep near a swampy land called Raudhah Sabkha."

"Wait here." Minutes later, he returned with a bottle of quinine and lifted the medicine to indicate that the woman take it. She looked at Si, who nodded. Si said, "The woman cannot take the bottle because her husband would beat her for receiving medicine from the hands of infidels."

"But this will help."

"She is afraid. The Muslim holy men say the way of the Christian is vile and against the Koran. They forbid such medicine."

"Do they have quinine?"

"No, they have no such medicine; they told the boy to drink water from a cup that had words from the Koran written in ink on the inside. The woman had him do this. Her son remains ill."

"Tell her to take the medicine. I will give it to you so it will be from your hands. Tell her you are Muslim."

Si took the quinine bottle and walked into the night. The woman lifted her son and followed. Around midnight Si returned and woke Frederick with a gentle push on his shoulder.

"What?" Frederick rubbed his eyes.

Si smiled. "The fever has gone. The medicine works."

chapter **44**

RICHARD WAS NO better the next morning. The night had been filled with fitful, painful sleep. A voice outside called Frederick and Si to the tent opening. Si pulled back the flap and saw an old, blue-robed Muslim man with a wide turban holding a steaming silver bowl. Ali stood by the man's side. Si held open the flap as they entered. Ali was smiling, something that made Frederick uneasy. A boy stood with them.

"Si, I am told that you have given great medicine for my son and it is the will of Allah that I now have to give your friend medicine for his eyes." Ali smiled again.

The old Muslim holding the silver bowl set it by Richard and then carefully pulled a damp cloth from the bowl and set it over Richard's eyes—eyes that were swollen and rimmed with crusted pus.

"Who . . . who is that?" Richard asked.

"A man has come to help you," Si said.

A minute later, the man removed the cloth and placed a hand behind Richard's head and lifted. Richard resisted.

"I think he wants you to sit," Frederick said.

Richard complied, groaning from the movement. The stranger placed the palm of his hand on Richard's back and pushed him forward so his face hovered over the bowl. The wafting steam rose to his face.

"What's that smell?" Richard's voice was weak. "It smells like garlic."

Si said something in Arabic. The old man answered and Si translated. "You are right. The doctor says it is boiled garlic and desert plants."

Richard's eyes remained closed. When the steam abated, the man in the turban snapped an order to the boy, who disappeared momentarily, then returned with another steaming bowl. The procedure started over. Four bowls later, the old man stood.

To Frederick, Richard's eyes still looked swollen, red, and irritated. They looked worse than when the procedures had started.

Si translated the words of the Muslim doctor. "Your eyes will be better tomorrow; you will be able to see again." He handed them a sack of garlic and a sheaf of desert plants. "Boil some of these every day and do what you saw me do."

"We will be traveling through the desert," Frederick said. "Water will be in short supply."

The Muslim doctor smiled. "Boiling should be with camel's urine. That is even better than water. The Frank will be cured in three days' time. Allah be praised and to his prophet Muhammed peace be upon his holy name."

The next day Ali returned to the tent of the sojourners and stood with arms folded in satisfaction. Richard was sitting up sipping tea and able to see slightly. "Are you well?"

Richard looked to Si for a translation. "He asks if you are better."

Richard nodded but said nothing.

"He is better but still has pain," Si said.

"We are grateful," Frederick added.

"Praise be to Allah. There is someone who looks for you."

Hearing the translation, Frederick said, "There is someone looking for us here? How could anyone find us after all the distance we have traveled?"

Outside the tent someone shouted, "Hello, my friends." The voice seemed familiar to Frederick. He rose and exited the tent, Ali and Si behind him. Richard joined them a moment later. From several yards away, Frederick saw Faris, riding on a long-legged camel. Faris tapped the beast on the shoulder and the camel buckled its knees, lowering itself to the ground in a dusty heap.

Frederick laughed.

Faris slid to the ground and dusted off his long blue robe. He grinned and held out his arms. "I am here to help you."

Frederick couldn't believe what he was seeing. "I don't understand. You refused to come with us."

Faris lowered his head. "The Bible teaches we are to help brothers who ask for help. I felt the Holy Spirit's strong guilt on my heart. I knew you may die without my help." He looked at Richard. "Many years ago your father, Paul Cooper, asked for my help. I did not go, and they are dead now. I do not want your blood on my hands as well. I could not live with such shame. It is my duty to help, even if I may be at risk. This is the obligation of all Christians, to help a brother in need. Ruth would have wanted this as well, I think."

"And you followed our trail out here?" Richard said.

"Yes. It is good that you have stayed here so long. My journey to find you was made easier."

"I've been ill," Richard said. "That is why we're still here."

"An answer to prayer is an answer to prayer." Faris smiled.

They stayed one more night to rest up for the long journey ahead. The following day Richard's eyes were almost completely healed—so much so that the sun's bright rays no longer hurt him. By Faris joining the caravan, it seemed that the journey was now blessed with some needed good fortune. Frederick whistled a cheerful old Austrian folk song the whole morning.

As the four men prepared to leave, Ali strode up and lifted Frederick's hand. He dropped the silver compass into his palm. Si stepped to the two men to translate. "A compass can only tell you which way to go. You will need more than a compass." Ali held out his hand and opened his fingers, revealing what looked like two dried grapes. "The Bedouin say that the best eyes are those of a wolf. A wolf always knows where to go, can see through the dark, and knows danger before it arrives. The Bedouin carry the eyeballs of a wolf with them at all times." He dropped them into Frederick's other hand. "To live in the desert, you should always have the eyes of a wolf."

Frederick thanked him. Ali looked at Faris. "And

you would be wise to keep your faith as a Christian locked in your mouth, for if these words of your God tumble foolishly from your lips, then not even wolf's eyes will keep you from death."

He turned and snapped his fingers. A boy scrambled forward. He held two blue robes. "Parting gift for the Franks."

The men slid on the robes, then each were handed an *agal* and *ghuttra* scarf.

Ali stepped back and nodded his approval. "You almost look like Arabs now. Your pants are an insult to Muslim men."

The caravan started toward the eastern hills. At the edge of the village, a grateful mother waved as the men passed. Her son stood at her side. A black-and-red veil covered with coins hid the woman's face but could not conceal grateful eyes.

For four days, Faris led them through the sun-blasted land of Arabia.

The distant horizon was an endless array of dry, craggy rocks and searing sand. Wadis appeared and disappeared in the yawning expanse. Sprigs of sage dotted the terrain. The land seemed devoid of all human life except for the occasional grouping of black woolen tents, home to the sinewy, sun-scarred Bedouin.

The territory they entered appeared just as white space on the old paper map they carried, but in reality it was a limitless vista of howling wind and biting sand. To Faris it was the land of his father. The thought worried him.

The acacia-wood saddle creaked under Frederick as the dry wind fluttered his robe. "A grand adventure, eh, Richard? During the war, all we knew was mud, rain, and more rain and more mud."

"I'm just happy to see anything at all. I thought for certain I would spend the rest of my days blind, unable to see my wife and the ocean below our cliff."

"You look much improved, friend."

"Thanks should be given to God," Faris said. "I have prayed this morning and praised His name for allowing me to find you and for all He has done for us. He is a mighty God indeed."

Richard chuckled. "Even I can say amen to that."

"Yes, indeed."

The time rolled past, one camel stride at a time. Minutes became hours, as they had the day before and the day before that. Each rode in silence; each was lost in his own thoughts.

Faris pulled his camel to a stop, then pointed to a peculiar mountain with twin, blackened snubbed peaks. "Jabal Musa—the Mountain of Moses."

chapter **45**

JULY 4, 1980
PHOENIX, ARIZONA

THE WORD *forgery* that he had heard from the detective reverberated in Gary's mind the entire ride to the Galaxy Motel. The echo did not stop until he was sitting at the scarred motel table in his uncle Daniel's room.

The old man sitting across from him seemed to have aged a year since Gary left. The place still reeked from foul breath, a stack of empty Chinese food boxes, whiskey on the carpet, and cigarette smoke on everything.

"So, what'd you find on your little jaunt to San Francisco?" Daniel slurred the question.

"I need to see your hands."

"My hands?"

"Let me see them, Uncle Daniel."

Daniel set his hands palms down on the table.

"Turn them over."

"What is this, boy? Since when do you care about my old, arthritic hands?"

"Just turn them over."

Gary pulled his uncle's hands close and studied the fingertips. A white line marred the end of Daniel's left index finger. "You have a scar, Uncle—an L-shaped scar on your fingertip."

359

"I got lots of scars. It comes from a life of hard work. Don't get many scars in college, I bet. Why are you so interested in an old, cut-up finger anyway?"

"How'd you get that scar, Uncle Daniel?"

Daniel yanked his hand back. "Why? It ain't important."

"Yes, it is."

"Why you interested in an old scar on my finger anyway?"

"Just tell me." The words came out louder than he'd intended.

"Okay, okay, I was working in the oil fields in Saudi Arabia, just south of Tabuk, and I cut it on some threaded pipe. A barb of metal sliced it. Bled awful, as I remember."

"There are no oil fields in the Tabuk area, Uncle."

"Where you going with all this, boy?"

"I called your former employer and was told there are no oil fields in the Tabuk area of Saudi Arabia." Gary stared into his uncle's rheumy eyes.

"Maybe they're wrong. Did you ever think about checking that out?"

"I already did. When did you cut your finger, Uncle?"

"This is just nonsense. A solid waste of time, that's what it is."

"When did you cut it?"

"Maybe 1978 or '79. Maybe it was 1980, I don't know for sure and don't give a—"

"Look at the Bible, Uncle." Gary pulled the old book from his backpack and set it on the table. "The bloody inscription has the words *R.C. Cooper* and a date of 1920. Now why would a man who is writing a death message in blood bother to write down the year?"

Daniel shrugged.

"Uncle, the blood is still reddish in color; the police said the blood smears are probably only months old."

"Police? Why did you bring the police into this?"

"They know nothing about you, Uncle. They only inspected the bloody marks and told me that they couldn't have been written in 1920. The detective also said the person who made these marks was left-handed and had a pronounced L-shaped scar on his fingertip."

Daniel curled his fingers.

"It seems more than a coincidence that you are left-handed and have a scar that matches the one in the Bible."

Daniel turned toward the wall. "What do you want from me, boy?"

"How about some truth? You really didn't work in the oil fields in Tabuk, did you?"

Daniel lowered his eyes. "Well, you got me on that one. I did work the rigs for years. That's the truth, son. But you're right. It wasn't in Tabuk."

"And you didn't find the Bible in a cave, did you?"

Daniel shook his head.

Gary leaned over the table. "Why? Why all the lying? Why are you writing messages in blood in an old Bible?"

Daniel rose and went for the bottle of Scotch on the nightstand, patting his pockets with one hand, searching for smokes. Gary sprang from his chair and snatched the whiskey bottle from his uncle's hand.

"Hey, what the—"

Gary didn't stop to listen. He marched into the bathroom and poured the liquor in the toilet.

"Gary, no! Why would you do a thing like that?"

"Sit down."

"Listen—"

"I said, sit down!" Gary pointed at the chair where his uncle had been sitting. Gary stayed on his feet.

"Okay, okay, so I lied a little. Ain't no reason to pour a man's booze down the crapper."

"Why would you lie to me?"

Daniel shut his eyes. When he opened them a minute later, he said, "Gold, Gary. It's that simple. I've been a drunk and a flat-broke bum a long time now, and this is the only way I can dig myself out. Can you understand that? I'm a desperate man who can't even afford rehab for the booze problem. With some money, maybe I could get a place to live that isn't a stinking dump like this motel. Maybe I could clean up my life. Maybe I could even live ten years longer . . . if only I had some money."

"This is all about money?"

"Money is the key to everything, Gary; you'll find that out someday." Daniel rubbed his forehead. "Only lucky thing ever happened to me was finding that Bible and the letters telling of where some gold might be."

"The letters don't mention a treasure, Uncle. You're lying to me again."

"No, I'm not. There were other letters in the Bible."

"What other letters?"

He nodded. "Two other letters in the Bible that I didn't show you. I kept those to myself. When I bought the Bible, it had some folded-up letters inside."

"You told me you found the Bible in a cave. Now you say you bought it?"

"Yeah. I bought it from a man in an antique shop outside Dubai. It was old, and I thought it might be worth something. I read somewhere that old books can be rare and valuable."

"Did you ask the man in the bookstore where he got the Bible?" Gary pressed.

"He said two men died in the desert building a water well: a German and a Arab. A big drilling rig fell on them, and in all the confusion the Bible found its way into the hands of a worker who took it to his shop and sold it. He said only Muslims ever go to his shop, so no one bought the book. He also said I could have it real cheap."

"Do you still have those letters?"

Uncle Daniel rose and moved to the battered dresser. He grunted as he yanked on a stuck drawer until it finally opened. He fished out two yellowed documents and returned to Gary. "These are them."

Gary carefully took the letters. "Why didn't you show me these letters before?"

"Maybe you would think it all a crazy scheme, the mention of buried gold and all, so I thought it best to keep these letters away from you. I knew that the more noble approach of finding the proper owner of a rare Bible would be more appealing for a Christian lad like you."

"Ruth!" Gary almost shouted when he saw her name.

"Best I can figure this letter was sent by this Ruth to our unknown R.C. Cooper."

Gary scanned the words. He saw *Emily in Wight.* "That's it, Uncle: Emily is in Wight. When you forged the words in blood *Emily in White,* it should have been spelled Wight. That's where we will find R.C. Cooper. He is or was related to Emily in Wight in England."

"I never was a good speller," Daniel muttered. "Gary, my boy, the letter from Ruth wrote of a map showing where gold can be found. An old parchment that tells right where it's hidden. The map is with this Emily. All I wanted you to do was find her, but I also needed to find out all I could about the Bible and all who have owned it over the years. I thought that maybe we could find us an old trail, from Tate to Ruth, and ultimately to Emily, who still may have the parchment telling us where the gold is hidden."

"You tricked me into doing all the legwork."

"Come on, Gary, I could never do it alone. Look at me. I'm just a dumb old bum. Can't even tell White from Wight, and you expected me to find my way in all this? Old men die, that's what they do. They eventually die from withering bodies, but they also die from dreams that never come true. I was young like you once, had the world by the throat. But I never lived past the next woman or the next bottle. I always woke up with a hangover and no money to my name. Somewhere along the line, I forgot how to dream and I gave up." He licked his lips. "But we have a chance here, boy. A chance to fill a lifetime of dreams."

"Uncle Daniel, you used me. Don't expect any sympathy."

Daniel lowered his head. "Can't argue there, boy."

"What about the gold scarab and gold ring that you gave me for graduation? Where did you get that stuff?"

"It's not worth much. I bought it all at a bazaar. They're trinkets—cost me maybe twenty bucks.

The scarab and the ring, fakes, just like me. Bought them in Cairo. Made the story real believable, didn't it?"

Gary pressed his lips into a tight line. "What about the cancer, Uncle Daniel? Tell me the truth. Do you have terminal cancer?"

Daniel looked away but said nothing.

Gary put his face in his hands. "I just can't believe you did this."

Daniel sighed. His shoulders drooped. "So now what?"

Gary rose and paced in the little room. After a minute, he stopped and faced his uncle. "I'll do this much: I will try and find R.C. Cooper or Emily on the Isle of Wight. Maybe, just maybe, I can find some information in the library. But first I'm going to send a fax to the police in England and inquire about some of those names."

"Police!" Daniel shot back.

"You got me into this, now I will get us out but I'm going to do it my way." He began pacing again. "I'm not doing all this for a crazy scheme to find gold. This Bible just may be a cherished heirloom for the family of R.C. Cooper, or whoever the rightful owner might be. You may be able to sleep at night, but I won't until I do the right thing here."

"Now I know you're not related to me, boy."

chapter **46**

JULY 31, 1920
JABAL MUSA, SAUDI ARABIA

FOUR HARD DAYS later, a tired Frederick, Si, Faris, and Richard arrived at a Bedouin encampment nestled at the base of Jabal Musa. Faris saw a woman kneeling over a lamb. She held a bloody, curved knife. Seeing the approaching caravan, she sprang to her feet, attached her veil with red, glistening fingers, then ran off.

A mangy dog bolted from a herd of dust-covered sheep and charged them, stopping a just a few feet away. It lowered its short chest, bared its teeth, and snarled. Faris pulled his camel to a stop in front of the now snapping animal and signaled the others to do the same. The camels grew agitated and their lanky legs shifted from side to side as the riders swayed and clung to their wooden saddles.

Men emerged from black wool tents and stepped into the heart of the late-afternoon heat. They held rifles and swords. Even across the several yards that separated them, Faris saw the men were emaciated: hollow cheeks; sunken eyes; sagging, sun-scarred skin. The only thing that looked normal was the black hair sticking out of red head scarves. Their faces were twisted in anger.

367

"We seem to have caused a disturbance," Frederick whispered.

Faris could hear the fear rising in his voice. Faris nodded but didn't dismount. "I doubt they have seen Egyptian blue robes and pale men."

A wild-looking man slowly circled Richard and Frederick, poking them with his finger as if to make sure that they were real and not ghosts.

Si raised a hand, motioning for the others to be still. Faris knew it was a good idea.

An older man with a white headdress scarf and a white robe embroidered at the edges with red and gold thread emerged from the tent. He looked wise and possessed a calmness and surety about himself.

"The clan leader," Faris said. "The emir."

Two cracked leather bandoleers loaded with rifle cartridges crossed his chest. He drew his sword from its ornate scabbard. He approached Frederick and raised the point of the blade to the man's face.

Frederick sat still as the man drew the sharp tip across his cheek. The emir stared with awe at Frederick's pink skin and deep blue eyes. A thin cut on Frederick's cheek oozed a drop of blood, but he remained still.

Faris studied the man in the white headdress. Something about him seemed familiar. The eyes, the turn in the mouth, the chin—"Uncle," he whispered to himself. The man with the sword was his uncle. Age had withered him, bent his back and lined his face, but Faris had no doubts. He cleared his throat and the man switched his gaze from Frederick to Faris. He stepped closer.

Faris took the initiative. "I am the boy who left this clan. I am the son of your brother." He paused. "I am Faris, Uncle."

The man lowered his sword, his face slack. A rush of fear exploded in Faris. His uncle might— would—feel compelled to kill him because of his Christian faith.

With a speed that belied his age, the emir reached up and pulled Faris from the camel. Faris offered no resistance; he just waited for the blade. It never came. Instead, the old man wrapped his arms around him in a lingering hug. Faris heard something near his ear. The emir wept—a haunting, joyful weeping. Long minutes passed before Faris felt his uncle's embrace release. He stepped back and looked into the eyes of a man he had not seen in decades.

"We feared you had died in the desert. How did you manage to live crossing the hot sands? You were such a small rabbit that went into a place filled with many hungry foxes." With his teeth glistening in the low sun, the emir added, "I see Allah has his favor upon you."

Faris took a deep breath. "The God of the Christians saved me." He recalled Ali's advice about leaving faith locked in his mouth. As wise as the advice seemed, Faris wouldn't mislead his uncle.

His uncle waved his hand as if dismissing the words. "Allah knows your heart is still Muslim, even though your lips betray him and his prophet Muhammed." He closed his eyes as if praying. "You are like a sheep that has become lost. That is all I know; a sheep who has now come home."

Faris smiled. "It is good to be home."

The emir lowered his voice. "We mourned your death but did so privately. Your father forbade even the mention of your name. It was as if you had never lived, but I never forgot you. I loved you as my own son. He did not even allow your mother her tears, but I heard her many times as she sat in the darkness weeping in the desert."

"Does my father live?"

The emir hesitated. "He died many years ago."

Faris flinched and lowered his head.

The emir turned and searched the faces of those who had gathered around him. He motioned to someone in the back.

Faris heard a gasp as the crowd parted. It was a shallow sound, trailing and frail. A woman bent with age wobbled toward them with arthritic stiffness. She shuffled to Faris and trembled uncontrollably. "Is it you? Is it you, my son Faris?"

Faris's heart tumbled at his mother's voice. Tears led to sobs as the two embraced. The sight of his mother drained his strength. In the windy desert, they kissed each other's tear-streaked faces. No one interrupted. Faris could smell her hair and skin. It was a smell of sweat and cooking smoke, grease, incense, oil, and cardamom, it was a smell he long remembered from his childhood and one that had not changed in three decades.

His mother stepped back and raised a hand to his face.

"Mother . . . mother." He began to tremble.

She sighed. "Faris . . . my boy . . . my Faris." Her tender voice quivered.

No one spoke. No one interrupted.

Finally, the emir said, "We will celebrate this wonderful gift of your return from the most merciful Allah and we will kill a lamb tonight—the fattest lamb. We will feast in celebration. Allah is benevolent."

That night the fire glowed as the women in the camp heaped on more dried camel dung. The beheaded body of the lamb turned on a metal spit, the flames licking the skin to a crackling brown. The lamb's head had been tossed to the edge of the camp, where growling and snapping dogs fought for their share. One by one the men sliced off glistening curls of brown meat that dripped with fat. Under the starry night, the women celebrated by ululating, *"Lee, lee, lee."* Men fired their rifles into the air. Each shot from the long barrels spewed yellow flames into the darkness.

371

Faris and the others sat around the fire. Richard leaned toward Faris. "I'm glad we're not the ones being roasted over the flames."

"The night is not over," Faris said smiling.

chapter 47

THAT NIGHT THE clan presented Faris with a new gray robe and a white head scarf with a black *agal,* and he sat on a carpet to the right of his uncle. Richard sat cross-legged on a carpet to the left of the emir and Frederick by him. Faris translated.

"Is the lamb to your liking?" the emir asked.

Frederick smiled as a trickle of lamb's juice ran down his chin. "It is wonderful."

Richard had been squirming most of the evening. He could wait no longer. "Do you know of men who look like us, white men who came here long ago to look for treasure? One of the men was my father. He came with another man named Edmond."

"Why did these men come to this place? No one of white skin comes here. It is a foolish thing to do."

"They came for gold."

"Gold?"

The clan leader thought, then in somber tones said, "Such men did come to this place. My father had them killed. I saw this with my own eyes. The men of the camp took them into the desert. That is where they remain."

Faris stopped translating and faced Richard. He could see the concern on his face.

"Will they kill us as well?" Richard asked.

"No, they consider you a guest."

"Do they know anything about the gold?"

"They know of the story of treasure, but they think it is only a legend started by old men around a campfire to please the ears of children. They do not believe that it really exists."

Frederick asked Faris, "Will the emir let us go to the place mentioned in the monk's document?"

Faris spoke to his uncle.

The emir raised a crooked finger, like a lecturing father. "Gold takes our eyes off of Allah. A good sword will save you, but not gold. A good well, a good camel, and a wife who bears many sons is all we need in the desert."

"Your people are thin and your camels are weak," Richard said. "I see no water for your camp. Your sheep are few, and I'm afraid some of the young boys will die before their time. We will share any gold we find with you."

The emir bolted to his feet. His face showed his anger, but he didn't speak at first. He seemed to be measuring his words. "Our people are dying. Your eyes do not lie. We have lost almost half our number. Five years we have lived under this drought. If Allah has willed that skies withhold their rain, then we must die—*enshala*. No rain will come to fill our wadis; no rain will catch in our wells, as Allah wills."

"The whites can pull water from the deep ground with pipes," Faris said. "Holes are drilled deep in the ground where the water waits, much farther than any man can dig with a shovel."

Richard smiled. "If we can find the gold, then we can help your people get pipes and drilling machines. We will bring men and equipment. Your people and your animals will have water to drink."

The emir said nothing.

Faris asked Richard for the Bible and opened it to Genesis 26:17. "Uncle, I would like to read to you from the Bible about the prophet Abraham."

His uncle looked puzzled. "You have the prophet Abraham in your Christian book?"

"Yes, the Bible also speaks about Isaac. It says that he moved his clan to the Valley of Gerar and that he settled there. The Bible tells of him reopening the dry wells that had been dug in the time of Abraham. He found water. Uncle, this is not magic. The men the whites will bring can dig deeper than Isaac could dig, they can put metal pipes down deeper and use pumps to pull up the water. It is the way of the whites. Our people will have water. This is a blessing."

The emir pulled his sword. "Can this gold buy these pipes? Can gold bring my people water from a dry, dead ground?"

Faris said, "Yes, Uncle, water will come to you like rain from a thousand black clouds."

"Maybe it is the will of Allah that you have come to this place; it is not for me to question his will." The emir paused. "I will take you to the gold and you will bring us many pipes."

Richard nodded.

The emir looked at Faris. "Our clan will grow strong again with good water." He looked at Frederick. "You then will stay with the clan. Your friend Richard will go to the white men and get many pipes. If the pipes do not come, then you will pay with your life for dealing in such treachery against the clan."

Richard started to protest, but Faris stopped him with a raised hand. "My uncle has ruled in front of his people. He will not change his mind on the matter. Frederick must stay if you wish to find the gold."

Frederick gazed into the fire. "I will stay. I know you will return. You did not abandon me in the war; you won't abandon me now."

Faris said, "It is done. The emir will take you to find the gold you seek, then you will bring back many men with pipes and machines."

The emir smiled and returned his sword to the ornate sheath. "Tomorrow we go to find this cave.

If the gold is there, I will count it a sure sign by Allah, praise his name, that I have done a pleasing thing in his holy sight."

Faris's eyes met Richard's and Frederick's. He could see the unspoken concern. He nodded. "It is a good arrangement. Do you agree?"

Frederick nodded. "Yes, I agree."

"I hope you know what you're doing, Frederick," Richard said.

Frederick chortled. "More to the point, Richard, I hope *you* know what you're doing."

chapter 48

AUGUST 1, 1920
JABAL MUSA, SAUDI ARABIA

THE NEXT DAY they prepped the camels, cinching the acacia-wood saddles to the beasts with leather straps, and engorged the huge goat-hair saddlebags with provisions.

Before they left, the emir glared at Si. "You are not to go into my land. I will not permit it."

"Why, Uncle?" Faris asked before Si could respond.

"He is Egyptian and a man of little character. He uses a whip on his camels and spurs their flanks. You can see marks on their hides. Arabian camels respond to a melody of kind songs, not a whip. They are a finer breed of beast. They deserve proper treatment."

Faris could see the anger on Si's face, but the man kept quiet. He knew the ways of the Bedouin. He also knew he was in no position to challenge the emir. His uncle's clan might be smaller than it once was, but it was plenty large to handle one angry Egyptian. After several minutes of trying to persuade his uncle to change his mind, Faris yielded and told the others. Si could do nothing but clench his jaw.

They spent another hour transferring their load from Si's camels to the emir's. No one complained aloud, but Faris could sense the tension. As soon as Si's camels were free, the Emir said, "I let you leave my camp with your head still attached. It is the best that I can do for you, Egyptian. Do not come back."

By the time the sun started its slide to the horizon, Richard, Faris, Frederick, and the emir had finished preparing the animals and headed north into the mountains.

Their late start gave them only a half day of travel and it seemed to Richard that evening came early. He sat in front of the tent he shared with Frederick, watching Faris cook over an open fire. The emir sat near Faris, watching his nephew. Through the first leg of the trip, their new guide had ridden several yards ahead of the others. Richard had the distinct feeling that having infidels so close made Faris's uncle uncomfortable.

"We can't get there soon enough, Frederick,"

Richard said. "I still think we could have pushed on for a few more miles."

"In the dark? That would not be wise. Besides, these people move at their own pace. There is no good in rushing them."

"Think of the gold. Think of the riches." He picked up a stick and poked the ground.

"Right now, all I can think of is a bath and a meal that includes fat German sausages."

"The gold doesn't call to you?" Richard asked.

"A great deal, but there is more to life than gold."

"Such as?"

Frederick turned to Richard. "Such as that lovely wife you left back in England. Such as the children you will have. You want children, no?"

"Of course I do. I'm crossing this cursed desert because of my wife. The money will provide us with a good life—better than I can hope for any other way."

"Perhaps," Frederick said. "But gold will not bring happiness. A man can be wealthy and miserable."

"A man can be poor and miserable, too, Frederick."

Frederick sighed.

"What is it, Frederick? What's on your mind?"

He gazed at the stars. "I was thinking about Ruth's letter to you. The one I delivered to you at your home."

"What about it?"

"She said you should not try to find the treasure. 'Better to seek God than gold,' she said."

"I recall her leaving it up to me. You're not losing heart, are you?"

Frederick chuckled. "No. I'm too deep in the desert to want to turn back now. No, my friend, I am in until the end." He paused. "But we must be wise enough not to lose ourselves in the process."

"No need to worry. Nothing is going to change me." He stood. "Now let's go see what Faris has been burning over that campfire."

Two more days passed; two days of ponderous travel; two days of suffocating heat by day and shivering cold by night. At last they arrived in a valley of supple red sands—a wide, chalk-rimmed vale of sun-bleached dunes sculpted by the unrelenting desert wind.

The caravan stopped and the emir pointed to a cave carved into the side of the steep mountain slope that formed one boundary of the valley. "As a young boy, I would often water our camels from the bitter black waters of the well there."

Richard gazed at the sight. Near the cave, a pair of wild camels knelt under the brow of a hill that cast a meager sliver of shade.

"I would bring a roped line of cow camels to drink there. Since I was still young, my mother accompanied me. She told me that no man could drink from the bitter waters and live very long. The well has the foul taste of salt and insults the tongue. Even the birds avoid such a poor well."

Richard asked, "Why are the camels able to drink from that place?"

"Camels are like no other animal. The female laps up the foul water and the next day her big, swaying udders are dripping with milk. Man cannot change bad water into good milk. Only the stomach of the desert beast can do that."

Faris smiled. "God is much like the camel—only our Lord can change a bitter dark heart into a heart of clear living waters."

The group plodded up to the cave on a trail of russet dust. The two indigenous camels held their place, undisturbed by the new arrivals. The pack camels knelt together.

Richard and Frederick rushed the last yards and plunged into the cave. Faris walked the distance. He arrived at the cave's entrance in time to hear Frederick shout, "It's here!" Frederick's voice echoed in the empty space. Richard moved to Frederick's side. Frederick had his eyes fixed on one wall—a wall with an ancient carving of seven candles in a lamp stand.

Richard spoke just above a whisper. "This is really it. I can't believe we're here, the very place my father lost his life, searching for it. All the miles, all the years, and here we are." He stepped to the cave wall and ran his fingers along the chiseled image. "Everything in the manuscript is here:

the red sands, the bitter well, the candle carvings, everything."

"Everything but a treasure," Frederick said.

"It's here. I can sense it." Richard dropped to his knees and began moving sand with his hands. Frederick joined him. At first they moved slowly, patiently, like archeologists at a dig site, but soon their digging became frantic.

Faris frowned as the men's greed took over. He stepped to the camels and removed two shovels. "Treasure will do you no good if you have no hands to carry it."

Richard and Frederick resumed work, digging as if their lives depended on it.

Then, *clink.*

"Wait," Frederick said. "I have something." He set the shovel aside and brushed at the sand with his fingers. A glint of gold. Frederick gently brushed away more sand. His hand trembled.

"What is it?" Richard asked.

Frederick pulled the object from the packed ground. "A bracelet. A solid gold bracelet." He held it before his face, then passed it to Richard.

Faris stood at the cave opening, next to his uncle, and watched in silence.

"It's been flattened." Richard turned the find over in his hands.

"Maybe it's flat because it's been in the ground so long."

"No," Faris said.

The men looked at him.

"You know the story of the golden calf?"

"Sure," Richard said. "Moses went up the mountain and was gone for some time. The people became restless and built a golden calf to worship."

"Not restless," Faris corrected. "They turned against God and made an idol from the gold they took from Egypt. Moses came down from the mountain and destroyed the golden calf, burned it, ground it to dust, made some of the Israelites drink water mixed with it. The rest was cast upon the waters of a brook."

"Well, this doesn't look like part of an idol," Richard said. "It looks like a deformed bracelet."

"What gold jewelry remained was trampled and left behind. The people were not allowed to carry it with them."

"So, three thousand years ago, some Hebrew stomped this underfoot, then many years later a Greek monk found the gold and buried it all in this cave?"

"Yes."

Frederick and Richard began digging again. Within seconds, they'd found a ring, then another bracelet, then a gold chain. They shoveled away more sand, and every few moments a new piece of gold, from a piece of jewelry to a cup, appeared.

Faris looked to his uncle, who gazed at the treasure. "You fulfilled your promise, Uncle."

"I have. Now they must fulfill theirs." He turned and left the mouth of the cave. Finding a wide stretch of shade, he sat and stared into the dry distance.

chapter **49**

A T FOUR THIRTY sharp, a long, black limo turned into the parking lot of the Galaxy Motel. The driver exited and opened the rear door.

Daniel hesitated as he bent and peered through the car's open door. He slipped into the back, sliding across the supple gray leather seat. He spied four full liquor bottles in a burl-wood rack. His red eyes fixed on the cut-crystal bottles marked with gold letters: GIN, BOURBON, SCOTCH, AND VODKA.

"Forget it, Uncle," Gary instructed as he slid in.

"How's 'bout one little drink? Just one?"

"I can smell the last one you had."

"But, Gary, this is quality hooch. Not cheap convenience-store booze. I bet it cost serious money and it's free to us."

"It is." The voice came from a woman with long, slender legs. She wore a smart-looking blue wool suit. She had a beautiful face, with auburn hair tucked into a tight roll behind a delicate neck. On her lap she held a stack of legal files.

Daniel raked back his greasy hair with a hand. "And what do we have here?"

She moved her eyes to Gary. "I have prepared some legal documents and think it best that I deal with the legal possessor of the Bible. I assume you are Gary Brandon, the one who contacted the police on the Isle of Wight, the one I called two days ago."

"I told you, no police." For a moment, Gary thought his uncle would bolt from the limo. He placed a hand on his knee.

"And I told you I was going to send a fax to England to help find the Bible's real owner. We are not the owners, Uncle, not in my mind anyway. The letter you found in the Bible mentions R.C. Cooper. He is, or was, the true owner."

"I bought the Bible and possession is nine-tenths of the law." He looked at the woman. "Isn't it, Ms. Uh . . ."

"Reed," the woman answered. "Ms. Shannon Reed, and yes you may be right on that, but the issue of ownership is not being disputed here. Gary is considered the rightful owner."

"Good." Daniel crossed his arms as if her words had vindicated him.

Shannon handed Gary the stack of papers. "These are very important documents that you should read. If a price for the Bible is agreed upon, then you will sign them and we will trade money for the Bible in question."

Shannon sat back and tapped her nose lightly, as if counting the seconds. "Gary, occasionally there are rare moments in our lives, slivers of time that define our destiny. For you, this is one of those times."

"Hey, what about me?" Daniel said. "Gary said you wanted to see both of us. I got a stake in this."

"That will be up to your nephew, Mr. Huff. He's been my contact on this matter."

Gary studied the papers, ignoring his uncle. After reading the last page, he said, "I am not sure I want to sell the Bible; it seems all wrong."

"I'm just the facilitator, not the purchaser. You will meet her at the airport soon and I am sure once you talk with her concerning the details of your Bible—"

"*Our* Bible," Daniel cut in.

Shannon shifted in the seat. "You gave the Bible to Mr. Brandon, true?"

"Maybe."

"My understanding is that you gave the Bible to your nephew. I'm certain there are plenty of witnesses who will testify that the Bible was given as a graduation gift."

Daniel licked his dry lips. "I suppose I did."

Shannon nodded. "I would like to know how you came upon the Bible. I assume it was legally."

Gary leaned forward as Daniel cleared his throat.

"Well, I don't see how that's any of your business."

"You better tell the truth, Uncle Daniel." Gary leaned over and whispered. "Lying only makes things worse."

"Okay, I found the book in a little bookshop in Dubai about a year ago." He told the same story he had confessed to Gary two days before. "I left the bookshop thinking I had made the purchase of a lifetime."

The corners of Shannon's mouth turned up. "I think you just may have."

Daniel returned a weak smile. "Well, after I read in the letter about the treasure map, I figured I would need to find out how I could get my hands on it. I am an old drunk and knew I could never find the clues that would lead to a Civil War soldier named Tate, or anyone else." Daniel turned to his nephew. "So I asked Gary to help."

"You *tricked* me into helping you, Uncle. Let's be honest about that."

"I was wrong." Daniel sulked. "How did you ever come to find this R.C. Cooper anyway?"

"Like I said, Uncle, I faxed the police on the Isle of Wight and they knew exactly who I was talking about. The next day Shannon called me and arranged a meeting. She represents someone who wants to buy the Bible for a sizable sum."

"How sizable?" Daniel asked as he looked at Shannon.

"You will be told in a minute. A woman named Carolyn Dawson will meet us at the airport. She has flown in from England today on Richard Cooper's private jet to consummate the deal."

Gary saw Daniel's eyes gleam.

The limousine traveled down East Buckeye Road to the airport and pulled to a gate near a section reserved for private airplanes. A security guard opened the gate and waved them in.

chapter 50

DECEMBER 12, 1920
JABAL MUSA, SAUDI ARABIA

IT HAD BEEN nearly five months since Faris and Richard left with camels bowed down from the weight of the resurrected treasure. Frederick spent his lonely days waiting for their return, living in a woolen tent at the edge of the camp. Veiled women brought his food. He never saw their faces—only their furtive glances at the strange white man. He lived like a castaway on an island in the middle of a sea of sand. The only joy in his long days was hunting quail and hiking the many mountain peaks that jutted into a cloudless indigo sky. The emir had instructed the men in camp to avoid him. The clan considered him an infidel and nothing more than collateral until the pipes were brought—if they were ever brought.

The days bled into weeks and those into long months of staggering solitude. He would have gone mad had it not been for Richard and Faris leaving him the Bible. He read from morning till night. In its pages he discovered the loneliness of Moses in the same desert, which had forged him into the kind of man who would lead a nation of people out of Egypt. The Bible soon made him realize that this same desert was the crucible needed to change him into the man God wanted him to be.

The wind carried a thin and distant sound. He paid it no attention. Over the months, he'd learned that the desert made unusual noises. Then he heard it again: a shout, a human voice in the distance.

Frederick crawled from his tent and faced the wind. "A caravan." He ran to the rise of sand dune and lifted his hand to shield his eyes from the dazzling sun. Camels approached from out of trailing clouds of dust.

Someone stepped to Frederick's side. "Faris," the emir said.

Frederick turned to the emir. "Water comes our way." Then he broke into laughter. The emir joined him.

The longest minutes of Frederick's life passed as he waited for the caravan to arrive. As it neared, he could see the camels laden with shovels, drills, pipes, and hand pumps. Behind them were more camels with men he took to be workers.

Faris rode a jolting, spirited camel into the camp, his face glowing with a smile that told all what was to happen. He waved his arms wildly to the return cheers of everyone. "We bring you rain from the ground!" he shouted. "Pipes! We have pipes."

Faris didn't wait for his camel to kneel. He slid onto the soft sand and ran to his uncle's open arms. "Pipes, Uncle. Pipes."

The emir hugged his nephew.

Frederick pulled his eyes away, to a man who rode a camel in the back of the pack. Richard tapped the beast's shoulders and the creature knelt. Richard dismounted, slapped off the desert grit, and stepped to Frederick with hand extended. "I told you we'd come back, my friend."

"I never doubted you."

Richard threw back his head and shouted, "We're rich, I tell you! We are both rich."

Faris heard the words and walked to Richard. "I must warn you that Sister Ruth was also wealthy, but she found peace only in her poverty, only by giving to others." He looked at both the men. Frederick felt as if his eyes were boring deep into their souls. He wondered if Faris knew something he didn't.

chapter 51

JULY 5, 1980
PHOENIX, ARIZONA

CAROLYN DAWSON WAITED patiently in the corporate jet for the limousine to arrive. She had traveled far and been given orders by her boss to acquire the Bible regardless of cost. Only the day before, on the Isle of Wight, she had quietly entered the darkened master bedroom of R.C. Cooper. The green glow from the oxygen monitor was the only light in the large room. She moved to her boss's bedside. Clear plastic tubes trailed from the old man's sunken face. A clock by the bed read 3:15 in the morning.

His eyes were closed, but she doubted her employer was asleep. For the past five years, he had complained about his nights, dozing off and on in blocks of random time, awakening from his fragile slumber only to nod off again in a repetitive, somnolent existence.

"Richard?" No response. She raised her voice. "R.C. They have found the Bible—the one from the war."

The old man's creased eyes opened and he drew in a raspy breath. "Where?"

"A young man in the States has it. He lives in Phoenix, Arizona."

390

"Arizona. In the U.S. He has the Bible? He has it in his possession?"

"Yes, sir. He found your name in it and a reference to Wight. He sent a fax to the police. They called."

"You've spoken with him?"

"Not yet. I wanted you to know first."

"Buy the Bible."

"Yes, sir. May I ask how much you are willing to pay?"

"As much as is necessary. I want the Bible." His words turned shallow. "I need the Bible."

Through the aircraft's window, Carolyn saw the limo park next to the business jet. Carolyn lifted the camel-skin briefcase from her lap, stood, and walked to the door being opened by the copilot, then descended the narrow metal steps.

At sixty-four, she looked and felt younger. A gentle breeze blew wisps of salt-and-pepper hair around her face. She wore classic attire from a shop on Old Bond Street. Hers was a world lived in stuffy business ledgers that constantly added up the wealth of another.

She approached the limo.

The limousine driver exited the car and opened the door to the rear sitting area. The woman slipped into the limo as if she had done so many times before. She sat next to Shannon and scanned all the occupants with disarming eyes and a no-nonsense expression.

391

"Hello, I'm Gary Branson and this is my uncle Daniel, Daniel Huff."

"Hi," Daniel said.

Shannon Reed extended her hand to the woman. "I am Shannon Reed. I oversee the company's legal interests in the U.S."

Carolyn gave the woman's hand a brief shake. "It is always nice to meet one of our many legal counsels around the world." She then returned her attention to Gary. "My name is Carolyn Dawson. A long time ago, my employer started a business called the Golden Well Drilling Company and has done quite well for himself. He is ill and the doctors say he will die very soon." She looked out the limo's window and on to the searing concrete tarmac. "Saudi Arabia is a very hot place, even hotter than here."

Shannon opened a refrigerator positioned between the rear seats, removed a green bottle of spring water, and handed it to Carolyn. She twisted off the cap and took a sip. "In the desert, water is more valuable than gold. A water well my employer drilled is still being used in Saudia Arabia today.

"My employer drilled only that one well, then lost interest in water. No money in it, he said. Later he became wealthy from vast oil leases. He's made a staggering amount of money from oil."

"What is your employer's name?" Gary asked.

"I think you may know. After all, you sent a fax to England asking about him."

"R.C. Cooper?"

"Yes. He has achieved many things. It's Sir Richard Cooper now. The queen knighted him several years ago. I am the only one who calls him Richard. It's a simple reward I earned from forty years as his personal secretary."

"I'm sorry," Gary said, "but apart from this Bible, I've never heard of him."

"He is a very private man now, considered a recluse by most. When he dies, I am afraid he won't be missed."

The comment confused Gary.

"You were quite clever to send that fax. Everyone there knows of the billionaire Sir R.C. Cooper. Sir Richard is one of the wealthiest men in all of England."

"Billionaire?" Daniel said.

"Many times over. Our company has investment holdings all over the world: refineries, mineral mines, shipping, and—" She stopped. "Well, that's not important right now."

Gary saw Daniel unfurl a big grin. "They're certainly important to me."

"What really matters," the woman continued, "is the Bible." She set the bottle of water in one of the drink holders. "Mr. Brandon, are you prepared to come to an agreement on compensation for the Bible?"

Daniel spoke up. "I have a little to say in this, don't I?"

"No, you don't," Shannon replied flatly. "We established that earlier."

Daniel wouldn't be put off. "What about all the gold mentioned in the old letters—all that gold just waiting in that cave over there?"

Carolyn raised a hand. "Gone. Sir Richard and his friend Frederick Von Scherling found and took it."

Daniel's confident expression crumbled. "The luck of my whole life. The Bible is not mine anymore, and the gold was found by someone else."

"Sir Richard wants that book back in his possession, and he will do whatever is necessary to have it. Trust me on this; he will stop at nothing."

"Is that a threat?" Daniel said.

"No, it is a simple and honest statement of will. He will pay handsomely if he can buy the Bible here and now. If he can't buy it, then he will find another way to get it. I'm not free to discuss those ways."

"How handsomely?" Daniel asked.

"As I have told you, Sir Richard is very old and a very ill man. He could pass away any minute. If he dies, then I am most certain the surviving members of the family will see little value in buying the Bible, which they all consider more a nuisance than an asset. I suggest we not waste time."

Gary spoke up. "Why does your boss want the Bible after all these years? It's important for me to know his reason."

"That is a good question, Mr. Brandon. Sir Richard thinks the Bible is the only thing that can save him from his rapidly approaching death. He believes the Bible saved his life in World War I. He sees it as the only thing that can save him now."

"So he is afraid to die."

"I think that is a fair assumption. Maybe there is more. I believe he is ashamed of his life. He's afraid to die but is more afraid to face God."

Gary thought. "I would like to hear the whole story."

Carolyn frowned. "It is not a pleasant tale, I am afraid."

"I want the truth."

"Truth? All right then, I suppose you deserve the truth. The wealth we make in this life comes with a burden of responsibility. Some never realize this until they are forced to their knees by a Divine hand.

"Richard knows that he has hoarded his money and never given a shilling to charity or the needy. Over the years, I've learned what a miser he is. Maybe he thinks by getting back the Bible he will somehow shield himself from God's disappointment and wrath. He sits in the dark most of the time now and says 'a dry rain cometh' over and over."

"So his marbles have come loose," Daniel muttered.

"Please, Uncle Daniel. Let the woman finish."

"Thank you. The thoughts of an old man with a large amount of money are difficult for anyone to understand. He has left a lot of destroyed lives along his path to make more money. Ever since he left Saudi Arabia, he has stepped on a lot of people as he's climbed the ladder of colossal wealth."

Gary said, "He can't be all that bad. He dug a well for the Bedouins once."

"True, my boss brought water to the Bedouins, but that was to fulfill a deal to get the gold he sought. He always did what he said he would— British honor and all that. The Bedouins received a few wells; Sir Richard got a cache of gold. The gold changed him. He never went back to help the Bedouins again, I'm afraid. He was always too busy working night and day to amass more and more wealth. In time, he alienated his family and lost most of what friends he had. I doubt if more than a dozen people will be at his funeral when he passes, and most of those will be lawyers representing the interests of estranged family members."

"You mentioned his friend Frederick. You said he found the gold with Sir Richard."

"True. Richard once told me that when he and Frederick drilled their first well in Arabia, Frederick cried as he watched the thirsty children drink from the pump's flowing nozzle. He quickly thereafter sold his share of the gold and drilled well after well until he was broke. Till the day he died, he and his constant companion, Faris, drilled with their own hands. Sir Richard told me they both died when a drilling rig fell on them."

"So your employer didn't help his friend financially."

"No. He considered it a financially poor investment to go after water when oil waited beneath the ground. I think it is one of the things that haunts him on his deathbed. His close friend spent most of his life helping others, while he only helped himself. His favorite saying was, 'The tiger in the jungle is the last to starve.'"

"Are you always this honest?" Gary asked.

She lowered her eyes. "No, but watching him eaten up with worry about the life after this one is making me take stock of my own life. As you may have noticed, I'm not young anymore. I may not be as bad as my employer, but that doesn't make me good. I am guilty of never having had the courage to stand up to Richard. I regret it deeply. It seems that we often become what we serve in life, good or bad—I have served the greed of a man for a long time now and am not proud of that fact."

"Fascinating," Daniel said. "How much will you pay for the Bible?"

"I am afraid that it is not how much we are willing to pay, but how much Gary here is willing to sell it for."

"One more question," Gary said. "How many people went to Frederick's funeral?"

"Who cares?" Daniel grunted.

"I do."

Carolyn fiddled with the bottle of water. "There were so many mourners at Frederick's funeral that they had to use a soccer field instead of a church for the services. But there was no funeral as such, just a memorial service. Frederick and Faris are buried in a paupers' cemetery in Egypt on each side of a woman named Sister Ruth. Across from the cemetery is a well that still flows with water. The well is owned by the Mother Mary Orphanage."

Gary spoke slowly. "A boy in the Civil War was a preacher and he carried this Bible. He died in the war. His name was Elijah Bell, but people called him the Bell Messenger. Before he died he handed the Bible to a new Messenger, the boy's killer, a man named Jeremiah Tate."

Gary flipped the Bible open and unfolded the old letter from the boy who'd died on the field of battle. "Tate passed it on. It's moved from hand to hand ever since then." He gazed at the old book. "It came to many, such as Ruth, Faris, and Frederick, who saved lives, but now in God's own providence, I feel the Bible rightfully belongs to R.C. Cooper."

Daniel snapped his head around. "What are you saying, boy? You better not be saying what I think you're saying. You going to give—"

"It's not mine to sell, Uncle Daniel. I don't own it any more than you do."

Daniel groaned. "Don't be stupid, Gary. We're talking serious money here."

"I know what's at stake, Uncle. I know what I'm doing." Gary held the Bible out to Carolyn.

She took the Bible and exchanged glances with Gary. "This is very generous of you, Mr. Brandon."

Gary shook his head. "No, it's not generous; it's just the right thing to do."

"Sir Richard instructed me to pay for the Bible, but since you renounce ownership . . ." She trailed off as her fingers touched the scarred and battered leather. "Maybe we can make a donation to some worthwhile cause in your name."

"You can do that, Miss Dawson? You said R.C. Cooper doesn't give to charities."

"You do have some worthy causes in mind that need help with money, don't you, Gary?"

Gary smiled. "Sure. There's a mission in San Francisco that some friends of mine want to refurbish, and oh, there's the orphanage in Egypt and there's the Bell Park in Petersburg that probably needs some new playground equipment or something, and there is also—"

Carolyn Dawson interrupted. "Fine . . . fine." She then looked at Shannon Reed. "We can easily arrange donations for those causes, can't we, Shannon?"

"I believe we can."

"If that's your wish, Mr. Brandon, then that's what we shall do."

"That is my wish," Gary said.

Uncle Daniel's face reddened like a turnip.

"Will one million dollars be an acceptable donation?"

"A million bucks?" Gary had to choke out the words.

"Very well, then—two million."

Gary said nothing. He couldn't.

Carolyn smiled. "You drive a hard bargain, Mr. Brandon. Fine then. Five million dollars placed in a foundation with structured accountability should help out a lot of worthwhile causes, don't you think?" She seemed giddy. "We'll arrange to have a foundation set up in your name and we'll fund that foundation with an additional endowment of one million dollars annually for operating expenses and ongoing revenue for giving." She looked at Shannon. "Make all the papers reflect that the family of R.C. Cooper will not be able to interfere with any of that money even after his death."

"I can do that," Shannon said. "But the papers need to be signed before he dies."

"Good," Carolyn said. "At least I can say I helped get some of his wealth to some good causes." She looked into the swimming dark eyes of Daniel. "Maybe we can do one more thing since we are on a roll here. You have a problem with alcohol, right, Mr. Huff?"

"What makes you say that?"

She sniffed the air. "I'm afraid it is most obvious."

Daniel slipped down a few inches in his seat but didn't reply.

"Well then, if you would agree to the following, Sir Richard will pay an endowment providing a lifetime trust for you that will supply enough money for you and your family to live comfortably for a long time. That is, if you follow all the rules designated by Gary. I can see that he cares for you, and after all, you did find and purchase the Bible."

Daniel stared at his nephew. "What kind of rules?"

"Okay . . . well, uh . . . let's see, Uncle Daniel, from now on no liquor, cigarettes, or gambling. This can be a new start for you. What do you say?"

Daniel blinked. "I can't just quit cold turkey."

"I'll get you the medical help you need to kick the booze and cigarettes. Oh, and another thing, I want you to go to church every week."

"*Every* week?"

"Yes, *every* week. What do you say?"

The old man wiped the sweat from his brow. "I guess I have no choice, do I?"

"No." Gary turned back to Carolyn Dawson. "The Bible is yours, I suppose."

Carolyn Dawson winked. "You know how to make a good deal."

"Ms. Dawson, I wasn't trying to take all that money—"

"I know. I suggested the deal that will make a big

difference to a lot of people in need. Maybe I can learn to live with myself."

Ten minutes later, Shannon handed her a hand-written page of the agreement. Carolyn signed it and handed it to Gary. "This will serve as an agreement. Even though it is not lengthy, it is binding."

Ms. Reed signed as a witness. "All done except for your signature, Gary."

"Will Sir Richard agree to all of this?" Gary asked.

"He has already agreed—I have power of attorney, and besides, he authorized me to pay whatever was necessary to obtain the Bible. He won't even notice the few million that will flow out of his coffers. You sign now, and Ms. Reed will set up the accounts."

Gary scribbled his signature on the paper and expelled a lungful of air.

Carolyn placed the Bible in the camel-skin case. "Thank you, Mr. Brandon. I feel that I have relieved a little personal guilt—no, a lot of personal guilt here."

Swinging her legs through the door, she exited the limo, then turned to Gary and motioned for him to follow. When Daniel started to move, Shannon Reed reached across the space separating them and anchored him in place with a tight grip on his shoulder.

Gary walked her to the jet. The engines began to whine in the hot, gusting wind. Carolyn had to shout over the increasing roar. "The book I have

. . . does it really have the power people say? Does it really save lives?"

"I suppose it does." He looked through the open door of the limo. "I'm hoping it will save one more life."

"And what about you, Mr. Brandon? You have a great deal of responsibility with all that money to give away. Are there any more miracles left over from this book for you?"

"God excels in miracles."

"Perhaps He does. Perhaps He does."

"Come to think of it," Gary said, "I need to hire some help, don't I? I mean, I have a foundation to run." A wide smile crossed his face. "There's this girl in Petersburg named Yvonne, and she would be great for the job."

"What is the name of your new foundation?"

"Name . . . I hadn't thought of that yet. All this is kinda sudden." His eyes drifted to the briefcase that held the Bible. "Maybe I'll call it the Bell Messenger Foundation."

"I like it. I like it a lot," Carolyn said, then turned and walked up the jet's steps, disappearing through the door. The door closed moments after she'd entered.

The whine of the engines drove Gary back to the limo. He watched the aircraft taxi to the runway. In a minute the jet was banking east over the Salt River, ascending into a column of dark, swollen rain clouds.

Center Point Publishing
600 Brooks Road ● PO Box 1
Thorndike ME 04986-0001 USA

(207) 568-3717

US & Canada:
1 800 929-9108
www.centerpointlargeprint.com